Burdens of a Saint

Book Two of The Guardian Series

Joan Hazel

ISBN-13: 978-1-939296-92-4

ISBN-10: 1939296927

Myrddin Publishing Group

Credits:

Editor: Irene Roth Luvaul

Cover: Joan Hazel

Contact us at: www.myrddinpublishinggroup.com

"Come on mom. You guys were about to start making out in the middle of the store."

Janet's body stiffened. "We were not!" All of a sudden, she could hear her grandfather's voice. "The scalded dog always hollers first." She shook her head. She wasn't a scalded dog.

Okay. Maybe she had wondered what it would be like to kiss Saint Wolfe's perfect lips. What if she did want to kiss him? She was a grown woman, and she could kiss whomever she liked. "I think you are exaggerating." She tried to sound innocent, but it wasn't working. "And what if I did find Mr. Wolfe attractive?" she conceded. "I can have a relationship with whomever I want."

Who was she kidding? Two more seconds and she would have thrown caution to the wind and Saint to the ground. That would have put a permanent crease in his prim and proper shorts!

.

ABOUT THE AUTHOR

Joan Hazel is the author of paranormal, contemporary and historical romance. Mrs. Hazel has enjoyed success as an opera singer and professor.

Currently she resides in Central Florida with her husband, and two fur kids, Izzy and Ellie.

Other works from Joan Hazel include:

The Last Guardian—Book One of the Guardian Series
What the Heart Sees—a Rubenesque Romance
Modern tales of Fantasy—only on www.smashwords.com

www.joanhazel.com

@guardianwriter

DEDICATION

To my dear friends, both new and old, whose unconditional love is a blessing in my life.

PROLOGUE

From the Parables of the Warrior Goddess

And so began the time of the Theriontropes upon the Earth. Allowed to exist as half human, half animal, their lives forever became intertwined with that of Haven and its guardians.

The All Father watched from atop his mountain fortress as shape shifters evolved and grew into a powerful race, acknowledging only the warrior goddess as their creator and worshipping her as such. He also watched as Loki's anger toward the Theriontropes grew.

Loki was the god known best for changing his form. If any god should be worshipped by such a race, it should be he. The Lord of Chaos's disdain for the shape shifters' lack of devotion to him seeped deep into his core. *How dare the Sisters of All Life and Knowledge create such an abomination?*

Filled with contempt, Loki stormed into the Temple of Creation so he might destroy the sister's gift to the warrior goddess while the traitors watched.

The three sisters encircled the Well of Creation. Knowing what lay in the god's heart, the sisters refused him access to the well and its contents.

Lightness spoke for the triumvirate. "Your presence is neither

1

requested nor welcome here. You may leave."

Angered by her defiance and offended that the youngest of the sisters would dare speak to him in such a manner, Loki pointed his staff in her direction. The tip blazed to life. His eyes narrowed as he steadied his hand and took aim at the young beauty's chest.

Darkness, the eldest of the sisters, placed her body before that of her sister. From under her cloak, she pulled a cord made from the finest gold threads. Holding the cord before her, Darkness removed her silver dagger from its sheath.

Fear came upon him, and Loki's eyes widened as he beheld the golden strand presented by Darkness. He knew his time among the immortals would come to an end should her dagger slip. Unable to control his rage, Loki hurled a flaming spear from the end of his staff with such force that it lodged in the ceiling of the cupola high above the heads of the sisters.

Darkness cackled in amusement at his anger, for no matter how fierce and cunning a warrior Loki believed himself to be, the sisters would always hold sway over him. To kill one of them would bring a fate worse than death upon him.

"Cease," Mother, the middle sister of the three, commanded.

Loki dared not look into the faces of the sisters. He didn't want to give them an opportunity to see into his thoughts.

Mother continued. "Hide your thoughts, you can't. Know your heart, we do. All actions, even those of a god, have consequences."

Darkness took over the sister's commands. "No harm shall come to Freyja's children by your hand, including those who watch over them."

"And if I choose to ignore your request?"

"We make no request, Loki," Lightness said. "If you choose not to heed our caution, you have only yourself to blame for your punishment."

Reluctantly, Loki bowed his head in acknowledgement of the sisters' warning. The sisters may have forbidden his interference, but they said nothing of anyone else doing so. With that in mind, Loki took his leave of the sisters.

CHAPTER 1

Saint Wolfe stared out across the ornate Italian gardens of his home, known as Haven. Haven was a place of respite and repose for all shape shifters and the only home Saint had ever known.

When he was barely two weeks old, Saint was brought to Haven by his older brother, Fergus. In those days, Haven was located in Scotland, not in Montana as it was now.

Saint had no idea how long he'd sat there, his gaze transfixed on the sunlight dancing across the reflecting pool, enjoying the aroma of the hot tea resting in the cup beside him. He felt comforted, surrounded by nature, and hidden from view of the main house. There he found solace.

Sadness filled Saint's heart as he thought of how much his life had changed in the past two-hundred-plus years. He had always been perplexed by those of his kind who enjoyed having an extended life span. In his estimation, semi-immortality was a drawback to being a shape shifter. So many he held dear had come and gone. It stood to reason there would be others, and unless he was dealt a wound from which he couldn't heal, he would live forever.

He wondered if maybe he should be more like his older brother, Fergus. As far as Saint knew, Fergus allowed no one to get close, but that wasn't his way.

For Saint, the goddess had chosen another path. His was a path of service, a life filled with doing what he must for the greater good of others, no matter the species. But after two centuries of watching over others, Saint feared he was approaching what Ghost called "burnout."

Saint wished. He stilled his thoughts. What was it he wished? He dared not voice his true feelings. There was no need to speak of things he knew would never come to fruition. He could curse the goddess and the Sisters of All Life and Knowledge, as the Fates were known in the world of shifters, but to what avail? Surely they knew what was best in cursing him to spend centuries without a true-mate by his side or children of his own.

Saint allowed the soothing voice of falling water to wash away his thoughts of family and home. It wasn't his place to question the sisters, something he would do well to remember.

Water poured from beneath the clawed feet of the massive stone griffin. The statue sat at one end of the reflecting pool, its unblinking gaze staring unwaveringly toward the main house of Haven, its great wings tucked neatly against its broad body. With one claw resting on the world, the beast watched silently over the gardens, awaiting the moment he was needed. With unfurled wings, the griffin would take to the air, ready to defend Haven, even unto his death.

At least that was the story Saint told himself. As a child, Saint thought of the griffin as Haven's private sentinel, going so far as to name the statue Liam. Often he mused if ever he truly needed a protector; Liam would spring to life to save him at Saint's command.

Saint smiled inwardly at the memory, definitely a childish fantasy. Yet it was one he still secretly hoped would one day come true. Not that Saint needed a protector. He simply thought a statue coming to life was a smashing idea.

Saint was rarely given to flights of fancy, but now he fought the urge to walk up to the statue and speak with it. Maybe, with everything Liam had seen and heard over the centuries, he could shed some wisdom on Saint's situation. Goddess knew there was no one at home he could confide in.

If he had to choose one member of his pack to speak with, it would be Mika Elkhart. Mika was the only other member of the Delta Pack who Saint considered like-minded. But Mika was busy adjusting to life with his true-mate, CJ Carson, helping her to become acclimated to life as the new guardian.

There was also the youngest member of his pack, Ghost Thorolfur. Saint shook his head at the thought. Ghost had his own problems. It couldn't have been easy to discover that after one hundred and thirty years, his twin brother wanted him dead and would stop at nothing to see that mission accomplished. Not to mention the fact Ghost's take on most situations was a bit unconventional. Mika was right. Fergus really should have taken Ghost's remote control away years ago.

Lastly, there was Fergus. The thought of speaking with Fergus about anything at the moment made him shudder. Fergus could be, for lack of a better word, obstinate. Who was he kidding? It was the perfect word to describe his brother. Of course, one could throw in stubborn, hardheaded, and positively medieval.

However, obstinate would do nicely, especially considering the subject Saint wished to address. All he would have to do is mention the name Bridget LeCœur, and Fergus would fly into a fit of rage. In Fergus's defense, Saint really couldn't blame him.

Throughout the world of shifters, certain packs existed with the core belief all other life forms, including humans, were to be used as food. Some of the worst packs Saint ever came in contact with actually raised humans like cattle. Though those packs looked and acted as if they were aristocracy, they were an abomination to the race of shifters. The practice was never sanctioned by any within the Theriontrope Foundation, the shifter's ruling organization.

Saint never expected to meet such individuals, and he definitely never expected to fall in love with one. The fact she happened to be the only daughter of the Alpha of such a group was a devastating coincidence.

"How could I have been such a fool?" Saint whispered, as he ran a hand through his dark auburn hair.

Absently, he let his hand fall to rest just above his heart. Like a vise grip, tightness lingered there and had since his return from the Underworld, where he and Mika had rescued the new guardian from captivity.

At times, the pressure was so great, the simple act of breathing seemed almost impossible. Had he been human, Saint would have suspected a heart attack. However, the continual changing and regeneration of cells during the process of shifting from human to animal made catching any illness virtually impossible.

When the pains first began, Saint had shifted. Changing into wolf form, he and Fergus raced the outer perimeter of Haven. He was sure once he shifted back into human form, the tightness would disappear, but it hadn't. That was when he realized the sensation had nothing to do with any physical ailment and everything to do with the emotional turmoil that lay beneath his calm exterior.

Saint never expected himself to want to be more like his adoptive brother, Ghost. But at the moment, he envied Ghost's innate ability to completely disregard certain things. The irritations of life slid easily off Ghost's thick hide, a quality that both annoyed and amazed Saint.

Taking a sip of tea, Saint allowed the warm liquid to flow over his tongue, tasting each individual flavor. This was one of his special blends meant to soothe and calm the nerves. He had designed it for Fergus many years ago. However, there was no amount of tea or meditation that could cool the anxiety that boiled in the pit of his stomach.

Over the centuries, like many of his kind, Saint learned to fear very little. Lack of fear seemed to be a character trait in most shape shifters, especially those who'd been alive as long as he and Fergus. It was a side effect born from the knowledge one was practically immortal. Unless a shifter sustained a mortal wound such as having their head severed or their heart ripped from their body, little could kill them. As long as shifters could alter their form, they would survive.

Saint considered the positives. Many times his life had been blessed by the goddess, and he firmly believed when the time came for him to transition from one world to the next, she would continue to watch over and protect him. He'd been Freyja's servant for too long for her to abandon him, which is why he had little doubt that he should make the journey to the Underworld.

CJ may have been Mika's true-mate, but Saint was the one with knowledge of the old text. He'd known it would take his familiarity with the Underworld or Hell, call it what you wish, to help rescue CJ.

He hadn't known what to expect. How could he? He certainly didn't expect to come face-to-face with the goddess Hel, nor did he expect her to be so beautiful and gracious. He also didn't expect her to be so willing to negotiate for CJ's return, as that wasn't her way. The mere fact she did so perplexed him still.

Saint swallowed back the anxiety that swelled beneath his perfectly starched collar. What had he done?

I will always protect you, the familiar voice of the Universe whispered to him, and he lifted his face to allow the cool morning breeze to caress his skin.

How he wanted to believe those words. He'd entrusted his life to the warrior goddess, and for centuries, she watched over and protected him. However, this was one time he wasn't sure her protection was possible. But no matter the cost, the continuation of his species was worth it. Fergus had taught him that much.

Saint closed his eyes and leaned his head back against the cool, stone wall of the grotto. Squinting through the leaves, he searched the clouds for an answer. The problem was, he didn't know the question. He only knew something beckoned to him. It begged him to return to the one place he dared not go.

"Saint!" CJ's voice splintered the silence of the morning. For her to call on him instead of her mate meant something was terribly wrong.

"Saint!" she called again with more urgency. Her footsteps thudded down the stone steps toward the grotto. "Saint, you've got to stop them before they kill each other!"

"Who?" Saint asked as he appeared beside her.

CJ yelped. "I'll never get used to you guys doing just popping in from nowhere," she fussed. "Never mind. It's Fergus and Ghost. You've got to stop them."

"What this time?" Saint sighed.

"I don't know. I was downstairs in the exam room doing inventory, and the next thing I know, there's a loud crash. I ran up the stairs and found the two of them at each other's throats. Seriously. Fergus had Ghost by the throat and was holding him about three feet off the ground."

"And Mika? Where is he?" Saint asked, as he took the steps quickly.

CJ followed close at his heels. "He went into town."

"Human or wolf?"

"Mika?" she stammered.

"Fergus and Ghost, are they human or wolf?"

9

"Human the last time I saw them. Why?"

"Then there is chance Ghost will survive," he answered flatly. Without waiting for CJ, Saint charged into the house and bounded down the hallway, stopping just outside the media room to assess the situation.

CDs and DVDs littered the floor where someone had turned over freestanding shelves. The artwork along the walls hung askew, and very little of the furniture was left intact. At the moment, Fergus and Ghost stood in the center of the room near an upturned sofa. Both men were bloodied and banged up, yet neither was ready to surrender.

A low, rumbling growl emanated from Ghost as he lunged forward, catching Fergus about the waist, driving the bigger man backwards. Fergus's body thudded hard against the wall, and he roared in frustration.

Fergus pushed away from the wall. With whirlwind speed, he flipped Ghost sideways, and without losing momentum, Fergus shoved Ghost above his head. Walking toward a window, Fergus paused in contemplation.

"Don't just stand there!" CJ yelled to Saint. "Do something!"

Saint hated to admit it, but he was torn. The storm between Fergus and Ghost had been brewing for quite a while, and frankly, he was tired of playing the peacemaker between the two of them.

His logical side said to stop them. It was the right and proper thing for him to do. Yet his illogical side told him to let the pair fight it out. Whatever troubled them needed to be brought out in the open, even if it meant they tore each other limb from limb. After all, they were shape shifters and would heal. The furniture, on the other hand, had taken enough punishment.

With more calm than he actually felt, Saint crossed the battle-torn room. "Let him go, brother." Saint spoke in even tones.

"Not until this dirty, little fice learns his place," Fergus grunted.

"Are you ever going to come into the twenty-first century? Really, who says fice anymore?" Ghost asked nonchalantly, which seemed rather odd, considering his present predicament.

"I say fice because that is what you are, a small, snappy, contemptuous little mongrel. No other word fits quite as well," Fergus answered.

"Your words mean nothing to me," Ghost spat. "I'm tired of standing in the shadow of the big badass Fergus Wolfe. Ass being the important word in that sentence."

Fergus lifted Ghost higher above his head. "Bastard!"

"Ora basta!" Saint commanded in Italian. "That's enough."

Ghost thinks only Fergus uses antiquated words. He has no idea the words I want to use, Saint thought. Even though the battle between his brothers had pushed Saint beyond his breaking point, he remained the epitome of composure.

He placed a calming hand on Fergus's arm. "You know you don't want to do this."

"By the gods, I want nothing more," Fergus spat.

Saint noted that neither Fergus's voice nor his body showed the strain of holding a fully grown man above his head. After nearly three hundred years, Saint was still amazed by his brother's strength and control.

"Then do it!" Ghost barked. "Throw me out like the garbage you think I am."

Ghost's last statement struck an odd cord in Saint, and by the look on Fergus's face, it did in him as well.

Did Ghost truly believe Fergus thought so little of him? Had the years caused Ghost to forget the sacrifices Fergus had made solely for him to live? Didn't he remember the countless hours Fergus spent teaching him to hunt or fish or read?

When Ghost was only ten, his twin brother Ævar tried to kill him by slitting his throat and leaving his body buried beneath the snow. Ghost's mother, Kenna, found him there, half-dead from blood loss and hypothermia.

That night, Kenna walked alone to a nearby village, and left her son in the care of strangers, until an emissary from the Theriontrope Foundation could retrieve the boy and bring him to the safety of Haven.

That emissary was Fergus.

At the request of the Foundation, Fergus traveled to Iceland to rescue the dying child. But when he got there, Fergus found Ghost's body ravaged by infection and fever. There was no way the child could withstand traveling by spatial shift in his condition.

At Saint's suggestion, Fergus transfused his own blood into Ghost. Already well past one hundred, the older shifter's powerful blood made the child well enough to be moved. As far as anyone could tell, there had been no other way.

Ghost was so frail in those days. He held little or no memory of his rescue, nor did he know the toll it had taken on Fergus, and he never would. Fergus swore both Saint and Mika to silence concerning Ghost's rescue. He thought the truth would be too hard for the child to handle.

Maybe it was the blood bond the two men shared, but over the years, Fergus had become more of a father to Ghost than a brother or mentor. He watched over Ghost and indulged him the way only a father would his son.

That is why Fergus's present treatment of Ghost seemed out of place. There was more going on than either man wanted to admit. If Saint could get Fergus to release Ghost, he would get to the bottom of things.

Without warning, Fergus whirled and threw Ghost across the

room. CJ ducked as Ghost slammed into the photo-covered wall nearest her and the door. Ghost's body fell to the floor, showered in broken glass.

Quickly, CJ rushed to his side, but Ghost pushed her away. "Is that all you have, old man?" Ghost asked, shaking the shards of glass from his hair and shoulders.

The pressure around Saint's heart increased, and he felt as if at any moment, it might burst. Taking in a deep breath, he tried to expand his chest as much as possible to relieve the tight band constricting his rib cage, but nothing seemed to help.

Saint stepped between the two men. He'd seen and heard enough. No longer could he stand by and watch his family tear itself apart.

"I've had enough," Saint said, voicing his thoughts aloud.

"You? This one has been a constant pain in my arse for the past hundred and fifty years, not yours," Fergus groused, and waived his hand toward Ghost.

Saint turned slowly toward his older brother. "You're right, brother. Ghost hasn't been a constant pain in my arse for the past one and a half centuries. That job has been equally shared between the both of you."

"Don't put me in the same category with him!" Ghost interjected.

"You." Saint spun on the younger man. "You've no idea what this man has done for you." He pointed to Fergus. "If it weren't for him...." Saint heard a low growl of censure issue from Fergus. Saint fought back his own words. "You," he pointed to Ghost, "you would be well served to hold your tongue upon occasion."

"Exactly," Fergus added.

"Don't think Ghost is the only one culpable in this," Saint snapped as he turned back to Fergus. "The two of you either don't speak or are at each other's throats, and I for one am tired of playing referee."

He had more to say to his older brother, so much more, but why bother? Saint could tell by the way Fergus adjusted the leather bracers about his wrist, nothing he said would change anything.

"If the two of you wish to rip each other apart, then so be it. But I refuse to stand by and watch. I don't care how you get this settled. I simply want it done by the time I return."

"Return? Where are you going?" Ghost asked.

Saint clamped his lips together tightly. He did not want to tell his family where he was going. They would only try to stop him, but in reality, there was no way he could keep his destination secret. Fergus could and would eventually track him down.

"Don't act as if you are going to leave," Fergus grumped. "This is your home. Everything you need is here."

"Not everything," Saint said, tugging on the hem of his immaculately pressed vest.

"Seriously," Ghost said. "You're not leaving, are you?"

"Actually, I am."

"And just where do you think you're going?" Fergus asked.

Saint paused, staring past his brother's head to the swaying treetops just beyond the gardens.

There really was only one place he wanted to go. Only one place he had thought of since returning from the Underworld. "It is time I returned to New Orleans," he stated, and left the room.

CHAPTER 2

Janet Beesinger stretched groggily as she rolled over in her large, iron bed. Through a single, opened eye, she glanced at the alarm clock on the night stand. The bright red numbers glared back at her. "Craaaaaaap," she said, as she threw back the covers, her feet landing with a soft thud on the rug. "Good thing my commute is only down the stairs," she mumbled, wrapping a well-worn chenille robe about her.

Throwing open the door to her bedroom, Janet looked about the hallway for any signs of her son. "Eric!" she yelled. "Eric, come on! You're late!"

"Late for what?" asked the teenager, as he stuck his head out of the kitchen door.

Janet wasn't sure why he looked at her like she had grown two heads, but she didn't have time to figure it out. She had less than an hour to get dressed and open her shop for business.

The opening was now pushed further back since she had to get Eric to school. *Crap!*

"What do you mean for what? School, of course. Now get a move on," she commanded, scampering down the hall of their small apartment.

Luckily for Janet, the apartment was upstairs above the building that housed her bookshop, My Spicy Cauldron. She inherited the building from her grandmother. Since she was a single mother, and raising a teenage son was not the cheapest proposition, living above the store was the practical and economical thing to do.

Eric always seemed hungry, and he grew out of clothes faster than any child she had ever seen. At fourteen, he stood almost a head above her. At the rate he was growing, he would be close to seven feet tall when all was said and done.

"Mom," Eric said, trying to get her attention, which was hard since she had not stopped talking since she woke. "Mom!"

"What, Eric?" she huffed over the sound of her house shoes scuffing against the wood floor.

"It's teacher initiative day. No school."

"Huh?" Janet grunted, still lost in her own thoughts. She wasn't sure she heard him correctly.

"I told you about it on Monday. Remember?" He drug out the last word into fourteen syllables.

"You don't have to be a smart—tail," Janet said, placing her hands on her hips.

Eric looked down at the ground and then back to his mom. "Sorry, Mom, you seemed confused."

Her head did feel a bit fuzzy. She hated being late for anything, and it always threw off her mojo. "Fine. Since you're home from school, you get to help me in the store."

"Ah, man."

"Don't 'ah, man' me. You know the rules. You want money, you gotta earn it."

"Yes ma'am," Eric said, trudging down the hall behind his mother.

Janet stopped and faced her son. There were days she found it incredibly hard to believe he was hers. Eric was a good kid. He never got in trouble at school. His grades weren't spectacular, but they weren't bad either. His worst trait was getting a bit mouthy at times, but overall, he was a good kid.

The day she had laid him in the bassinet next to her bed had been one of the happiest and scariest days of her life. Like all new mothers, Janet was positive her son was the most beautiful baby in the whole wide world. He had cotton-white hair and the deepest sapphire eyes. Everyone said his eyes would change color as he grew older, but she knew better. Just like she knew his blonde hair would never really darken. He was a gift from the gods, and he was hers.

Janet remembered the fear of sitting alone in the tiny bedroom of her apartment at the time. There, listening to the sound of Eric's breathing, Janet felt the weight the next twenty years and what they would bring. It seemed she cried a lot in those first few months. It was just she and Eric, ready to take on the world. Luckily, she had a handful of really good friends who were there when she needed them.

But looking at Eric now, Janet saw he was worth every tear and all the trouble she had gone through. In her opinion, Eric was still her beautiful, perfect baby boy. *Only six more years*, she thought and then what?

"What?" Eric asked, stopping in front of his mom.

"Nothing," Janet sniffed.

"You got that look again."

"What look?" she asked, pulling a towel from the linen closet.

Eric flipped a swatch of shaggy, blonde hair from his forehead. "I don't know. Kinda sad, I guess."

"Not sad. It's just...well, sometimes I just can't believe you're my son. That's all."

"Geeze, Mom," Eric said, pushing his hands into his pockets.

"Don't go gettin' all mushy on me."

"Too bad. I'm your mother. It's what we do," she said, wiping a tear from her cheek. "Now, let's get the store open, then you can run to Mattie's and get us breakfast."

Eric eyes lit up. "Really?"

Mattie's Pastries belonged to one of Janet's best friends, Mattie McClure. The day Janet and Eric moved into the upstairs of the bookstore was the first day the two ladies met, and they had been friends ever since.

Janet had little time to fix breakfast and get dressed. However, she could always go for take-out.

"Can I get a giant cinnamon roll with the cream cheese icing?" Eric asked, sounding more like the little boy she used to know instead of the teenager he had become.

"Let me think about it," Janet said, as she walked into the bathroom and shut the door. She knew there was nothing to think about. She would give in and let him have one, along with anything else he wanted to eat, which, here lately, seemed to be everything in sight plus some. No wonder her grocery budget was going through the roof.

"Darn it," she cursed at the round-faced clock. She had wanted to look her best today but instead would have to opt for the quick change. She grunted in disgust at the thought of the calendar on her counter. For some reason, she had circled today's date with a red marker. Beside the number, she had written the words *"Your life changes today."*

Actually, it had been Janet's alter ego, Princess Ryhinni, who had written those words. *Princess Ryhinni knows all, sees all.* At least, that is what her business card said.

From the time she was small, Janet had been able to see into the other realm. She could hear things no one else heard and see things others no one else saw. For Janet, the spirit world intertwined easily with the real world. Being born with second sight, as Janet's grandmother called it, was a gift, and one her grandmother sought to exploit.

Despite her mother's protests, Janet's grandmother dragged her from city to city and town to town. Janet was forced to perform private readings or séances for wealthy clients her grandmother always seemed to find.

In the beginning, Janet found the trips exciting. She had seen most of Europe and the eastern shores of the United States by the time she was sixteen. But as she got older, Janet wanted nothing more than to stay in one spot.

She couldn't remember being at the same school for more than four months at a time. Eventually, her grandmother gave up even trying to enroll her. Instead, she home-schooled Janet, which truly wasn't all that bad. But what pained Janet most was not being there when her mother passed away, and deep inside, Janet knew she would never forgive her grandmother for that.

Eventually, Janet rebelled. She left her grandmother and moved back home to New Orleans. What better place for a psychic? She spent years eking out a living reading palms and tarot along Jackson Square.

Janet needed something that would set her apart from the other fortune tellers and palmists. During that time, Princess Ryhinni was born. What better shtick than the channeled spirit of a century-old exiled Princess and mystic?

Stepping from the shower, Janet wiped the steam from the bathroom mirror. She stared at her foggy reflection and wondered if Princess Ryhinni was right. Would her life actually change today and if so how? She rarely predicted anything about her own life. That was the problem with being psychic. You can see things for everyone but yourself.

There were occasional instances when you know something is

going to happen, but you have no idea what. Janet called those moments her cosmic teasers, and in her opinion, they stunk.

"As long as Eric's safe," she whispered. Silently, Janet offered up a prayer of protection and thanks as she rubbed the silver pendant of Thor's hammer known as mjöllnir that hung about her neck. Now she could start her day and accept what was to come.

CHAPTER 3

"Saint," Fergus called, as he followed his brother up the grand staircase of Haven that led to their sleeping quarters. "Saint, stop!"

Saint refused his brother's request. For more than two hundred years, he had followed almost every order Fergus had given. Not only was Fergus his older brother, but he was also Mika, Ghost and his pack leader. Rarely, if ever, did Saint disobey an order, and for him to do so should alert Fergus to how far he had been pushed.

Pausing at the top of the stairs, Saint turned and looked at his brother. No emotion showed in Saint's forest-fern eyes. Over the years, he had become adept at not showing his emotions. He learned the hard way letting people know how you felt would only get you hurt.

Without a word, he continued on toward his bedroom.

Opening the door, he looked about the sparsely furnished room. Since his time studying with the Dominican monks, Saint learned to need little in the way of possessions, and his room reflected that philosophy. It was nothing like Fergus's room, lavishly decorated with heavily carved Renaissance furniture, or Ghost's bedroom, which housed a vast assortment of Viking artifacts any museum curator would froth at the mouth to have.

Saint took stock of his possessions. To the right of the door sat a plain oak dresser and a shaker-style mirror. To the left lay a pencil post bed covered with a patchwork quilt. *My room is as plain as I*, he thought.

Underneath the window was a small desk and chair in the same no-nonsense style, piled high with books and papers. The only ornate item in the whole room was a statue of the goddess Freyja that rested directly across from his bed. Saint couldn't remember a time the statue hadn't watched over him.

He had no idea where the statue came from. Like most of the furnishings at Haven, the statue simply appeared. It wasn't until the last guardian, Charles Stone, had been murdered and Haven began to rearrange itself that Saint even questioned how things came to be there.

Again Saint touched his chest. Never before had he felt a pain such as this, and in his heart, he knew the only way to rid himself of the discomfort was to allow it to lead him, in hopes it would go away.

He pulled a leather travel bag from the closet and began to pack. He could feel Fergus glare at him from the doorway. "I know you have something to say, brother," Saint said, "so say it."

Still, he dared not look in Fergus's direction. Instead he busied himself with picking out clothes, which was not too taxing considering he had worn the exact cut of suit for more than a hundred years.

My wardrobe, yet another hold over from the Dominicans, Saint thought, as he pulled a couple of pairs of black trousers and long, black dusters from the closet. Dressing all in black was a trademark of the Dominican order and the reason they were known as the Black Friars.

Saint arranged the clothes in the satchel with great precision. "Really, Fergus, either speak or leave, but don't stand there with your chest puffed out and glower at me."

"I am not glowering," Fergus finally said, as he dropped his arms to his sides.

Saint slanted his head first one way then the other as he studied his brother's features. "Actually, I am pretty sure you are," Saint said, walking to his dresser. He picked up a silver-handled hairbrush from where it rested on the top of the dresser. With great care, he ran the boar bristles through his shoulder-length, auburn hair to smooth it down.

Placing the brush aside, Saint lifted the antique hair clasp he had worn since he was a teenager. He gazed down at the ancient item in his hands and lovingly traced the pattern with the pads of his thumbs.

The design was an intricate Celtic knot woven in bronze and laced with a strip of leather. The leather had been replaced many times over the years, and the once orange-red of the bronze was now a dark brown. The meaning of the clasp's design had been long forgotten and lost in time. It bore the crest of his mother's clan and was forged long before either Fergus or Saint was born.

He thought of the parents he never knew and a brother who risked his own life rather than allow the infant Saint to die. There was no way Saint could ever repay all Fergus had given to him. He, Mika, and Ghost all had Fergus to thank for their lives. That fact alone was enough to earn Fergus not only each man's respect and loyalty, but also their love.

Saint looked again to the time-worn clasp. He remembered the day Fergus had taken it from his own hair and given it to him. "May the spirit of our mother protect you always, bràthair," Fergus told him, as he placed the object in Saint's hand.

That was the night before Fergus went on one of his first missions for the Theriontrope Foundation. The Foundation was the closest thing shifters had to a governmental system. It was responsible for helping those in need and bringing justice to those that don't follow the rules. It just so happened that for the last two hundred and fifty years, Theriontrope's main enforcer had been Fergus.

When Saint was a boy, Fergus began his work for the Foundation. At first, the missions were simple. Either he would carry missives from one pack to another or see to a shifter's safe passage. Nothing too taxing.

Through the years, Fergus's skills grew, making it easy for the Theriontrope to send him on increasingly difficult and dangerous missions. Whenever Michael Grey, the head of Theriontrope, called, Fergus always answered. But no matter where Fergus went or how long he was gone, he would telepathically contact Saint. It took Saint a while, but he finally understood Fergus did so to alleviate a child's fears of being left alone.

However, one night in particular, Fergus called Saint to his room. He was preparing to leave on a mission, and somehow Saint could tell Fergus feared he may not return.

Saint could see it in his mind's eye as if it were yesterday. He followed Fergus to an ornately carved armoire that stood along the south wall of Fergus's bedroom. Inside the wardrobe, clothing, books, and assorted items lay in disarray, and he gawked at the mess as Fergus reached in and pulled out a long knife and sheath. Saint knew the item on sight since it was something Fergus had forbidden him to touch. It was Fergus's fighting knife, a perfectly balanced, fifteen-inch blade with a handle made from the horn of stag. At first, he thought Fergus was going to give him the knife, but instead, Fergus placed it back inside the cabinet.

Still unsure of his brother's intentions, Saint stood by pensively as Fergus reached behind his neck and untied the leather thong that held the bronze clasp in place. The polished metal glinted in the dim light of the candles as Fergus looked down at the object in his hand. Saint would never forget the sadness that passed across his brother's face in that moment. It was probably the closest he ever came to seeing Fergus shed a tear.

Handing the tie to Saint, Fergus explained it once belonged to their mother and that the knot work represented Wolf Red, the clan from which they were descended.

Until that point, Fergus spoke very little of their mother, but there in the stillness of the night, he spoke for the longest of times of their mother's kindness and of their father's undying devotion to his family.

According to Fergus, Saint looked like their mother, which was a statement Saint found quite odd considering how similar he and Fergus appeared, especially when Saint reached adulthood. There could never be any mistake the two were brothers.

"Never forget that she loved you, Aodhàn," Fergus had told him, calling Saint by his given name.

"But if she loved me so much, then why did she choose to take her own life?" Being young and naïve, Saint had to ask.

"She just loved our father more."

That was the last statement Fergus ever made about their mother. Saint knew no matter how many years passed from the time of their mother's death, it would always weigh heavily upon Fergus. She had been so stricken with grief at the death of her husband, she took her own life. Barely a few weeks old, Saint was taken by Fergus to Haven.

He could only imagine what Fergus had gone through to get them to safety. The brothers had never really spoken about the incident. At the time of Saint's birth, Prince Charles had placed a bounty on all wolves. From adult males to pups, Prince Charles demanded the eradication of the species.

Fergus told Saint their mother begged their father not to go hunting as a wolf, but he wouldn't listen. He argued that he could move with more stealth as a wolf than as a human. When he'd not returned, Fergus knew what had happened. His father had been killed by a local farmer.

Frang, Fergus and Saint's father, was the last wolf to be killed in Scotland. He was also the last of their clan other than the brothers.

We are a dying breed. The thought occurred to Saint that unless Fergus found a mate, their clan would completely disappear.

A part of him held out hope that one day he would find someone to fall in love with. But there never seemed to be enough time. There was always one more mission to take on or one more riddle to unravel.

"Saint?" Fergus's voice brought him back from the past, a place he had frequented quite a bit lately.

With great ease, Saint placed the clasp at the nape of his neck and tied the leather thong.

"Yes, dear brother?" Saint asked, taking the brush across the room and placing it in the bag with the rest of his belongings.

Fergus sat on the bed next to Saint's luggage. "Don't do this. I beg of you."

"What exactly do you think I am doing?" Saint watched Fergus unsnap the bracer on his left arm to readjust the fitting. It was an unconscious habit Fergus had when upset or agitated, and as far as Saint knew, it was his brother's only "tell."

"I am not exactly sure," Fergus answered once he had finished fidgeting. "But I do know somehow Bridget LeCœur is involved, and if she is involved, then no good can come of this."

"Bridget has been dead for nearly seventy years."

"Exactly. Which is why you should let this thing be."

"There isn't a thing to let be."

"Do you think me a fool? You think I don't know why you were so damned determined to travel to the Underworld?"

Saint stared straight into Fergus's flame-colored eyes. "I went to

26

bring the guardian back. Nothing more, nothing less."

Fergus became still. "The guardian may have taken you to the Underworld, but you can't deny Bridget somehow fit into your plans."

Saint slammed his satchel shut and walked across the room to stare out the window. Whether Fergus believed him or not, Bridget had not been at the forefront of Saint's decision in going to the Underworld. He would be lying if he denied thinking about her once he had gotten there, but bartering for a single soul had been difficult enough. There was no way he would try for two.

The journey to the Underworld had taken a toll on him greater than he allowed anyone to know. He told no one the details of his conversations with Hel or that, since his return, a pressure lay about his heart, and no matter what he tried, the pain refused to go away.

Nor had he said anything about how with every twinge of pain, he could still feel the Queen's icy touch upon his skin. These problems, this pain, belonged solely to Saint, and he would not burden any of his family with them.

No. The price to bring CJ back was already too high. There was no way he could have made a deal for another soul, not even for Bridget.

Fergus's face seemed to be the same unwavering mask he always wore. But Saint noticed the minute changes in the hard-set lines of his eyes.

"Do you forget that woman almost destroyed you when she was alive?" Fergus questioned.

"I forget nothing," Saint said. "I remember all too well what she was capable of...and yet...."

"And yet you still love her."

Saint looked out the window. He watched as a single, brown oak leaf wafted its way to the ground. He thought how much alike he and the leaf were, both drifting aimlessly, both alone. "I can neither confirm nor deny your statement. In truth, I am unsure of my feelings," Saint answered.

"Then, prithee, brother, why must it be New Orleans? If a vacation is what you seek, then go to New York. You could spend a week or so touring the museums.

"In fact, we could all go. Mika and CJ might like some time in the city. There is always Broadway or your favorite, the Metropolitan Opera. We could get Mika to see what is being performed. I'm sure there is something playing that you would enjoy seeing."

Saint was touched by Fergus's suggestion. If only it were that easy. Although his brother could probably spend hours in the armor collection of the Metropolitan Museum, Saint could not see Fergus taking in a Broadway show.

"And who would we leave in charge of Haven?" Saint asked. "Ghost, perhaps?"

"Bah!" Fergus exhaled his answer.

"And therein lays the reason we cannot all go."

"But...."

"No, Fergus. It must be New Orleans, and," Saint held up his hand, "I must go alone. I will keep our link open so you can reach me if need be."

"Your mind is made up then?" Fergus asked.

"It is."

"Then so be it," Fergus said, extending his arm to his brother. "May the goddess keep you safe in your journeys, bràthair," he added.

Saint grasped his brother's forearm in the way old warriors had done for centuries. "And also you, my brother."

Releasing his grasp, Fergus walked stiffly to the door. Saint wanted to say something to him, something that would alleviate the concerns he could feel rolling about Fergus's head.

"Fergus," Saint called to him.

"Yes?"

"Promise me one thing."

"For you, my brother, anything," Fergus said.

"Don't push Ghost away."

Again, Fergus adjusted his bracers. "I don't know what you are talking about."

Saint smiled softly. "Now who is playing the fool? I see what you are doing, and now isn't the time for Ghost...."

"Ghost is a bloody pain!" Fergus snapped.

"Only because you allow him to be."

"Hmpf." Fergus grunted and crossed his arms over his chest.

"You know me to be correct, but that is a conversation for another day. Simply promise me you will not allow him to leave Haven so long as I am gone."

"Ghost is a grown wolf, Saint. If he wishes to leave...."

"Promise," Saint pressed.

"Fine," Fergus groaned. "I promise. Only don't take too long on your quest, for if he can't leave, and he does not curb that tongue of his, then I may very well kill him before your return." With that, Fergus slammed the door and left.

There were times Saint wished he could beat some sense into his brother's thick head. Ghost was and would always be their annoying little brother. Fergus had allowed him to be so, and in some ways, Saint thought Fergus liked it that way.

Today went beyond anything Saint had seen before. It was as if Fergus was purposefully pushing Ghost from the pack. Saint stopped to examine his thoughts. *Was it possible? What reason could Fergus possibly have to push Ghost away?*

"Preposterous," Saint mumbled. There could be no possible reason for such a thing. Yet, from the way things appeared, that was exactly what Fergus was doing, but why?

If there was ever a time Ghost needed the shelter of Haven and the protection of his pack, it was now. Ghost's twin, Ævar, was set on killing him. It was revenge born from a childhood rivalry. So now was definitely not the time to allow Ghost to leave.

Shaking his head to clear his thoughts, Saint pulled open the top drawer of his desk. He removed a wallet and passport and stopped to check that both were in order. Seldom did he need cash or to prove his identity, but he never knew when he would need either. Especially since he had no idea how long his trip would take. He had to be prepared for anything.

Saint concentrated on the space between the foot of his bed and the statue of Freyja. In his mind, he pictured the small, enclosed courtyard of Jean Lafitte National Park. It would be the perfect place for him to transport into New Orleans. Seldom were there more than two or three people roaming within the old stone buildings, and even if someone did see him appear, they would pretend they didn't. Saint concentrated more intently. He imagined the old cobblestone courtyard and close quarters toward the back wall.

Slowly the molecules of air in his room began to swirl and shift, as the space between the two places began to merge, creating a wormhole. Grabbing his gear from the foot of his bed, Saint stepped into the vortex and, with a wave of his hand, vanished.

CHAPTER 4

Blinding rage ignited behind the wintry stare of Ævar Thorolfur as he glared across the large mahogany desk at his friend and mentor, Lucas Darkwater. White hot energy danced along his skin, beckoning him to transition into his animal form. As an Arctic wolf, Ævar could easily leap across his desk and rip out Lucas's throat with his teeth. He could almost taste Lucas's warm blood upon his tongue and feel the satisfying snap as cartilage and bone gave way beneath his powerful jaws. The image only served to whet his appetite for retaliation.

Closing his eyes, Ævar tilted back his head and twisted his neck first one way then another, willing his lungs to take a deep, calming breath. To battle the ancient Viking sitting across from him would not be the best of ideas. He had seen Lucas drive a four-foot-long sword hilt-deep into the earth. With that in mind, Ævar forced his ire under control. No need to do anything rash.

For Ævar to say he felt betrayed would be an understatement. Lucas was the reason Mika, Saint, and CJ had become trapped in the Underworld. All Lucas had to do was leave them there as promised. Two members of Delta Pack and the new guardian, all within Ævar's grasp, and Lucas let them go. How hard could it have been?

His and Lucas's original plan had been so perfect. He had no idea how the spell Lucas had given him had actually worked or how he had enticed the Queen of the Underworld to hold CJ's soul. Lucas's magic was ancient and powerful, and long ago Ævar realized not to question it.

When Lucas appeared with the small vial of murky, green liquid, he had no idea what it was for. Lucas called the liquid Hel's kiss. The purpose, he explained, was to allow the drinker to steal a person's *hame* or soul. All it would take was one kiss on the lips, and the victim's soul would be transferred to the one bestowing the kiss. Ævar expressed concern about getting close enough to kiss CJ. Of course, Lucas had an answer for that also. "Not a problem," Lucas said. "The new guardian knows your brother, but not well enough to know his mannerisms. Since you and Ghost are identical twins, getting close should not be difficult.'

As usual, Lucas was correct. Ævar had been able to get close to CJ and kiss her while his brother and Mika Elkhart watched. A cruel smile curled Ævar's lips at the thought of Lucas's plan. There was no way the guardian's soul would ever be returned. Once Saint led the charge into the Underworld, there was little left to do except wait. Fergus would be so distraught at the loss of his pack-mates, he would make an error in judgment and lose his head.

That would leave Ghost with no one to protect him. Then Ævar would have no interruptions in assuring his brother's demise. With everyone gone, control of Haven and the world of shape shifters would fall to him and Lucas, of course.

"How could you let them go?" Ævar asked, leveling his ice-blue stare on Lucas. "We had all of them." He banged his fist against his desk. "How could you just let them walk away like that?"

Lucas's deep green eyes twinkled in amusement at Ævar's irritation. His flame-colored hair was tied elegantly at the nape of his neck, and as with all shape shifters, Lucas didn't appear to be more than thirty-five or forty.

His long legs stretched before him, Lucas sat motionless across from Ævar. "It was not I, old friend. The goddess obviously had her own ideas where the monk was concerned," Lucas answered, his voice as well manicured as the rest of him. "Remember, patience in all things will yield greater results," Lucas said, flicking an imaginary piece of lint from his expertly tailored trousers. "You must look at the larger picture."

"I thought I had been," Ævar huffed.

"Perhaps. But what you fail to see is the picture has changed. We must now adjust our focus. That is all." Lucas rose to his feet. "You could kill every member of the Delta Pack, including your brother. You could even kill the newly appointed guardian, but what would that really get you?" Lucas asked.

"It gets *us* control of Haven," Ævar answered.

Lucas moved to the large bank of windows that overlooked the water below. "Think about it, Ævar. Does ridding our lives of Delta Pack and the guardian really give you what you want?"

Ævar looked up at the man towering above him. "What are you saying?"

"A headless army runs away when the enemy is bearing down upon them."

"I am in no mood for your games today, Lucas," Ævar answered, crossing his arms over his chest.

Normally, he would play Lucas's game, but not today. For once, Ævar could truthfully say his brain hurt. "For the love of Thor, would you please just say what you mean?"

Lucas visibly tensed at Ævar's statement. In all the years he had known Lucas, Ævar never understood his friend's consternation at the invocation of Odin, or any of the gods, for that matter. From birth, shape shifters were taught the story of how they were created by the Sisters of All Life and Knowledge as a gift for the goddess Freyja. They were taught to revere and honor the Norse gods, just as Christians were taught to revere Christ or the Buddhists were taught to honor Buddha. Still, Lucas's irritation was always apparent.

"Very well," Lucas acquiesced. "I am saying that the only way to truly bring an end to Delta Pack and the guardians is to bring down Theriontrope. Not the other way around."

Ævar could only stare at his friend in disbelief as Lucas's comments battled for understanding in his head. "Grey?" Ævar chuckled. "You want to kill Michael Grey? You can't be serious!"

Lucas smiled wryly. "Michael Grey *is* Theriontrope. Think about it, Ævar. Through the centuries, what has been the one constant where Haven and the guardians are concerned? The name may have changed, but the man is the same."

"That's impossible," Ævar argued. "That would mean that Grey was...was...."

"Immortal?" Lucas broke in. "Do you not remember the old teachings? The stories of Freyja sending her emissary to watch over shape shifters and the guardians?"

"Kenna told me those stories years ago. I assumed they were merely myth. An old wolf's tale."

"Your history, *our* history," Lucas corrected, "is the stuff of legend and wolf's tales, as you call them."

"You actually want me to believe that Grey is, what? Descended from the gods?"

"Not descended from, but sent from. He is Freyja's personal servant."

If what Lucas said was true, if Michael Grey was, in fact, the personal servant of the goddess... No. It was impossible.

Ævar's mother had told him the stories of the warrior goddess, and how all the sisters needed to create shifters was three drops of her blood. Three drops. One for every order of shifter: canine, cat, and bear. The story even told that Freyja wept in fear for the safety of her newly created children. From those tears, the guardians were created.

Still, Freyja was not satisfied, so to watch over them all, she sent Valborg, her most trusted servant.

Could Michael Grey be that servant? After all, he had been at the helm of the Theriontrope Foundation since before Ævar was even born, and that was more than one hundred years ago. If what Lucas said was true and if Grey was linked to Freyja, then to kill him would be a slap in the face of the goddess. It was nothing short of blasphemous. Ævar moved a few paces from Lucas, just in case a stray lightning bolt zinged his direction.

"Obviously, this proposition is too challenging for you at the moment," Lucas said with an elegant wave of his hand, causing the space he touched to swirl and shift, transforming into an open doorway between Ævar's office and wherever Lucas wished to go. "Sever the head, Ævar," Lucas said, as he stepped through the portal, "and the rest, as they say, will take care of itself."

Ævar stared dumbstruck at the spot his friend had vacated. Was Lucas right? Did Michael Grey hold the key to the downfall of Theriontrope? If so, how would one go about killing an immortal, especially one that was linked to Freyja?

Over the years, Lucas had come up with some pretty daft ideas, but this was complete lunacy even for him. Ævar shook his head violently. He would never even consider such a thing. Plus he knew from experience that particular philosophy didn't always work.

Once before, Ævar tried to destroy Delta Pack by capturing their leader. Even now, Ævar felt a bit of pride at being able to hold Fergus prisoner. Ævar had been sure that with the head of Delta Pack out of the picture, the elite force would crumble. Who else would be able to lead the famed Theriontrope enforcers?

Certainly not Mika. He was not the Alpha type.

There was the other Wolfe brother, Saint, but as far as Ævar knew, Saint would rather spend time with his nose in a book than leading the pack.

That left Ævar's twin Ægir, or Ghost, as he had been renamed. Ghost may have been first born, but Ævar knew himself to be the stronger of the two. In the words of the witch, "Would the sun allow the moon to outshine him?" Moreover, there was no way Michael Grey would allow an egocentric womanizer such as Ghost to take over the pack. Not that it mattered, since without Fergus to protect him, Ghost didn't stand a chance.

Ævar thought back to Lucas's suggestion. *Sever the head....* As much as it pained Ævar to disagree with his old friend and mentor, destroying Michael Grey was not the best way to bring the demise of the Delta Pack, but what was?

He had already tried to destroy Fergus. Thanks to a traitor in his midst, that didn't turn out the way he had planned. Mika and Saint were also within his grasp, but for reasons he would never understand, the goddess Hel allowed them to live.

Lucas was going about this whole thing wrong. He was not killing a snake. He was taking down a pack. And how does one take down a pack? The weakest among them must be culled out, which means he must, once again, try to end the life of his twin. *Ghost must die.*

Ævar hadn't forgotten his last attempt on Ghost's life. He had left nothing to chance, or so he thought. Who knew Charles Stone had a daughter who, like her father, was a guardian, but there was another way. A way his brother wouldn't see coming. He had toyed for quite a while with the idea of hiring a professional, and he had the perfect one in mind.

A wicked light flashed in his cold, blue eyes. Checking his Lange & Sohnë pocket watch for the time, he made a brief calculation. If he was correct, he should be able to get in and get out of the hospital without anyone being the wiser. Ævar created a circular pattern in the space beside him. The molecules shifted and swirled, opening a wormhole beside him, and without a second thought, he stepped inside.

CHAPTER 5

"You can't let him go," Fergus overheard CJ say, as he neared the kitchen. He could tell by the gentle tone of her voice, Mika had returned from his earlier errand. Over the past few months, Fergus had observed how the tone of CJ's voice seemed to change when she spoke with her mate, as opposed to the others in the pack. It was a peculiar aberration, but one he found endearing

Fergus noted how day by day, CJ had grown more and more comfortable with Mika, and the thought of their being true-mates. Although he had no personal experience to draw from, Fergus could at least be thankful that, for one of his brothers, both love and family were a possibility.

Secretly he longed for a woman to look at him in such a way.

Was love supposed to be like that? Fergus's heart ached in the knowledge he would never find such joy. The gods didn't smile on one such as he, but, if they did, there was little doubt in his mind the woman he would choose.

How many nights had his dreams been filled by the girl with the haunting blue eyes? *Ísold.* Her name whispered across his mind and into his soul. It had been years since he last saw her, his beautiful specter in the night.

      Try as he might, Fergus was unable to stop her image from floating through his memory, and the memory of how he came to meet her.

      He should have listened to his gut that night. Everything within him yelled not to follow the tiger into the underground tunnels. He could hear Saint's voice asking him to wait for backup, but as the Christian Bible said, "Pride goeth before destruction, and an haughty spirit before a fall."

      Full of his own ego, Fergus charged into the darkened passageways without thought of his own safety. He had battled all manner of shifter over the years. How hard could it be to subdue a tiger? All he had to do was get close enough to hit her with a tranquillizer dart, radio Therion Control, and wait for transport.

      He tracked the animal through the labyrinth of tunnels that twisted beneath the city. Engulfed in darkness and shadow, his line of sight was compromised, giving the tiger the advantage. He called upon his wolf senses, picking up the sound of padded paws whispering against concrete and stone, but there was little time for him to react.

      Within seconds, the tiger was on him. Her roar, a deafening battle cry, reverberated off the arched walls. Pain shot through his shoulder as her incisors pierced muscle and sinew. Kicking with all his might, Fergus made contact with what he assumed was the animal's midsection.

      A light flashed, blinding him completely. Deep, stinging heat radiated from his upper thigh, sweeping throughout his body. The acrid taste of bile rose in the back of his throat, as he realized it was he that had been tranquilized.

      He awoke in chains with no memory of how he had gotten there. His entire body ached from lying on the icy floor. Dim lights hung overhead, casting minimal light about the room. His body weak from exhaustion and dehydration, it took all his strength to stand.

His only thought throughout his continual torture and interrogation was the protection of his pack. Hiding his thoughts from his brothers, he refused to allow them any knowledge of burning pain raging through his body. There was also the possibility Delta Pack would be walking into a trap. The only option Fergus had, was to shut down the common telepathic link shared between he and the others, but in doing so, he prohibited his pack from finding him.

Still, he had known there was no way Saint would give up on him. It would only be a matter of time until he was rescued, so he waited and prayed to the goddess for Theriontrope to find him before he went mad. Had it not been for the girl with the sapphire eyes, he would have.

Often Fergus wondered what had gone through Ísold's mind the first time she saw him. She should have feared what she saw. Most females would have run at the first sight of him.

Chains intertwined with silver barbs wound about Fergus's wrist and forearms, forcing him to stand on tiptoes. With every twist of his arms or slouch of his posture, the barbs tore deeper and deeper into his flesh. Blood poured down his shoulders and back where a silver-tipped cat o' nine tails had ripped the flesh from his body. His hair lay in thick, black mats where the blood had dried between his beatings.

Half out of his mind from pain and drugs, his thoughts jumped from one place to another like a squirrel leaping from branch to branch. There was no sense of day or night, only unrelenting pain and confusion.

Oh, how he begged for Darkness, the taker of all life, to come and take him. Instead, the Fates decided to send him salvation wrapped in a vision of indigo and gold.

He felt Ísold's presence the moment she appeared in his room. Energy, warm, soft, and feminine curled about him, comforting him unlike anything he had felt before or since. A gift from the gods, she walked out of thin air and into his prison cell. And for only the second time in his life, Fergus thought angels possibly existed.

From beneath his dark auburn lashes, Fergus saw the girl as she stepped into view. The breath stilled in his lungs as she drew nearer. Hair the color of coal framed her soft, round face, partially concealing the most memorable eyes any man would wish to get lost in. She was warmth and grace and beauty, and she watched him for what seemed an eternity.

She should have been repulsed by him as he hung there. Instead, she seemed mesmerized at the sight of him. Somehow, Ísold had the ability to look past the pitiful creature before her, to strip away all the blood, pain, and darkness that filled him to find the man he could be. The man he wanted to be. Even now, the memory of her compassion was enough to bring him to his knees.

It was many years later, and Fergus still didn't know who his captor had been or what he had wanted. His interrogation lasted for days at a time before receiving any rest. The questions were always the same and never made sense. Then again, did anything ever make sense to a person who was being tortured? Sometimes, in the stillness of the night, he could still feel his own blood as it poured down his arms, warm and wet, as hooks bit deeper and deeper into his flesh.

Enough! Fergus commanded his thoughts to cease. He was becoming as bad as Saint about woolgathering. Ísold belonged to another time and another place, and unlike his brother, Fergus would do well to remember such.

Fergus felt three sets of eyes on him as he entered the kitchen. Mika leaned his hips casually against the counter nearest the kitchen sink, pretending to oversee CJ as she tended to Ghost's wounds.

Fighting the urge to groan, Fergus contemplated what he should do with the youngest of his pack. Ghost had been under his care and tutelage

41

since the day Fergus rescued him from Iceland and brought him to live at Haven. No matter how irritating or exasperating his pupil had been, Fergus had never laid a hand on Ghost until recently. The fact he had done so twice within the past few month pained him more than he would care to admit.

Fergus grimaced at the sight of the large purple bruises along Ghost's jawline. He would never forgive himself for those, but, as usual, Ghost had the most damnable way of saying the wrong thing at the wrong time. Sometimes Fergus thought Ghost did it on purpose.

A twinge of guilt struck Fergus, and he fought the urge to look away. Shifting his attention to CJ, Fergus watched as she hovered near her patient. Cotton pad in hand, she cleaned the minor cuts and scrapes Ghost had sustained in the fight. Ghost hissed loudly and jerked his face away when she touched him.

"Suck it up, wolf!" she snapped. "You two tried to break each other apart, and you're going to whine over a little antiseptic?"

"I'm not whining."

"Of course not," CJ said, looking carefully over Ghost's wounds. "Big baby," she muttered.

Fergus raised an eyebrow at her tone. It was nice to have a female living at Haven again. The last female to do so was CJ's grandmother, and that had been more than fifty years prior.

In the beginning, Fergus worried the adjustment of living with four shifters might be too difficult for CJ, but after the way she handled Ghost, he realized she fit in perfectly. He was sure no woman had ever spoken to the youngest of his pack in such a way. CJ just might be the thing they all needed.

"What are you mad at me for?" Ghost protested. "I didn't do anything."

CJ placed her hands on her hips. "I'm not getting into this with you, but you would think after one hundred years, or however long you've been alive, you would learn when to keep your mouth shut."

"You mean my incredibly kissable mouth, don't you?" Ghost tried to give her one of his ain't-I-adorable smiles but ended up wincing in pain from the split in his lip.

CJ rolled her eyes. "Seriously, you guys," she said, putting away the first aid kit. "You can't let Saint go. It just feels wrong."

"Saint is ancient among us, Wicahpi," Mika said, using his pet name for her. "He can care for himself."

"Mika is right," Fergus added. "Besides, I am afraid it is too late. He has already left us."

CJ pulled Ghost's face closer for one final inspection. "What do you mean 'already left us'?"

"He left moments ago and there was little I could do to stop him," Fergus stated.

"He just popped out? Right like that? No goodbye? Nothing?" Ghost asked. Fergus heard the disappointment and anger in Ghost's voice, but what was he to do? Saint was almost as old as Fergus. After all these years, surely Saint knew how to handle himself. At least, that was what Fergus had to keep telling himself.

"But New Orleans?" Ghost asked. "What about New York? He loves the Metropolitan Museum. You know how nostalgic he gets in the Hall of Reliquaries."

Fergus narrowed his gaze at Ghost. Could Ghost have somehow picked up on his and Saint's earlier conversation? He had never admitted to such ability before, but still.... Fergus shrugged. "I suggested that. However, he would have none of it."

"What is wrong with New Orleans?" CJ asked. "I love that place."

"Let us suffice it to say, Saint has history there, and it isn't necessarily a happy one," Fergus answered. "He believes he needs time to think through a few things. I'm sure he will contact us if need be."

Fergus rummaged through the refrigerator. He wasn't actually hungry. He simply needed something to keep his mind from thinking of his brother, among other things.

Plus, he wasn't sure who he was trying to convince more of Saint's self-sufficiency, himself or the others. *Saint can take care of himself.* "Besides, it isn't possible for him to run into certain individuals."

At his words, the room became silent and still. Two things Fergus learned not to trust when his back was turned. It could only mean one thing. There was a conversation going on that he was not privy to.

Not all shape shifters had the ability to use telepathy; however, all four members of Delta Pack did. The pack seemed to share not only a common link, but also links from each individual to another. It was a skill that came in handy in their line of work.

Without even trying, he was able to hear Ghost's thoughts. Something Fergus attributed to the blood transfusion he gave Ghost as a child. Most of the time, his connection to Ghost's thoughts annoyed Fergus greatly. Then again, it could also be quite useful. He wasn't proud of the fact he could eavesdrop on conversations...but desperate times and all.

Fergus closed his eyes, tuning his thoughts into those of Ghost.

You said you were going to tell him about you-know-what, he heard Ghost say.

And if we are wrong? Mika asked.

And if we're not? Ghost asked.

I see no need in worrying Fergus unnecessarily.

Fergus heard enough. It wasn't in his brothers' character to keep information from him. It was bad enough to discover Mika's secrecy over the guardian. The subject was still a source of irritation for Fergus. It was of little consequence Mika's deception was for a good cause. However, Fergus wouldn't tolerate any further subterfuge from his family. As pack leader, he needed to know when one of its members was in trouble. The fact that Saint was his baby brother did little to help the situation.

"What?" Fergus said, as he slammed the refrigerator door, startling a yelp from CJ. "What are you two not telling me?" His disapproving gaze shot from one man to the other. Something in their manner reminded Fergus of when the men were boys and he caught them behind the stables playing betting games with the stable hands.

At the time, Mika and Ghost were about thirteen and the perfect age for mischief. Fergus watched from a distance as Mika stood with his back to the group. Ghost would then ask the workers to choose a card from the deck and show it to everyone in the group, including Ghost. Then, using their private connection, Ghost would tell Mika which card the guy had chosen, and magically, Mika would guess the stable-hand's card.

By the time Fergus interceded, the pair had swindled the men out of close to a week's pay each. To punish them, Mika and Ghost were made to take over livery duties for that week. The stable hands were given a week off with double their pay. Fergus was still unsure who thought up the scheme, but he would have put his own money on Ghost.

"Tell him," Ghost finally said.

"Very well." Mika moved protectively toward CJ, placing his body between her and Fergus. "When Ghost and I landed in Florida, there was another shifter at the terminal," Mika said, as he snaked his arm around CJ's waist.

"Another of our kind being there should not come as a surprise considering the terminal is owned by Theriontrope," Fergus reasoned.

Mika nodded. "I had the same thought at first. The night was dark and rainy when we landed, and I assumed it was the electricity in the air making me uneasy. Then I caught a glimpse of a woman watching us. When she realized I had seen her, she took off running. We pursued, but before we could get to her, she disappeared inside a wormhole."

Uneasiness settled in the pit of Fergus gut. "A female?" he asked, wary of the answer.

"Try Bridget," Ghost blurted.

Fergus stiffened. *Impossible.* Bridget died in an explosion sometime during World War II. At least, that was what Michael Grey had told him. Surely Grey would not have lied about something so serious. Then again, he had lied about CJ, and once again, Fergus's faith in his employer faltered.

"Are you positive?" Fergus clenched his jaw.

"No. I can't be positive. That is why I thought it best not to worry you," Mika answered. "But if it was not her, then this woman could have to be her twin."

"Oh, for Thor's sake, Mika," Ghost said. "The woman waved at us. You know it was her."

Fergus took in a deep breath and released it slowly. Was it possible? Could Bridget still be alive and, if so, was that the reason for Saint's return to New Orleans? Surely his brother would not be so foolish as to go chasing after her.

"Is there anything else you two have been keeping from me?" Fergus challenged.

"No, my brother," Mika answered. "We only wished not to alarm you."

"I fear that sentiment comes too late. Consider me alarmed," Fergus said striding across the room.

"I'm coming too," Ghost announced and jumped to his feet.

"No," Fergus commanded. A loud "oof" sounded from behind

him, as Ghost charged into Fergus's back. "You don't even know where I am going."

"You're going after Saint, aren't you?"

"Actually, no," Fergus said. "I have a call to make."

"Then you're going after Saint?"

Fergus stopped and counted to ten. "It is possible, but much hinges on Grey's answers." He held up his hand for Ghost's silence. "Even if I do follow Saint, you cannot go."

"Come on, Fergus. You can't keep holding a grudge," Ghost argued.

The larger man looked down at his protégé. "Actually I can." Fergus watched the anger and frustration spark behind Ghost's pale blue eyes. "However, this has nothing to do with any grudge." Fergus laid a hand on the smaller man's shoulder. "Saint made me promise I would not allow you to leave Haven while he was away."

"Why?"

"That I don't know. He simply told me it would be for the best."

"But Mika—what do you think?" Ghost asked. "Do you think I should be held prisoner here?"

Mika crossed his arms over his chest. "Haven is your home, not a prison."

"So you agree with Saint?" Ghost asked Mika again, completely ignoring Fergus.

"Ours isn't to question Saint's wisdom, brother," Mika said. "He hears what even I can't. If he believes you should remain at Haven, then you must heed his warning."

Ghost seemed to mull over Mika's words carefully. "Fine," he shrugged. "If Saint wants me here, then here is where I'll be."

"A wise decision. I will let you know what Grey has to say," Fergus said and strode from the room.

Although Mika and CJ were mere feet away, Ghost felt increasingly more uncomfortable and alone. Seeing his friend so happy caused him to wonder if he would ever lucky be enough to find a woman who looked at him the way CJ looked at Mika.

It wasn't as if Ghost lacked for the company of women. He learned at a very young age that most women—correction—all women, found him attractive. Could he help it if his striking Nordic looks were irresistible to the opposite sex?

His attractiveness was his greatest asset and his biggest curse. He would not deny that fact nor feel guilty about it. That was simply how things were.

In fact, he could go down to Mad Mooney's tonight and hook up with any one of the women there. Was that truly what he wanted? A hookup?

Emptiness crept its way back into Ghost's heart. He was unsure when the restlessness set in. He hated the feeling, but it was one he had grown accustomed to. No matter how many conquests he made, none of them seemed capable of easing his loneness.

Only once in his adult life could he remember finding an inner peace. That was the day Ariel had touched him. The smallest of brushes from her hand and his world became free of any discomfort.

Gooseflesh erupted down his back at the memory of her fingers buried deep in his fur. Maybe one day, he would see sweet Ariel with her luscious curves and pouty, kissable lips. Maybe one day, he would find a woman who would see him as the answer to all her dreams not just sexual ones. Who was he kidding? Fergus would develop a sense of humor before that day ever came.

Most wolves and coyotes may mate for life, but not Ghost. He was the proverbial lone wolf. For him, a wife and family were not in the picture. He may be the one all the women wanted to take to bed, but he wasn't the one they wanted to take home to Momma.

Yep. The more Ghost thought about it, the better a night at Mad Mooney's looked. It had been a couple of weeks since he had seen Collette. She usually worked the bar on the weekends and was always up for a good time, and that was exactly what Ghost needed at the moment, a little fun to get his mind off things.

Sure, Saint may have warned for him not to leave Haven. Then again, that could have been Fergus being Fergus. Mooney's was close to home, and if he really got in trouble, Mika was only a shout away on the old telepathic grapevine.

"Hey, CJ," Ghost called from the doorway.

"Yes?"

"Do you think your friend Ariel will be coming to visit anytime soon?"

CJ's brows knitted together as she thought over his question. "No. Not that I know of. Why?"

"Oh, no reason. Just a question," he murmured and walked away.

"What was that about?" CJ turned in Mika's arms to face him. The love in his honey-colored eyes still sent shivers through her body. She had no idea what she had done to deserve a man such as him, but she thanked every god she could think of that she had.

"Obviously, there is something about your friend he found appealing," Mika said, brushing his cheek against hers.

"Really? You think so?"

Mika pulled her closer. "You sound surprised, Wicahpi."

"Maybe a bit."

"Is there a reason Ghost should not find her company enjoyable?"

Mika murmured and kissed along the curve of CJ's neck to her collar bone.

"I may not know Ghost well, but Ariel just doesn't seem his type," she said.

"I don't know. I think she's exactly Ghost's type. She is breathing, isn't she?"

"That is terrible," she said, trying not to give in to the feel of Mika's hot breath on her skin. She loved the way little bits of electricity seemed to dance in the wake of his touch upon her body or the way his waist-length hair fell in a silken curtain upon her skin as he lay above her.

CJ's pulse quickened as thoughts of their lovemaking played in her mind. "If you don't stop, you are going to embarrass yourself," she whispered breathlessly.

I am not the one having thoughts of us in our bed. That is you, Mika said, using their private link.

Stay out of my head, Elkhart, she teased and was rewarded with his dark laughter inside her mind.

Maybe you should send for your friend, Mika said, trailing hot kisses along her jawline to take her lips with his. His mouth was insistent and inviting, and CJ gave herself willingly to him. There was no place on earth she would rather be than where she was at this moment.

Did you hear me, Little Star?

Yes, CJ sighed.

So you will call your friend?

Mmm hmm, she answered, not really listening to what he said. "Wait, what?" she asked, pushing against the solid wall of his chest. "Call Ariel? Why?"

"I assumed you would want your friends here to help you," Mika said.

"Help me with what?" CJ asked, pulling back so she could see him more clearly.

"Our wedding, of course."

"Wedding? Excuse me, but I don't remember your asking me."

Mika gazed lovingly down at her. "You are my mate. There is no question."

"That's a rather smug attitude, don't you think?" CJ teased.

Mika smiled at her as he took her hands in his and placed them against his chest. CJ could feel the steady rhythm of his heart as it beat in time to her own. There was no question in her heart or mind that Mika was her mate. She had known it the first moment their eyes met at her clinic back in Florida. They were meant to be.

"Do you not wish for a wedding?" Mika asked.

"It's not necessary. I am yours and you are mine. I don't need a piece of paper to tell me what I already know."

"Am I to assume you don't want this?" Mika asked as he looked down at CJ's hand.

CJ followed Mika's gaze to her left hand and the ring that rested on her finger. Her mate was truly magic. She had no idea how he placed the ring on her finger without her notice, nor did she care. Tears welled in her eyes as she looked at the dark green stone that seemed to change to red before her eyes.

"Mika, it's...it's beautiful."

"It's Alexandrite to match the green of your eyes. However, if you truly feel we don't need a wedding, I can take it back," he remarked and reached for the ring.

CJ jerked her hand from his. "Don't you dare!" She turned her hand first one way then the other to watch it change colors. She had never been the type of woman to ooh and ah over jewelry. She had no idea of carats or cut. Heck, the only reason her ears were even pierced was because her mother had it done when she was an infant. Still, she stared transfixed at the square-cut stone of green set in silver. "I love it," she whispered, fighting back tears of joy. "Almost as much as I love you."

CHAPTER 6

More than fifty years had passed since Saint walked the old stone streets around Jackson Square. So much had changed, and yet, even with Hurricane Katrina, much had stayed the same. "And that," he spoke to himself, "is the beauty of New Orleans."

Once upon a time, Saint thought to call the Crescent City his home. He believed New Orleans would be the place where he grew old. He would leave Delta Pack. Marry. Have children and raise them on an oak-lined plantation just outside the city. His new pack would learn to love the wonderful melding of cultures that were the soul of the city. However, that was not the will of the goddess.

Taking in a deep breath, Saint adjusted the grip on his satchel and began to stroll down Decatur Street toward Toulouse. Pausing, he looked over his shoulder, checking the second story windows of the shops he passed.

No matter how hard he tried, Saint couldn't shake the feeling Bridget was still with him, watching from above, and yet, even he would have sworn he had seen her in Florida only a few months ago.

When CJ was attacked by Ævar, Saint was summoned to her aid. After a cursory exam, he decided the best way to help CJ was to take her back to Haven. It wasn't until he stepped into the wormhole that he happened to glance to the large branches of an oak tree that snaked above his head. There, blended amongst the leaves and Spanish moss, stood a woman. She had a stillness only a shifter could possess.

Saint searched the leaves quickly until her found her face. He looked deep into the woman's eyes. It may have been years since he looked into those ebony eyes, but as sure as he breathed, Saint knew those eyes belonged to Bridget LeCœur.

It was nice to think that even in death, Bridget cared enough for him that she should choose to spend her eternity watching over him. Too bad his summation was mere folly. Bridget never loved anyone enough to be compelled to watch over them from the afterlife, not even Saint.

He tried to ignore what he saw, thinking her merely his imagination. He seemed to be able to do that from time to time, see people or spirits others could not. He knew the difference between real and imaginary, and the woman he had seen was definitely real.

So where did that leave him? Saint had no idea. He only knew the voice of the Universe had led him back to New Orleans. Back to where it all began and ended.

Continuing along Toulouse to Bourbon, he paused in front of what is now the Inn on Bourbon. Melancholy overtook him at the memory of the old French Opera House that once stood there. He had spent many nights there. Opening night of the opera season was the highlight of Creole society. The crème de la crème were always in attendance.

It was on such a night he was introduced to Bridget, during the intermission of Les Huguenot. Saint could not say he fell in love with her at first sight. His feelings were not that easily given.

Saint could still hear the swishing of silk and petticoats as the women glided down the staircase. The light scent of rose or lilac wafted with each flutter of their fans.

How he missed the days when people dressed to be received in public. In his opinion, the worst thing to ever happen to fashion was when women began wearing trousers in public. It was an antiquated view, but then again, so was he.

Phantoms from a bygone era, he lamented inwardly and moved on.

"I was a fool," Saint mumbled with a shake of his head. He should have known better than to think a woman like Bridget would fall for him. Saint considered himself to be a simple man. He needed little more in life than the necessities. If Abraham Maslow and his hierarchy of needs were to be believed, then Saint would not be considered much evolved. He snorted in derision. Of course he was evolved. Was there ever any question?

Bridget was, for lack of a better term, spoiled. Being the only daughter, she was doted on by her father. Whatever Bridget wanted, she got. It mattered little who or what was damaged in the process.

Saint paused again in his thoughts. Absently, he looked at the weathered sign above his head. "My Spicy Cauldron, Curious Goods and Books," he read aloud. *What an odd name. Rather old world. No one used the phrase Curious Goods anymore, did they?*

The hair along Saint's forearms prickled as a gust of wind billowed down the street. Bright gold and magenta leaves swirled around Saint's legs and body, engulfing him in a tornado of color. This was not simply a random act of nature. The animal inside him sensed it. There was an unnatural movement to the leaves. It was if they moved in concert, not one changed place or dropped to the ground.

He sucked in his breath as sharp pain pricked the back of his hand. Then, as quickly as the whirlwind came, it moved down the sidewalk and disappeared around the corner. Saint studied the droplets of blood forming on the back of his hand. Removing the white handkerchief from the inside breast pocket of his coat, he wiped the blood away and thought little more of it.

Saint knew this part of the city well, especially this particular storefront. Years ago it had been an apothecary shop. The owner, Mr. Fortis Beesinger, became a dear friend to both Saint and Fergus. From time to time, Saint would find his way there for a game of chess or spirited debate on the politics of President Grant.

Fortis was an ally to all shape shifters and supporter of the Theriontrope Foundation. He was also known as a student of Voodoo and became the source for many medicinal herbs Saint might be in need of.

Sadness settled over Saint at the thought of yet another friend lost to time. With each passing year, the number was becoming too great to count. He wondered what would become of CJ and Mika, since she was human and Mika was not. True, guardians did possess a longer life span than most humans. Still, they were not immortal or invincible. Illness and death would come to guardians the same as any other human.

Eventually the couple would have to deal with the difference in their life spans. Maybe once he returned home, Saint would check the old scrolls. It was possible something was there that could aid them in some way, but, that was a problem for another day. Thank the goddess a human mate was one problem he didn't have to deal with. At least Bridget had been a shape shifter, even if she was a sociopath whose father used humans as cattle. Saint shuddered at the thought.

Glancing again to the sign, he noted the old-style script and flaking, red paint. At the very bottom of the sign was a crescent moon, one of the symbols of Theriontrope supporters.

"Interesting," he mumbled with a tilt of his head and peered through the window. A wide array of crystals and fairy figurines were interspersed with books, the titles of which ranged from Chakra reading to gluten-free baking. Reading over the titles, Saint wondered about the person who now owned the shop. If the window display was any indication, the owner had to be a bit eccentric. But this was New Orleans, and eccentric was commonplace, if not a bit mundane.

He also wondered if use of the Theriontrope symbol had been on purpose or an accident.

Saint examined the large display of elves, gnomes, and fairies in the shop window. He always found it comical the way humans depicted the Fey. *If they only knew.*

Saint began to leave when, out of the corner of his eye, he caught a glimpse of a small, faded sign in the bottom corner of the window. "Princess Ryhinni, knows all – tells all."

Saint pondered over the poster. *Princess indeed!* Everyone knew truly psychic humans were a rarity. Of course, the guardians were human and could be extremely psychic. But most humans who proclaimed any ability to see the future or speak with the dead were charlatans, plain and simple.

The thought that he and Mika, or any shifter for that matter, was psychic or connected, as he preferred it to be called, was easy for him to accept. He lived that connection on a daily basis, but a human? *Preposterous!*

It wasn't that humans were incapable of being psychic. They merely lacked the patience and belief to become so. It was a double standard. He knew. Yet, Saint could not help himself.

Oh well, he thought as he began to leave, but whether for nostalgia's sake or mere curiosity, he turned back to the little store. He could almost feel an invisible string pulling his body, tugging him toward the shop and whatever lay inside.

With conscious effort, Saint forced his body to stop. He had no idea what caused his actions. There was nothing within the little store he could possibly need. All the same, Saint could not get his body to move in any other direction than that of the bookstore.

Tiny bells tinkled as the door to the shop flew open. Saint looked up in time to step out of the way as a young boy rushed past, nearly toppling him to the ground.

"Eric!" a woman yelled from the open door. "Where are your manners? Say 'excuse me.'"

The young boy screeched to a standstill. Brilliant blue eyes stared up at Saint from beneath a fringe of shaggy, blonde hair, and for the briefest of moments Saint caught a glimpse of Ghost as a boy.

"Sorry," the boy said.

"And?" the woman pushed.

"And I will be more careful in the future." Eric shook the hair from his face, to have it land perfectly back into place.

A whole lot like Ghost, Saint thought. "I am fine," Saint said to the young boy, "but thank you for the apology."

Eric replied with a shrug. "Can I go now, Mom?"

"Go," she answered, but the boy had already begun to trot away. "But straight to Mattie's and back. You hear me!" She called after him. "Do you hear me?"

Saint saw the boy wave to her over his shoulder and continue on his sprint.

"I'm really sorry about that," the woman said as she turned to Saint. "Never stand between a growing boy and food. He wolfs everything down these days."

"I remember," Saint mumbled, thinking of both Mika and Ghost as teenage boys. The two bested both him and Fergus when it came to eating, and still could.

"Oh, you have a son?

Saint detected a touch of sadness in her voice, though he could not understand why.

"A son? No."

"But you said—oh, never mind. It's none of my business."

"I have two younger brothers," Saint volunteered. "They were in constant competition to see who could eat the most." *Or run the fastest or shoot the straightest,* Saint added in his head.

Saint left the thoughts of his brothers to look at the woman with whom he spoke. The ground beneath his feet jerked as the world around him seemed to cease its spinning, or maybe, for the first time, it began. He wasn't sure quite sure which one it was, but in the moment he looked into her deep brown eyes, he could tell this woman would always be a part of his life.

Silently he cursed the gods. Of course the Sisters of All Life and Knowledge would complicate things. It was their way.

"Would you care to come in?" asked the woman.

Don't give in. You have things to do. "I really must be going," he answered, even though his body refused to walk away.

"Are you sure?" She smiled up at him. "I was about to make myself a cup of tea. If you would you care to join me. It's the least I can do since my son tried to flatten you."

Saint's brain told him it was a bad idea to accept her offer, while every cell of his being told him this was where he needed to be. *Fates be damned.* There was someplace he had to be, and he refused to allow them to stop him. Still, he did want to see how much the store had changed over the years, and a cup of tea would be the perfect excuse.

"Yes. I would fancy a cup of tea.."

The scent of juniper and aged paper greeted Saint as he entered the store. He was surprised by how little the small shop had actually changed. Scroll-worked shelves lined the walls behind the sales counter. The bottles and tins once housed there had been replaced by statuary from various religions, the most prominent of which was a large statue of Thor, and if he had noticed correctly, the woman wore an amulet of Mjölnir about her neck.

A small set of stairs led to a raised platform in the back of the store, where two overstuffed chairs and a table invited patrons to curl up and read. To the right ran rows of bookshelves crammed full. He found it interesting when, for no apparent reason, the discomfort around his heart began to ease.

"I hope you don't mind," she said, going to a whitewashed hutch near the stairs. "I blend my own teas. It's something I started doing years ago."

Saint peered over Janet's shoulder as she opened a small white jar. Inhaling deeply, Saint caught the scent of mint, rose hips, and orange zest. *What a delightful surprise.*

"Is everything okay?" she asked, her face mere inches from his.

"Quite," Saint answered. His mouth went suddenly dry, and he shifted uncomfortably with the awareness of the warmth of her body. "I...I realized I have not introduced myself." He stepped back. "Aidan Wolfe, at your service," he said with a small nod of his head. He wasn't sure why he used the Americanized version of his given name. It just slipped out.

"Oh goodness, where are my manners. I fuss so much at Eric, I just seem to forget...," she rambled. "I'm...sorry...," she said, offering her hand. "I'm Janet. Janet Beesinger."

Taking her hand in his, Saint could not help but look deep into her eyes. An indescribable peace swept throughout his body. It was unlike anything he had felt before, and if given the chance, he would never want to leave.

Saint jerked his hand away, trying to ignore the spot where the warmth of her touch still lingered upon his skin. He looked about, doing his best not to look in Janet's direction. "Beesinger, did you say?"

"I know." Janet went back to the tea. "It is an unusual name, but I like it. Much more interesting than say Jones or Smith, don't you think?"

"Yes." Saint took care to avoid physical contact with Janet. It wasn't that he didn't want to. He definitely did. Saint ran a finger around the edge of his tabbed collar. He found it strange that the neck of his shirt felt tight when it had been fine moments before.

Janet was not what he would consider tall since her head barely reached the top of his shoulder. Her deep mahogany hair was loosely pulled back from her round face. In Saint's opinion, the woman appeared too young to have a son the age of the boy called Eric, who he guessed to be about fifteen. Then again, Saint knew looks could be all together deceiving.

He wondered if it was possible for Janet to be a descendant of Fortis Beesinger. After all, this was once his store. *Beesinger could possibly be her married name.* She did have a son after all.

"Beesinger is your married name?" From the look on Janet's face, Saint could tell he had struck a nerve.

"No," she answered sharply. "I've never been married, and before you ask, Eric's father isn't in the picture."

"My sincere apology." Saint straightened. "That was incredibly forward of me. I didn't mean to pry."

Saint noticed her ridged posture began to slacken. Whatever darkness clouded her demeanor quickly rolled past. "No...I'm sorry," Janet said. "You would think after all this time; I would not be so sensitive."

It had been more than a century since he had been alone in the company of a woman he found attractive. That was unless you counted his walks with Hel in the Underworld. Closing his eyes tightly, Saint tried to shut out the image of the beautiful blue goddess who ruled the dead. Her words played a continual loop in his head.

"So we have reached an accord?" the goddess had asked, a polite smile curving her lips as she looked up at him. Saint's blood still chilled at the remembrance of her words, and he fought to push away the thoughts of the frozen goddess. Saint hadn't told anyone of his deal with Hel. There was no need to tell the others. He didn't want live with the knowledge his actions caused others despair. It was better that way.

I should leave, Saint kept telling himself, but chivalry dictated he stay put. It would be inconsiderate to run out just as he had gotten his tea.

It may have been the fact he had once spent countless hours in this building, or it may have been the lilt of Janet's southern accent as she rambled on, but being near her made the small bookstore seem as intimate as any bedroom. Yet it felt so right.

Saint's jumble of emotions confused him all the more. It perplexed him how it was possible to feel awkward and comfortable at the same time?

By the goddess, these thoughts are ridiculous.

Saint searched for a topic of conservation to take his mind off the mesmerizing pulsation of the pendant that lay at her throat. Finally, his sight landed on the yellowed flier taped to the door. "This Princess Ryhinni, how does one go about meeting with her?"

Janet cast a wry glance his way before speaking. "You don't strike me as a man in need of the Princess's services."

"And why is that?"

"Usually people come to see the Princess when they are searching for something. Their life path. An object. Absolution. But you, Mr. Wolfe...."

"Please. Call me Aidan," Saint requested.

"Aidan?" Janet tilted her head. "But that isn't the name people call you."

Saint was baffled. There was no way this woman could possible know people didn't call him by his given name. "You are correct. My name is Aidan, but most everyone calls me Saint."

He waited as Janet studied his features, assessing him. Normally, he despised such scrutiny, but with Janet, it felt natural.

Janet looked at Saint over the top of her cup. "Which name would you rather I use?"

In truth, Saint liked the way Janet turned his name from two syllables into three. It had been ages since anyone called him Aiden, and he was unsure he would answer if anyone called him by that name.

"Saint will be fine."

"Very well, Saint. You don't seem like a man who loses things easily nor is in need of forgiveness."

"Really? And why is that?"

"From your dress, I can tell you are too fastidious and precise a man to let things get away from you."

"And absolution?"

Janet's eyes glimmered with amusement at his question. "Let's just say your aura shows little in the way of impurities."

Saint couldn't help but allow a spark of delight at her words. Janet was right in her observation. He was too organized to lose anything, but a person was not a thing. Sometimes, the pain of loss was too great. How many friends had he watched die over the years, and how many more were to come?

Tightness constricted Saint's chest again, snuffing out any relief he had once felt.

"Are you all right?" Janet asked, reaching for him, yet not touching.

"It is nothing. Merely a passing thought of an old friend." He took a long sip of tea.

"This Princess, I would very much like to meet her."

"I take it you have a question for her."

"You tell me." It was not his intention to issue a challenge, but in essence, that was exactly what he did.

She sputtered. "You...you think I'm the Princess?"

"Are you not?" he asked, stepping closer. *Odd,* he thought. Only a moment ago he wanted to get as far from Janet as he could, but now...now, all he wanted was for her to touch him again and take away the torment in his soul.

"Possibly, but...."

"Then help me," Saint whispered. "Tell me if I shall find what I seek." He watched Janet's mouth as her lips tightened and released. Her heartbeat pounded in his ears. He noticed her pulse quicken at his accusation. The delicate aroma of orange blossoms lingered upon her skin, and he fought the urge to step even closer to drink in the scent of her.

"Very well. Give me your left hand," she commented and sat her teacup aside.

He placed his cup next to hers. "Left? Shouldn't you ask for my dominant hand?"

A single corner of Janet's mouth tipped upwards. "I did."

Without further hesitation, Saint placed his hand in hers. Peace spread from his fingertips throughout the rest of his body. He felt the tension release from his arms and torso, allowing him to breathe without constraint.

Janet brought his hand closer to her face, turning it first one way, then another. Saint noticed the subtle variations in the color of her hair. Some strands were dark brown, some tinged with red, some gold. Even in the dim light of the bookstore, her hair glistened in a way that begged him to loosen it from its restraints so he could watch it fall about her shoulders.

"You are a very old soul," Janet said, not taking her eyes from his hand.

"You think so?"

"Definitely." Her voice sounded distant. "I have never seen a hand quite like yours. You are both complicated and simple at the same time."

"Is that normal?" he asked, observing the delicate fingers of her hand as they traced the individual lines that ran across his palm. Next to his hands, Janet's seemed childlike, and from somewhere deep inside, an overwhelming urge to protect her welled up within him, pushing itself to the forefront of Saint's generally guarded emotions. Clearing his throat, he attempted to quell those feelings.

"May I see your other hand, please?"

Saint placed his hands, palms up, side by side. He was both amused and fascinated with her. It wasn't so much his need for her to answer his question as it was the desire for her closeness. Maybe desire was too strong of a word. Need? No, that wasn't the right word either. For once, Saint's extensive vocabulary failed him.

"That's odd," she said.

"Problem?"

"Oh, no, it's just…most people's hands are similar, but there are always slight differences, unless both hands are complete opposites, which mean they are either hiding something or not living up to their potential," she answered. "But yours...yours are perfectly symmetrical."

Saint detected fascination in her voice. He could read the confusion in the delicate lines of her face and understood that whatever she saw in him was different than anything she had seen before. "And this is unusual?"

"Very," Janet whispered. Her moist breath wafted across his hand.

"So what does that mean, exactly?" he asked, in an effort to keep her talking.

"It means the face you present to the world is your true self. No lying, no subterfuge. You, Saint Wolfe, are exactly who you were meant to be. Every twist, every turn of your life, good or bad, is as it should be."

Of course, he was who he was meant to be. Who else would he be? What a blanket statement. She might as well have said, "I see a person in your life whose name has an 'A' in it." Obviously, she was as much of a phony as he suspected. *You are who you were meant to be. Bah!* Now would be a good time for him to gather his belongings and go.

But still, everything about his life was as it should be. Nothing had ever been chance, and all had been in service of the goddess. Maybe he could wait a moment or two and give the princess a bit more time.

Who was he kidding? There was only one human who had ever been able to read him, and she had been an exception. Come to think of it, he had found her connection to the Universe uncanny also. Often she had commented how he had the hands of an artist and the soul of a poet and the heart of a warrior. Saint never thought too much about any of those things. He was simply who he was. He was neither a poet nor a warrior and definitely not an artist. He wasn't even exceptional. He was simply Saint.

Janet was exceptional. He hadn't noticed it until they were tucked away from the noises of a waking city. Whatever *it* was, Janet had it. Again, the appropriate word slipped through his grasp. *Too bad Fergus was not here,* Saint mused. *Surely he would find my loss for verbiage amusing.*

Janet spoke in hushed, distracted tones. "You search for someone, a woman. One you have waited many years for."

"Longer than you can imagine," Saint murmured and closed the gap between them. He felt a gentle vibration dance between her skin and his. For some inexplicable reason, Saint wanted to know if it was his nearness that made her nervous or if it was merely a coincidence. *Could she possibly feel the same way?* Maybe he should step closer and find out.

But there are no coincidences. He heard the voice inside him say.

Saint tried to block out the voice. He was in New Orleans on a mission. The last thing he needed was to get sidetracked by the Universe and a beautiful woman who smelled of peaches and hyacinth.

Have I ever led you astray? the voice asked him.

You brought me here to find Bridget, Saint insisted.

Are you sure?

"She is near," Janet said, her voice bringing him back from his argument with the Universe.

"What? Who?"

"The woman you seek. She is very near."

"Impossible," Saint returned, and pulled his hand from hers.

"It isn't. You will meet her, and it will be soon. If you haven't already."

Saint clasped his hands tightly behind his back. "I am sorry, Princess Ryhinni or whatever you call yourself. In this, you are wrong."

"Believe what you want," Janet shrugged. "I should have known better than to agree to read you since you were determined not to believe me, no matter what I said."

"I beg your pardon?" Saint asked.

"You heard me. So arrogant," she mumbled, and began to clear away the tea. "Your kind thinks they are the only ones connected to the spirits or the Universe or the gods. Whatever *you* want to call it."

Janet pushed past Saint. Without giving him another glance, she stormed across the room, past the front counter, and disappeared behind a brightly striped curtain.

Frustration swept through Saint like a wild storm. He should walk from this building never to return. He had things to do and worrying about Janet Beesinger was not one of them.

Knows all indeed! Saint snatched his satchel from the floor and slung the worn strap over his shoulder. It was a mistake to ask the princess to read him. Slowing his movements, Saint tuned his hearing to the noises behind the curtain. Janet hadn't stopped mumbling since leaving the room, and he found her fussing endearing. His reticence at her statement had little to do with her and everything to do with Bridget's death.

Saint wanted to believe Michael Grey wouldn't keep secrets from him and the pack. However, Grey's track record wasn't too good at the moment. He did hide his knowledge of CJ Carson and the fact that Theriontrope had watched over her for 30 years. Were those not lies by omission? Saint tried not to question the wisdom of Theriontrope or of Michael Grey, but he wondered how many more secrets had been kept from him and the others.

Was it possible Bridget was one of those secrets?

Against his better judgment, Saint placed his satchel upon the counter and followed Janet behind the curtain, only to find himself standing inside a small, ornately decorated room. The room was not one he remembered from years past, and he surmised it must have been added at some point to serve as an office, but now it appeared to be Princess Ryhinni's reading room.

The dimly lit space was decorated with fabrics of deep scarlet, purple, and gold, giving the room a tented effect. In the center sat a round table covered with a cloth of deep gold and purple. One chair faced the doorway. Another sat directly across from it. In the center of the table, on a raised pedestal, was a rather large crystal ball. Resting nearby was a deck of Tarot cards. The only thing missing was a rainbow-colored turban.

Looking to his right, Saint noticed two large wingback chairs, flanking an antique gaming table. There was something familiar about the table, and he wondered if it was the same table where once he and his old friend, Fortis, once played chess.

Saint leaned low over the crystal ball. Not that he knew anything about scrying. He had tried it before but had never found it beneficial. Still, he stared into the milky colored orb, searching for any clue as to why he had gone on this infernal quest in the first place.

"I thought you had left," Janet said, as she came back into the room.

Saint shot up, hitting his head on the small crystal chandelier that hung low above the table. *Drat!* He was never clumsy. This woman placed him ill at ease, and he disliked it immensely.

"I beg your pardon?" He smoothed a hand along the top of his head.

"I said, I thought you left," she answered coldly.

"I take it this is the Princess's room?"

Janet crossed her arms over her chest. "Why are you here, Mr. Wolfe?"

Saint was surprised by her cool demeanor, and for some reason he didn't understand, he found he wanted nothing more than to kiss the disdain from her face. *Kiss her?* Shocked by his own reaction, he put distance between them. "I am here on business."

"Of course you are." Janet sighed. "Well, so am I, and mine is running this store. So if you will excuse me, I need to get on with my day," she said, walking toward the curtain that separated them from the rest of the world.

Saint followed. "Please forgive me. I apologize for taking so much of your time."

Janet did not hesitate as she opened the door. "Good luck to you, Mr. Wolfe. I hope you find what you're looking for."

Saint knew somehow he was to blame for the tears welling in

Janet's eyes. He should leave before he made things worse, but Janet's unhappiness tore at him. There had to be something he could do to rectify the situation, even if it meant coercing her to talk to him. "Janet…would you happen to have a room I could lease for a few days?" *By the goddess, where did that come from?*

Janet sucked in a deep breath. "What? What makes you think I would have a place you could stay?"

Saint shrugged. "Forgive me, but I saw the sign lying on the counter." He pointed toward a letter-sized sheet of paper with the words "ROOM FOR RENT—INQUIRE WITHIN" typed in a large, bold font. "Is the room still available?"

"No," she blurted. "I mean…yes. I mean…." Janet huffed.

"It can't be both. Unless the room is available but you prefer not lease to one of *my kind.*"

"I didn't mean it like that," she said. "The room is still available. I assumed you would rather stay at the Crowne Plaza or someplace like that."

"No," he said, trying to appear nonchalant. "I believe I will be much more comfortable here with you and your son." Saint pulled the wallet from the interior pocket of his coat. Retrieving ten one hundred dollar bills from inside, he handed the stack to Janet.

"What's this?" she asked.

"One month's rent."

Saint was unsure what Janet's silence meant, but he figured she had one of two options. She would either say yes or no. Frankly, he was not sure which one he would like best.

"Okay. Fine," she agreed, much to his relief. "Follow me."

Without so much as a peep, Janet led Saint up the staircase to her and Eric's apartment. Stepping on the top stair, Saint realized little had changed since Fortis had lived there. He recognized many of the furnishings as those that belonged to the shop's original owner. What was once considered common to an era was now considered antiquated, much like him.

"Here you go," Janet said, opening the door to a sparsely decorated room.

"Thank you." Saint lay his satchel upon the bed.

"Are you sure you wouldn't be more comfortable in a hotel?" she asked.

A smile slipped across Saint's lips at her question. *Is this woman trying to be rid of me?* "I assure you. I will be fine."

"Okay. Just…erm…let me know if you need anything else."

"I will. Thank you."

With a soft click of the door handle, Janet left him. Saint wanted to assure her no matter the condition of the room, it would be fine. He considered any time he slept on a bed and not on the ground a luxury.

It was not as if he needed much since he didn't plan on spending more than a few days. The room had most creature comforts—a bed, desk and chair, and dresser. It even had a private bath. From the lingering scent of Janet's perfume, Saint assumed this was once her bedroom. He was unsure of her financial situation but concluded she must have given up her bedroom out of necessity.

Once she and Eric are with you at Haven, they will want for nothing, the voice of the Universe said.

In all his years of study and dedication, Saint had never quite figured out who the voice belonged to, but questioning its omniscience was not something he was inclined to do.

Saint smoothed the lines of his coat as he hung it in the closet. He needed to take his animal form. It was the best way for him to heal the abrasion on his hand.

Undressing completely, Saint called forth the red wolf. Golden light emanated from Saint's midsection. He imagined the light splitting into a million particles spinning faster and faster until it burst into a shower of golden sparks. The sparks converged and collapsed into each other, morphing into a large, red wolf.

With a yawn, the wolf jumped onto the bed. He didn't remember ever being so tired, but sleep hadn't been a friend to him over the past few months. So his exhaustion stood to reason.

Saint had no misgivings that his return to New Orleans would yield a city he was unfamiliar with. The world often seemed to progress around him. He had seen the invention of automobiles, electricity, computers, and cell phones, everything humans now believe to be a necessity.

If only they would unplug from the world for fifteen minutes a day and just be. He doubted most people would even want to hear what goes on in their own hearts and minds.

If only humans would listen and build the connection between them and the divine, he thought.

Hypocrite. The word zinged into his thoughts. He found it interesting that his thoughts had taken on a tone and quality similar to Janet.

Excuse me? He rebutted. *Me, a hypocrite?*

Yes. Hypocrite.

In what way?

You prattle on about how humans need a greater connection to the Universe, yet you don't believe it is possible. That is being a hypocrite.

Saint rotated his ears forward and backwards. Could Janet actually hear his thoughts? *Preposterous.* Humans were incapable of doing such. Well, except for Mika's mate CJ, but that was different. Unlike CJ, Janet was not a guardian and positively not his mate.

* * *

Janet walked numbly down the stairs. *What just happened? Why did I leave that notice on the counter?* Although she had cleaned out the room and gotten it ready to lease, she had not fully decided to do so. She could have said no. She should have said no.

She had noticed him standing in front of her store while she was on the phone with Mattie. Before she could stop Eric, he was out the door and charging down the street. She was so embarrassed when he almost plowed the poor man down.

"Poor man," she scoffed. Very little about that man seemed poor. He could have worn a potato sack, and everything about him would have screamed wealth. *Damn shape shifters!*

Your life will change today. Janet thought of the words circled in red ink on her calendar. "I don't need this kind of change," she spoke toward the heavens, and she meant every word.

The last thing she ever expected, wanted, or needed was for her life to become entangled with a shifter, but there was no denying her attraction to him. Redheads had never been her thing, but for Aidan Wolfe she would make an exception.

Janet groaned. Could she help it that from his crisply starched collar to his immaculately shined shoes, Saint Wolfe was the sexiest man, shifter or not, she had ever seen? If given the chance, she would deny him nothing. Janet blushed at the thought.

Within seconds in his presence, Janet felt the silver threads of her life unraveling and intertwining with his, connecting them for all time. Janet bit her bottom lip. *Did he feel it too?*

"No. No. No," she commanded, as she slammed her palm down upon the counter. There was no way this could be happening.

She tried to follow in the footsteps of her father and grandfather, to help shifters. That's why she placed a small crescent moon on her sign. "I should have taken down that damn sign!" she grumbled, thinking about the ragged shingle above the entrance to her bookstore.

She had been around shifters most of her life and understood the powerful, physical attractiveness of their species. All of them were gorgeous.

Two types of shifters normally entered Janet's world. There were the young ones, less than a century old. Usually, they had very little money and in many ways, seemed almost feral.

Then there were the old ones. It was easy to distinguish them by their carriage and demeanor. Their movements were slower, more deliberate, as if they had all the time in the world, because they did. They were the ones with wealth, prestige, and power.

Judging from Saint's appearance and behavior, he was a member of the second group, and if Janet had to wager a guess, she would place him at well over a century, possibly pushing two.

Most of the shifters she met were good people, but there were a few who had crossed her path that were pure evil. Then again, she reasoned, the same could be said for many humans.

At the moment, Janet's heart was not longing to be near a human. It was crying out for a shifter she knew very little about, other than the few things Princess Ryhinni had picked up on.

If only humans would listen and build the connection between them and the divine.

Hypocrite. The word jumped into Janet's mind before she had a chance to realize what happened. How dare he talk about wanting humans to be more connected to the divine and yet he doesn't believe it possible?

Excuse me? She heard him say. *Me, a hypocrite?*

Yes. Hypocrite, she answered back.

In what way?

You prattle on about how humans need a greater connection to the Universe, yet you don't believe it is possible. That is being a hypocrite.

Janet felt more than heard a humph. She considered how crazy it was to believe Saint was actually carrying on a conversation with her inside her head, but she had to admit it was kind of fun, even if he believed it to be preposterous.

CHAPTER 7

For months, Fergus had sensed the dark clouds of turmoil that billowed within his brother. He could readily see through Saint's placid facade and increasing solitude, and he would bet his left hand Bridget had something to do with his brother's mood. She was the only one who could ever put Saint in such a state of melancholy. Yet no matter how hard Fergus pushed, Saint refused to speak with anyone about what really happened in the Underworld.

If Mika and Ghost's suspicions were confirmed and Bridget was alive, there would be nothing left for Fergus to do than hunt her down and rip her throat open. It was only out of love for his brother that she was allowed to live the first time.

With super-human speed, Fergus bounded up the stairs, making a sharp right turn and ending up before the floor-length mirror at the end of the hall. Its bronze frame filled the wall, giving him a perfect view of his entire body as he counted each measured step in an effort to gain composure. *Damn Michael Grey! How could he have not told them? Was that not the job of the director of Theriontrope? To assess threats and have Fergus eliminate them?*

Reaching toward the mirror, Fergus made the sign of the runic symbol Berkano, the symbol represented Freyja and those connected to her.

The symbol was ancient and held more magic than most, except the oldest, realized.

Slowly, the silver behind the glass bent and swirled before melting away and bringing into focus Dr. Michael Grey's office. The director of the Theriontrope Foundation sat with his back to the mirror, unaware he was being watched.

No matter how much Fergus wanted to reach through the mirror and pull the director of the Theriontrope Foundation through, he knew Saint would not approve, especially if he throttled Michael Grey within an inch of his life.

"Grey!" Fergus barked.

The small thump of Michael's chair alerted Fergus to the fact he held the element of surprise. Michael spun in his chair. "Fergus, my friend. What—"

"A friend does not base said friendship on half-truths and lies."

Michael moved to stand before the large mirror that covered the entire height and breadth of the wall of his office. Made of ornately crafted silver and obsidian, the mirror was an ancient form of communication between Grey and the Delta Pack, among others.

"I have no idea what you are talking about."

"Bridget LeCœur," Fergus said through gritted teeth. "I accepted your lies about the guardian since I believed it best for Mika and for Haven. But how by the grace of Freyja could you not tell Saint that she-devil was still alive?"

"Impossible. Bridget was killed years ago," Dr. Grey stuttered.

Fergus stepped closer to the mirror, his nose coming within a cat's whisker of touching the glass. He studied the look of confusion that lingered on Michael's face. "Don't toy with me, Grey. I am not of good humor. You know how things between her and Saint ended. The happiest day of my life was the day I received word she was dead."

For Fergus, no truer words had ever been spoken. If he remembered correctly, he danced a bit, out of Saint's line of sight, of course.

"I remember well what she and her pack did," Grey said.

"Then you can understand my angst when I hear rumors she may still live."

Dr. Grey shook his head. "You saw the photographs and read the reports the same as I."

White hot anger zipped through Fergus. He wanted to believe Michael Grey. Truly he did, but after what happened with the last guardian, he was unsure he could ever trust Dr. Grey again. Too many questions still lingered.

For starters, if Bridget was alive, why would she have followed Mika and Ghost to Florida? Was she keeping tabs on his pack and if so, to what end?

Acid churned in the pit of Fergus's stomach. "Mika and Ghost believe they saw her."

"When was this?"

"When they retrieved the guardian."

"Could they have been mistaken?"

Fergus pulled back the reins on his temper. "My question is with you, not them. You are the head of Theriontrope. Is it not the duty of your office to know the whereabouts of all shifters?"

"I am not omniscient, Fergus. There is always the possibility someone kept his or her identity hidden."

Fergus became disturbingly still. Even his breath stilled to the point his chest neither rose nor fell. "Grey, if you are truly my friend, I need to know. Is Bridget LeCœur still alive, and if she is, where might she be?"

"What difference would that make?" Michael Grey asked.

"Saint has felt it necessary to return to New Orleans without the company of me or the others." Fergus entwined his arms across his chest.

"You saw the photos after she died. No shifter can survive decapitation. Has Saint been contacted by someone claiming to be Bridget?"

"No, and I need to make sure it stays that way."

"You don't mean...."

"Remember who and what I am, Grey," Fergus butted in. "Nothing or no one will stop me from finishing the job I started years ago, and this time there will be no question of the bitch's death." With a swipe of his hand, Fergus disappeared behind the polished surface of the mirror.

A chill ran through Dr. Grey's body. It took most all his control not to flinch as Fergus's arm swept across the mirror. He didn't like the underlying accusation in Fergus's tone, but in all fairness to Fergus, his reticence to accept anything Michael Grey had to say was understandable.

He had never wanted to hold back the truth where CJ Carson was concerned, but it had been for her own good. In the end, everything worked out the way it should.

Bridget LeCœur was a different situation. As far as the Foundation was concerned, she was deceased. She had been decapitated by flying shrapnel during an air strike over Germany during World War II. Dr. Grey shook his head. It simply wasn't possible that she lived.

Fergus's last statement resonated inside Dr. Grey's head. The leader of Delta Pack never made idle threats. If Bridget was still alive, then she wouldn't be for long once Fergus found her.

Lifting his head, Dr. Grey studied the intricately carved wolf, cougar, and bear that adorned the frame of the mirror in his office. The relief stared down in accusation. If his benefactor used the mirror to spy on him, then she would have heard the whole of his and Fergus's conversation.

The distorted reflection of the goddess's portrait caught his eye. He had painted the image of her long ago, and no matter how hard he tried to capture Freyja's beauty, he felt his attempt had fallen short.

Michael swung the painting to one side, revealing a retinal scanner. Leaning forward, he allowed the small beam of blue-green light to map the contour of his eye. With a soft click, the door unlocked.

The room flooded with light as he entered, revealing row upon row of file cabinets. With purpose, he made his way through the labyrinth, stopping at the cabinet marked LeCœur. Pulling open the middle drawer, he thumbed through the multicolored folders until he found the one entitled LeCœur, Bridget.

The file contained most everything there was to know about the woman, including black and white photos of her mangled body. Taken at different angles, the photos served as proof of her death. No shifter could survive decapitation. It was simply impossible.

The hair at the back of Michael's neck rose as the ions in the atmosphere around him hummed with energy. As he suspected, his benefactor had arrived. Quickly, Dr. Grey closed the file drawer. Even though the woman would tell him to take as long as he needed, he hated to keep her waiting.

Dr. Grey stilled at the sight of her. No matter how many eons he had served the goddess Freyja, he would consider her beauty to be without parallel.

Normally when she appeared in the human realm, she dressed as one of them, in a suit of dark blue and decadent pumps, but not today.

Today she dressed as she would in Asgard. The violet of her gown accented the green of her eyes, and her blonde hair hanging loosely about her shoulders framed her face, almost hiding her favorite necklace, Brísingamen.

Dr. Grey stopped before her. "Is it true? Is she alive?"

"You have no greeting for me this day?" she asked in silken tones.

"Please forgive me, Goddess. I am bit distracted at the moment."

"So it would seem." Freyja draped her body across the settee nearest her. "Come." She patted the cushion beside her.

Always obedient to her wishes, Michael sat down beside the goddess. "It would give me no greater pleasure than to tell you Fergus made a mistake and that Bridget indeed walks in Helhiem. However, that would be a falsehood."

"I have proof of her death here." Michael shook the folder.

"There are forces at work here, Grey, forces I cannot control."

"How is that possible? You are a goddess."

She smiled softly. "But I am not the only one. Asgard is filled with gods, and I do not hold rule over them, especially not over the goddess of the Underworld.

Michael fidgeted in his seat. The mere thought of the ruler of Helhiem was enough to bring anxiety. "What does Hel have to do with this?"

"When Bridget died, her soul went to Helhiem, as it should have. However, she begged to be returned to the world of humans."

"And the Queen of the Underworld obliged?"

"Hel is as obedient to her father as you are to me."

Michael pinched the bridge of his nose, trying to relive the pressure building there. "You want me to believe that Bridget LeCœur is alive because Loki took pity upon her?"

Freyja said nothing.

As Saint would say—"preposterous", Grey thought. *No matter how devoted Hel may be to her father, the Sisters of All Life and Knowledge surely would not let him delve in their world.*

"And the sisters allowed him to play with fate in such a way?" Dr. Grey asked.

"So it would seem. For what reason, only they can answer."

Michael could not help the feelings of resentment and betrayal that washed over him. How could his goddess have lied to him?

"I did not lie to you, Grey," she said, answering the question he didn't dare voice. Freyja moved toward him. "No more than you lied to Fergus about the new guardian or those other little secrets we keep."

Eyes the color of Grey's name drilled into the goddess. "How am I to do my job when you don't hold up your end of the bargain? What else have you chosen not to tell me?" His voice rose in timbre, indicating his agitation.

"What right do you have to question my decisions? I am the one who placed you here, and it is by my grace alone that you still walk here in Midgard," she whispered.

Michael's jaw hurt from the strain of holding back his tongue. What right? What right! As her charge, he had every right. She owed him that much. How was he to do his job without having the necessary information?

The hem of Freyja's gown brushed the tops of his shoes. The heat of her skin danced upon his cheek. "Need I remind you, you belong to me and as such shall serve me until I release you from your obligations?"

"Forgive me, my goddess. I meant no disrespect."

"Of course." She pulled back. "Now that the wolf is out of the bag, what are you prepared to do about it?"

Michael took a moment to ponder the situation. He thought of Fergus's most recent words. "I will finish the job I started years ago." Maybe it was best to let that happen. Bridget and her pack were a scourge within the world of shifters. If Fergus could rid the population of all those that hunted humans, it wouldn't upset him one bit.

Anxiety, red-hot, burned in the pit of Michael Grey's stomach. Loki brought Bridget back from Helheim? No matter how many ways he looked at it, Grey couldn't see her resurrection as a good thing. Every thought, word, and deed that came from Loki were solely for his gain.

"I believe the best solution is to let Fergus do what he does best."

Freyja nodded and motioned toward the mirror, opening a doorway into Asgard. "Then it is settled," she said, stepping through the glass. "Rest assured, Grey, none will stand in his way."

With Freyja gone, Michael drooped in his chair. Fergus must be called. The leader of Delta Pack would hunt her down and take great pleasure in her demise, of that Grey had no doubt. But before he made that call, he should find out where Bridget might be. With any luck, she would be in Zimbabwe or some other location far, far away from Saint.

Taking the telephone from its cradle, Grey dialed the number he knew all too well. New Orleans was still a city of shifters and, as such, required someone to keep an eye on things. That someone was Kellas Scott. If Bridget had so much as stepped a toe within the city limits, Kellas would know.

"Kellas," Dr. Grey said before Kellas has a chance to say hello. "I hate to dispense with the niceties, but I need to know if you have come across some information."

"There is much I see and hear," Kellas answered, his Scottish accent now tainted with inflections of Cajun.

"I am sure there is, but this is about someone in particular."

"And who that be?" Kellas asked.

Dr. Grey sighed. He never expected to hear Bridget's name again, let alone be asking about her. "I need to know if you have any information regarding Bridget LeCœur." Dr. Grey's question was met with silence.

Kellas was one of the ancients in the shifter community. Not that anyone would know by looking at him. Like all of his kind, Kellas stopped physically aging while in his forties, yet he carried himself with the quiet confidence of a soul as old as time itself. One of Kellas's most admirable traits was his ability to answer a question without answering it.

"Nah, I no see Bridget," Kellas finally answered.

Ah yes, Dr. Grey thought, *Kellas's patented way of not actually answering my question.* "First, cut the accent and, second, why do I hear a 'but' in your statement?"

"I may have heard something about a certain she-wolf roaming the streets of my fine city," Kellas said, dropping the accents as requested.

Michael groaned, laying his head against the back of his chair. "I was in hopes of a different answer."

"Then I am sorry I didn't have better news."

"You can't change the facts. Expect to hear from Fergus Wolfe. I am sure he will be contacting you soon."

"His presence will be welcomed."

Michael's head roared. Bone weary, he knew the next call he had to make, but first he needed peace. Every muscle along the line of his shoulders ached. His job had taken too many years and too much out of him. If he had known the implications of his actions those eons ago when he accepted his goddess's request, he would have told her no.

Would it not have been better for him to serve within her palace than to spend an eternity away from his homeland? There was a chance, however small, had he remained in Asgard, he could have had a normal life.

Maybe the goddess would have granted him the ability to wed and have a family of his own. As it was, he had nothing to show for his lifetime of service other than memories and loneliness.

The sound of the birds beyond his window faded to silence as slumber overtook him. The dreams came quickly, and so he found himself returning to his childhood. Standing scarcely inside the mouth of a cave, a young boy looked out at the raging storm. Thunder and lightning bounced off steep mountain walls, making it impossible to leave.

"Come here, child," a voice creaked behind him.

Spinning about, he saw a woman. Haggard and stooped with age, she stepped nearer.

"I said, 'Come here child.'" She reached a gnarled hand toward him.

An icy wind swept across his face, chilling him to the core and forcing his eyes to fill with tears. Clenching his fists at his side, the young Grey stood his ground. He must be strong for the goddess. She wouldn't cry. He wouldn't cry. He moved forward, his feet a slave to the old woman's command.

As Grey stopped before her, the woman's ebony eyes bored into his soul. No matter what happened, he wouldn't give into his fear.

"A boy your age should not be wandering these caves alone. How come you to be here?" she asked.

"I live in the house of the goddess Freyja." Michael lifted his chin in defiance.

"So you do. That does not answer my question. How do you come to be here?"

The young boy looked again to the cave opening and the raging storm without. There was something familiar about the old woman, yet she scared him more than any warrior ever could.

The old woman huffed as she sat upon the closest boulder. "Boy." Her voice bounced along the cave walls.

"I…I was in the goddess's hunting party. When the storm came, I was unable to keep up with the others."

"So Freyja took a child to the hunt?" She leaned on a staff as crooked as her own body. "Ah, she know not you were there, did she, boy?"

How had the crone known? He had been told repeatedly to stay home, that the hunt would be too dangerous for a child his age. But he wasn't a child. He was seven turnings old. He knew how to ride a horse and to wield a knife. What he lacked in size he more than made up for in skill.

Michael Grey's body jolted awake. He hated when that happened. Rolling his neck from side to side, he worked to muster the will to call Fergus. With any luck, someone else would answer. Grey stilled his hand as he reached toward the mirror.

The din of a thousand rivers rushed toward him, filling his office with sound. The timbre and intensity increased to deafening proportions, forcing him to place his hand over his ears. Closing his eyes, he willed himself to wake. Surely this was still part of his dream.

You had no choice, Valborg, his ancient name rode upon the noise. *You were chosen. Your path was set.*

Jumping from his seat, Grey searched the room for the owner of the voice. "Who is there?" He yelled into the emptiness. The floor tilted and rolled beneath his feet. He was caught in the centrifuge of time and space, moving neither forward or backward. Placing a hand over his mouth, he fought back the nausea as he tried to focus.

As quickly as the tumult began, it ended. Michael looked down at the uneven ground beneath his dark leather shoes. He noticed his hands — adult hands. No longer a child, Michael Grey the man now stood before the woman. She was Darkness, the oldest of the Sisters of All Life and Knowledge.

Her dark eyes glistened in the dim light of the cave as she spoke. "Even as a boy, you were headstrong."

"Forgive me, Darkness. My memory isn't what it once was."

Darkness cackled at his comment, and he knew she didn't believe him. Michael may have been a boy the first time they met, but coming face-to-face with one of the fates would forever be ingrained in his mind.

"I now ask the man the same question I asked the boy," she began. "What is your name, child?"

"Michael Grey," he answered without hesitation.

Again she laughed. "That is the name you gave yourself. What is your given name?"

"My given name is Valborg."

"Given by whom?"

This wasn't a conversation he wished to have. Not even in a dream.

"It was given by the goddess when I was but a child."

"Understand the meaning of your name, do you?"

Michael bowed his head and fidgeted beneath the old woman's gaze. There was no need for him to feel shame, yet he did. He needed to wake up.

He could almost hear her bones creak as she pulled her worn body to its complete height of maybe five foot. "Forget your name, forget your purpose. Your name was chosen because you were chosen."

"What do you mean, I was chosen?"

"Nothing is done without our knowledge. We give our blessing or our curse. Remember your name. Remember your calling. Doubt our wisdom no more."

Michael's eyelids flew open. He lay facedown upon the Oriental rug near his desk. With care, he rose to his knees, stopping to rest his elbows on the chair before rising completely. Exhaustion washed over him. What had Darkness meant? Of course he was chosen. Freyja personally chose him to serve her.

But what had she meant about remembering his name and his calling? He would never forget what it meant—protector on the battlefield. He wanted to believe the goddess had chosen his name out of some sense of connection to him. Now he wasn't so sure.

CHAPTER 8

Apple-y lay upon her stomach, flipping through the latest *Haute Couture* magazine. Feet clad in Louis Vuitton black and white mules swung in lazy circles in the air. Licking her finger, she flipped another page.

"Apple-y look better in red than her," she hissed before turning another page.

She loved pretty things and prided herself on the fact she had the figure to pull off any design out there. Maybe her master would let her be a model one day. He had the money and ability to make it happen for her. He might let her if she behaved while staying in the hospital. She would ask him about that sometime.

Apple-y hated the hospital. Her master said it would be a good idea for her to get away from people and relax, but how could she relax? He said she had become too excitable after her last job. Apple–y hadn't thought she became too excitable. She thought her master would be happy with her work. He never told her not to kill anyone.

She rapped well-manicured nails against the silken page of the magazine. What was it the military men had called it?

Collateral...collateral...something. Not important, she thought. *Stupid man should have never opened door.*

But he did, and here she was, stuck in a place scented with blood, fear, and adrenaline. All three were intoxicating to her. Was it her fault that any of those aromas could cause a girl like her to lose control? Never mind what happens when all three were mixed together.

Apple-y turned her head toward the door. Using her preternatural skills, she homed in on the faint squeak of rubber soles against tiled floors. She could make out soft grunts of exhaled air as Jerry, one of the nurses, walked by. She crinkled her nose. Jerry's cheap cologne permeated her nostrils, and Apple-y pinched her nose, refusing to breathe until he was well past her room.

Oh, how she loved playing cat and mouse with the humans. She especially loved watching them squirm as they waited on her to take her medication. It was Jerry's fault that most of the nurses and orderlies feared her. How dare that sweaty man put his hands on her?

A smile quirked at the corner of her mouth as she remembered the look of terror in the man's face as she morphed into a tiger and stalked him about her cell. His screams were music to her ears. By the time the others came to his rescue, Apple-y was back in human form, sitting upon her bed, the complete innocent.

After that, everyone left her alone. She would see them when they brought her medication in a small, plastic cup. She would always smile nicely and take what was offered. They would watch her and check her mouth to make sure she swallowed them.

What they didn't know was Apple-y never swallowed the pills. She would hold the medication in the back of her throat until the orderlies were out of sight, then regurgitate the capsules and flush them down the sink. If she was feeling particularly nice, she might give them to another patient.

Apple-y fancied herself a Madame Curie searching for the perfect element to cure all maladies. She was a ground-breaking researcher, testing her hypothesis. It interested her how the same medications could affect people differently. Some became comatose. Too bad the last person she shared her medication with ran headlong through the second story window. *Oh well*, she shrugged.

The fine hairs along Apple-y's body began to rise. She lifted her head and caught the scent of ozone in the air. Swinging her lithe body into a seated position, she made a quick check in the mirror. She had to be sure every sleek, black hair was in place, and her favorite lipstick, Revolutionary Red, tinted her pouty lips.

Excitement bubbled beneath her breast. Her master was coming. No longer would she have to stay in this place.

The air swirled and shimmered, manufacturing a vortex from nothingness. She fidgeted in anticipation as the image of her master came into view. Apple-y couldn't contain her excitement. Barely had her master stepped from the wormhole, before she launched into the air to jump into his arms. Wrapping her arms and legs around about his body, Apple-y smothered his face with kisses.

"Master finally come for his Apple-y," she purred. A rich Russian accent tinged her English. "She beginning to think you love her no longer."

Ævar laughed heartily as he allowed her leeway with her show of affection for him.

She slid her body down the length of his, reveling in the feel of body-to-body contact. "Did you bring Apple-y present? She like when you spoil her." Pulling back slightly, she looked into his crystal eyes. "You no bring present?" she asked. Her bottom lip protruded.

"What have I said about speaking in the third person? You need to use I, not your name." He tapped her on the tip of her nose.

"Apple-y…I have problem with that. Master know how hard for Apple-y…I to remember." She dropped her head to look up at him through dark lashes.

"I do know," he lowered his tone. "But it's something you must always work on."

Apple-y pulled away from him. She knew he didn't mean to hurt her feelings, but it always bothered her when her master showed displeasure.

Call it love. Call it loyalty. Call it something altogether different. Apple-y owed Ævar her life.

Growing up in an orphanage, Apple-y had no memory of her life before the age of eight. It was as if she woke up one morning living in an institution with forty other children. She never fit in or tried to make friends. In her mind, she knew they would always leave her.

She had been on her own for only a short time before Ævar came to her rescue. Damp warmth flowed down her cheeks, bringing her back from the edge of her personal abyss.

"I do have a present for you," Ævar said, wiping away an errant tear with the pad of his thumb. "But I don't have it with me."

"Then how Apple-y…." She stopped when she caught the scolding look on his face. "Then how I get it?"

"You will get it when you finish the job I have for you."

Apple-y clapped her hands together excitedly. "Ooh, master have job for Apple-y."

Ævar nodded.

"Okee dokey." Apple-y ran to the closet, pulling out a small suitcase. She always kept one fully packed for when her master would come to get her. A broad smile lighted her face as she turned back to Ævar. "Apple-y ready."

CHAPTER 9

A damp chill ran through Ísold's body as her bare feet landed on the marble floor. Dark as a starless night, the hall stretched out before her. With a deafening thud, the door closed behind her. The reverberations brought her nerves into complete attention.

Her hands worked their way along the expanse of the door. The smooth surface sliding beneath her fingers. Hard and cool to the touch, it reminded her of the silver challis she often used when scrying for her stepbrother.

Murmurs from off in the distance filled her ears. At first, she thought it to be running water, but as she closed her eyes and listened, she could make out words.

"Come, child," the voice beckoned "Come. See to mother."

"Mother?" she whispered. To Ísold, the voice held no similarities to her mother's voice. Then again, it had been more than thirty years since she had seen or spoken to her mother, so she was unsure if memory served her well or not.

Ísold leaned her small frame against the door. The sound of her heart thumped inside her head. The slamming of the door had left her only one choice, to follow the sound of the voice. Unexpectedly, Fergus Wolfe's face flashed before her eyes.

It was not the haggard, drawn face she remembered last seeing in the tunnels beneath the prison. This Fergus was plump with life. His amber eyes filled with determination, just as they had been all those years ago. She remembered how even in the face of his own impending death, Fergus never allowed fear to falter his resolve.

Calmness washed through Ísold's mind and body. It amazed her how much she remembered of the man when he spoke not at all. Pushing away from the door, Ísold stood as erect as possible. She had no idea who or what waited for her at the end of the hall, but whatever it was, she would meet it without fear, just as her Red Prince would have done.

With unfaltering steps, Ísold made her way toward the opposite end of the tunnel and the faint pinprick of light she saw there.

Her eyes burned with the intensity of her gaze as she focused on the speck. With each step, the illumination brightened until, at last, Ísold emerged through a narrow doorway. Craning her neck, she followed the length of the column to where it merged with the ceiling. Ísold was mesmerized by the twinkling of the vaulted stones above her head. The ceiling sparkled with the brilliance billions of multicolored gems.

Ísold's body continued its journey, though her mind was lost in the heavenly display above her. Warmth wrapped around the upper part of her arm and shook her gently until she brought her attention downward.

Before her stood a woman barely as tall as she. A shock of silver white hair haloed around her head and mirrored the glint of silver at her waist. "Welcome, child," the stocky woman in black said.

"What is this place?" Ísold asked.

"Important that is not." The woman shuffled around the large vat in the floor. "There is no need to fear me, child. No harm will come to you."

Looking into the vat, Ísold saw herself asleep in the Castle of White. Many times before, she had walked the In Between, but that was before she had be locked away from the world and her powers by her captor. "I am not afraid," she answered.

The old woman cackled. "Like your brothers you are."

A pang of sadness wrapped about Ísold's heart. How much she had wanted to be like her brothers. Not in looks, though she was always envious of their eyes. Mostly she was jealous they were changelings, and she was mortal. As far as Ísold was concerned, she and her brothers were complete opposites.

"Your day will come," the woman said in a sing-song voice. "A message we have for you."

"We?"

"My sisters and I give you many messages. Some you tell. Others you keep. This one you shall keep."

They are the ones who give me the messages? What else can they do? Could it be? Ísold's hand flew to her throat. Disappointment filled her as her fingers touched the clasp of the torc about her neck.

Forged from silver and horsehair, the torc possessed the ability to block almost all of Ísold's powers as a seer or seðnor, as she was known by her clan. Her jailer had placed the choker around her neck to control her, stripping her of all but the gift of prophecy.

"Can you...?" Ísold looked to the woman. "Could you remove this for me?" She lifted the torc slightly.

"Could? Yes. Will? No." The old woman took the silver dagger from its sheath.

"But...."

The woman held up her hand for silence. "Nothing happens in Abred of which we are unaware. All is as it should be."

Abred, the land of the mortals. Ísold remembered the word from her teachings. "What good could come from my being locked away?" Ísold asked, stepping toward the woman.

"Question not the way of things," the woman said, moving toward Ísold. "In time, the answers will come. Your conviction is strong. Your will is strong. Remain as you are, and all will be answered in time."

Tears burned Isoldes eyes. This had to be a cruel dream set forth by the gods to torture her. Had her brother grown so strong in his own magic that he now had the ability to torment her even in her sleep? How she had once prayed to have dreams again, to be able to walk the In Between as she had done before being locked away.

Since the day Ævar placed the torc about her neck and locked her away in the *vígi hvítur litur*, the Fortress of White, Ísold had ceased to dream. She spoke with no one except the servants, and she only spoke with them when necessary. Her one true friend was Cassius, and she saw him on those rare occasions Ævar allowed him to visit.

But recently, her ability to dream had returned. Overjoyed, Ísold thought the dreams a blessing, a delightful respite from the loneliness and cold of her prison. She enjoyed dreaming of the brother she never met. She only hoped that he was as wonderful in person as he was in her dreams. It would break her heart to know he was anything like his twin.

But dreams like that often brought her only misery. It hurt her to know her brother knew nothing of her existence and that she would never be able to meet him. The sound of rustling fabric caught Ísold's attention. The woman held her hand palm upward toward the ceiling, and Ísold watched as a single strand of silver descended from the vast space above them. Writhing like an airborne serpent, the thread spiraled and dipped until it hung suspended before the woman.

With greater speed than Ísold could imagine, the woman slashed the thread in two. The separated pieces fell into the vat and, with a hiss, dissolved into the liquid contained there.

"My sisters and I have a message for you. Remember it well, but tell no one. Not even your brother."

"Why give me a message when I can do nothing with it."

A cackle cracked from the old woman's throat. "Are you ready?" she asked, ignoring Ísold's question. "Good."

Fog now clouds the daughters fair; of Earth and water, of fire and air.

Four there are and two be found; Earth and fire by thread be bound.

Gentle treasures hidden not from sight; to remain in darkness be not their plight.

The breath of life a specter needs; a heart of ice great strength impedes.

Lightness binds and darkness severs; a mother alone brings souls together.

Ísold woke with a start, almost falling off the edge of the well-worn chaise lounge. She pushed back the hair from her face and tried to steady her breathing.

The dreams came too often now. Dreams of people, places, and things she had never seen before. She had dreamed of them so many times now that she had begun to think of them as real.

What was it the old woman had said? *Four daughters?* Ísold searched her memory, repeating word for word what the old woman said. She still didn't understand why she would be given a prophecy she would be unable to share.

Ísold looked at the large row of windows above her. She was not good at telling time since it meant so little in her world. Nonetheless, she was positive it had been months since Ævar and Cassius were at the Fortress. That was the day she told Ævar their brother was still alive.

Ísold touched her throat as the memory of Ævar's hands, wrapped about her throat, came flooding back. She had begged for Freyja to allow

97

Darkness to take her so that she might live for eternity in Fólkvangr with the man she so desperately loved, her Red Prince. It wasn't until after helping him escape that she learned her prince's name – Fergus Wolfe. Ævar had held Fergus captive for years.

While walking the space that lay somewhere between wake and sleep, Ísold found Fergus. appeared not to be breathing and for a moment, she thought him dead. Then he opened his eyes, and in that moment, Ísold knew they would be bound for all time.

Watching Fergus be tortured day after day was more than her young heart could bear. Enlisting the help of Cassius, she devised a plan to help her prince escape. Somehow, Ævar discovered she was the mastermind behind the breakout. For her crimes against him and their pack, she was sent to live out the rest of her life at the Fortress.

Before Ísold's banishment was to begin, Ævar placed an enchanted torc about her neck. Supposedly made from the mane of Sleipnir and cursed by a witch, the torc was like nothing she had seen before. Its sole purpose was to bind Ísold's own magical powers. No longer was she able to walk the spaces between sleep and wake, nor was she able to cast spells. The only influence she held in the realm of magic was that of second sight. Any other powers she may have ever possessed would forever lie dormant.

Ísold felt the smooth, cold surface give way with a sickening crack as she stood. Her breath stopped. Looking down, she pulled back the long skirt of her emerald dressing gown. Tears filled her eyes at the sight of Fergus's photo crushed beneath her foot.

A gut-wrenching sob tore from Ísold's throat. It was the most precious and cruel gift Ævar had ever given her. He was the one who told Ísold that Fergus was killed on one of the many missions he went on for the Theriontrope Foundation.

As so many times before, Ævar had deceived her. The photo was proof of his deceit and that Fergus still lived. How vicious her stepbrother could be. It would have been better if she had never known the truth, if she had died believing Fergus did not live, that he had not broken his promise to her.

"If you are not my dream, then by the goddess, I swear I shall return for you," he had told her. How many years had it been and he had not come for her. But according to Cassius, no one knew she lived. Only he and Ævar had knowledge of her whereabouts.

Now the precious frame that protected Fergus's photo lay in ruin. *What have I done?* she wondered, and slid a slender fragment of glass from the frame. Maybe if the goddess would not grant her most fervent wish, then she would do it herself. Who was there to know or care? The servants would be glad that she was gone. Ævar would only be upset his personal oracle no longer held answers for him. With the exception of Kenna, her mother, and Cassius, no one else would care, especially not her red prince.

"Hana rau dòglingr." She whispered the name she had called him since their meeting as she placed the cold glass against the supple underside of her wrist. Tears streamed down her cheeks, blurring her vision. This was it. Finally she would have the relief she longed for. "Goodbye, my prince. I will always love you," she said as she closed her eyes and pulled the sharp edge across her wrist.

She waited for the sting of cold air hitting the open wound, for the metallic scent of blood warm and sticky as it fell from her wrist, but none of that came. Wiping her eyes with the back of her sleeve, Ísold stared down at her wrist. Nothing was there, not even an impression of where the makeshift blade lay against her skin.

Ísold cried out in pain as she ran the tip of her finger across the same blade and drew blood. *How was that even possible?* she thought.

"Miss Ísold?"

Ísold jumped at the sound of the maid's voice.

The maid shuffled toward her. "Miss, you've hurt yourself. I'll go and fetch some wrapping."

"It...it's not necessary," Ísold called after her, but it was too late. The maid was already somewhere along the hallway.

A shadow moved across Ísold's face, taking her attention upward. She moved to get a better view of the bank of windows high along the wall. There, beyond the glass, was the eagle she had once seen perched upon the wall of the Keep.

The large bird stared down at Ísold. She felt more than heard chanting fill her body. The rhythmic words were a language she couldn't understand, yet they mesmerized and cradled her aching soul. As she stared into the eagle's jet black eye, her feeling of despair seemed to melt away.

"Who are you?" she whispered. She knew it was impossible, but the eagle seemed to give her a knowing wink before taking to the sky.

CHAPTER 10

Ghost stared at his refection in the mirror. The deep purple shirt he wore perfectly accented the icy color of his eyes and silver-streaked hair. *Perfection,* he thought with a smile. But his smile disappeared as he caught a glimpse of the faded scar beneath his jawline.

He hated the scar. It was a daily reminder of his twin and the hatred his brother felt for him.

Although most people completely ignored it, he never would.

Painful memories of the family he was denied filled his mind. Ghost was only ten the last time he had seen either of his parents. He remembered waving to them as he and his brother, Ævar, left their small village to play and fish in the woods of Iceland.

Looking back now, Ghost understood why his younger brother was so eager for only the two of them to go fishing. Ævar had begged and pleaded with their father to allow them to go to the river alone. He promised they would not stray too far from the village and their regular fishing spot.

How could his brother want him dead? They were only ten. What ten-year-old dreams of killing his brother?

Ghost? Is everything okay? Fergus's voice jolted his thoughts

With a sniff, Ghost wiped the back of his hand across his cheek.

Fine, Fergus. Everything is fine.

Very well, just remember what Saint said. And as quickly as Fergus's voice filled his mind, it was gone.

Damn, Fergus. Ghost thought of the fight he and his leader had earlier. There was a moment of panic when he thought Fergus would truly throw him from the window. Luckily, Saint had intervened.

With a huff, Ghost ripped the shirt over his head. Saint had told him to stay put, and he wouldn't go against his brother's wishes no matter how much he wanted to. Instead, he would be a good boy and find something else to relieve his boredom.

Normally, he would watch a movie or catch up on a television show he had missed while on assignment. But for once, he couldn't think of a single movie or show he wanted to watch.

Pulling on an old t-shirt, Ghost kicked off his shoes and picked up his drumsticks. "Time for a little one-on-one with the Peart," Ghost murmured as he headed to the music room.

He would put on his earphones, block out the world, and live his fantasy of being a rock and roll legend. Ghost perused the collection of CDs. "Ah, a little Rush might be the best medicine," he mumbled, pulling out the CD. There was nothing better than playing along with Neil Peart to take his mind off of things.

The first strains of *Spirit of the Radio* filled his ears and closed out the rest of the world. Geddy Lee sounded great as always, as Ghost's mind began to soar. Far above Haven, Ghost's thoughts flew out into the openness of the Montana skies. Beat for beat, he and Neil were in perfect unison. The first track ended, moving seamlessly into *Freewill.*

Midway through the song, Ghost realized something was not quite right. He shook his head, trying push out the sound of a second voice creeping into the song. Of course, the voice stopped during the instrumental part, but as soon as Geddy started back up, so did the voice.

He opened his eyes and looked about the room, thinking maybe somehow CJ had entered the room and joined the song. He was alone. Ghost ripped the headphones off in an effort to clear the sound. *This is nuts. There has to be something wrong with the CD.* But even as the thought came to him, Ghost knew it was wrong. He had played that particular CD a hundred times without ever hearing that particular sound.

He would change CDs. That's it. Something different.

Pulling The Who from the rack, he went straight to *Who Are You.* Surely no one would be singing with Roger Daltrey. The wan, wan, wan of the synthesizer began and then the crash of the symbols. Before long, he was halfway through the song with no additional vocalist.

Sticks flying and colliding with cymbals, Ghost was back in the zone, his mind and spirit soaring free again. Then from nowhere, a soprano voice chimed in with "whoooooo are you," repeating the words over and over. It wouldn't have bothered him so much except she was off-pitch.

"What the...." Ghost snatched away the headphones and threw them across the room. Never before had he even ventured to believe in ghosts, as in spirits and hauntings and such, but now he was not so sure. The only thing he was sure of was whatever the heck was going on, he didn't like it.

Disgruntled, Ghost flipped off the stereo and left the music room. Frustration seemed to be commonplace for him these days. The fact Fergus and Saint practically forbade his leaving Haven did little to alleviate that mood. Now the one thing he liked to do most was being interrupted by a...a what? A phantom? He was not connected to the Universe in the way both Mika and Saint were, and even if he was, he highly doubted the Universe would spend its time singing classic rock music.

He also never heard the voices of anyone other than his pack, especially not a woman. Well, there was CJ, but she was now a member of his pack and a guardian, so that made sense. The other didn't.

I must be going insane. What other explanation could there be for what he was experiencing?

"Are you okay, brother?"

It wasn't until Ghost heard Mika's voice that he realized he had wandered into the study. "Hmm?" Ghost grunted.

"You seem distracted. Does something trouble you?"

Ghost gazed out the wide expanse of windows to the open courtyard with its lush gardens and fountains. Saint always seemed to find comfort there. *If Saint were there, what would he do? Make a cup of tea, sit by the fountain, and meditate.* Ghost scrunched his face at the thought of tea. That was Saint and Fergus's thing, not his, and meditation required too much effort.

He looked about the high shelves at the vast array of books housed there. Maybe reading? Nah. Nothing really interested him. It was hard for him to believe Haven would ever feel confining or constricting, yet at this moment, it did.

"We need a mission," Ghost said flatly.

"*We* need a mission?" Mika raised an eyebrow in question.

"Fine. I need a mission," Ghost said.

"Restless?"

Ghost plopped down in one of the dark leather, wingback chairs across from Mika. "Yes. No. I don't know."

Mika closed the book he was reading and placed it on the ornately carved table beside his chair. "There is more to your mood than boredom.

What ails you?"

Ghost rested his elbows on pale denim-clad legs. A stern look washed over his face, taking the sparkle from his usually mischievous eyes. "When you hear CJ, telepathically, I mean, what does it feel like?"

"Feel? I don't understand your question."

"How does it feel? Does it make you happy? Do you feel anxious? Do you feel at ease? How does it make you feel?"

Ghost didn't want to admit it to himself, but he actually liked the mystery voice. Aside from it being tonally impaired, the singing held warmth that seemed to weave in and out of his heart, bringing him peace. It intrigued and frightened him more than anything else ever had. Only once before had he felt such utter calm and tranquility, and that was when he met CJ's friend and co-worker, Arial.

"I feel love."

"What does love feel like?"

"It feels like love."

Ghost slumped back in his chair.

"Not the answer you were looking for?" Mika asked.

"Not exactly." Ghost picked at the frayed hole in the knee of his jeans. He didn't dare face Mika's assessing gaze.

"What brought on this question?"

"Never mind. It was stupid anyway." Ghost stretched as he rose from the chair. "I think I'll go for a run." He pulled the t-shirt over his head and kicked off his shoes.

"Would you like some company?"

"Nah. I kind of want to be alone."

With a courtly nod of his head, Mika told Ghost he understood.

"Would you mind closing the door behind me?" Ghost asked as light began to emanate from the core of his body. The air in the room became charged with electricity as his body exploded into a thousand tiny lights. The lights expanded outward, dancing about before converging into the form of a solid white wolf.

"No catch phrase this time?"

The wolf peered up at Mika. *Nah.* He shrugged. *For some reason, I'm just not in the mood,* Ghost answered telepathically. With a running leap, Ghost was on the ground and racing as hard as his body would allow into the woods of Haven.

Mika felt CJ's arms wrap around him, and her body press against his back. "Was that Ghost?" she asked.

"Yes."

"I thought Fergus and Saint said for him to stay at Haven while they were away."

Mika turned to face CJ and placed his cheek against the silkiness of her hair. "They did."

"Is it safe for him to be out there alone?"

A pang of jealousy shot through Mika at CJ's concern for his pack mate. He knew it was unwarranted, yet he couldn't help himself.

"Stop." CJ pushed playfully against the broad expanse of Mika's chest. "Ghost is the last shifter you should be jealous of."

"Does that mean there's another I should worry about?"

"I'll never tell."

Mika could feel CJ smile as she teased him. The Great Father was right to choose her as his mate. There was no way he could love another the way he loved this woman.

"If you feel you need to follow Ghost, then go," CJ whispered to him.

"Ghost can take care of himself. Besides, it isn't as if he is leaving Haven."

"Are you trying to convince me or yourself?"

Mika hugged her tighter. "In truth, I don't know. Ghost is nearly as old as I. Fergus trained him just as he did me. Still...." Mika's voice trailed off in the direction of Ghost's exit.

The warmth of CJ's body left him as she pulled away. "Go after him. You know you want to."

Did he want to or did he need to? There was a fine line between the two. His pack mate was safe within the confines of Haven, was he not? Of course he was.

CJ was right. Mika was trying to convince himself Ghost would be fine. So if Ghost was safe, then why did Mika have an overwhelming urge to follow? Unwillingly, Mika left her arms. "You know I can deny you nothing."

"I know." CJ smiled up at him, warming his heart in a way nothing else ever could. Within moments, he changed from man to coyote.

CJ opened the doors for him, allowing him access to the terrace. Lifting his muzzle to the sky, Mika took in the scents around him. Catching Ghost's scent, Mika took off after his brother.

CHAPTER 11

Apple-y perched on the edge of Ævar's desk. Her lithe legs swung back and forth in rhythm with the grandfather clock that stood along the far wall.

She was bored. Very, very bored. Looking over her shoulder, she scrutinized the woman standing near Ævar. Miranda, Ævar's secretary, adjusted her weight from one foot to the other, glancing nervously at Apple-y.

Making human's squirm it was one of Apple-y's favorite things to do.

Apple-y looked the woman up and down. She wasn't attractive enough to be a shifter. In fact, Miranda was a bit on the frumpy side for Apple-y's taste. Still, the woman spent more time with her master than Apple-y did. That fact alone was enough to bring out her jealousy.

A small, almost imperceptible growl rolled in the lowest depths of Apple-y's throat. There was no better time than now to let this person know her place.

"Stop, Apple-y," Ævar said, without stopping what he was doing.

"Apple-y do nothing," she answered, giving a final, scrutinizing glance to Miranda.

"Mmm hmm," Ævar grunted. With one last scratch of pen on paper, he closed the folder and dismissed his assistant, who, Apple-y noticed, almost ran from the room.

"Apple-y no like that person. She need to go."

Ævar leaned back, locking his hands behind his head. Apple-y enjoyed when her Master posed for her, leaving the most vulnerable part of himself exposed to her. His body was so open and inviting.

Using her tigerian reflexes, Apple-y straddled his legs. Each hand wrapped around his biceps. She had never forgotten the solid feel of his body and slender muscle and tendons gliding beneath skin. Languidly stroking her cheek against his, she reveled in the experience of his clean-shaven skin.

"Maybe let Apple-y have fun with her? Just a little scare?" she pleaded.

A soft chuckle vibrated in his throat, and she found pleasure in his amusement. "You can't eliminate every female from my life. Miranda has a job to do and I need her."

A pang of jealousy shot through Apple-y. What did he mean he needed that person? She was merely an assistant, and assistants were as common as grass. Everyone knew that. Not that she cared what her Master thought. Obviously, he cared little for her opinions. She needed to remember that.

Ævar's powerful arms held her solidly in place even though she tried to wiggle away. "What is going on in that head of yours?" he asked.

"Nothing," she sniffed, refusing to meet his gaze.

"Apple-y. Apple-y, look at me."

"Nyet," she answered in her native Russian.

Taking her face in his hands, Ævar tried to force her submission, but she jerked away. She wouldn't give him the satisfaction of having physical control of her. She felt a chill as he removed the warmth of his touch. Only now would she look at him.

"*Da?*"

"There's no need for jealousy." Ævar's voice wafted across the gentle slope of her throat. His breath warmed the delicate skin beneath her ear. "Miranda has been with my company for years and is very loyal. If you kill her, than I would be forced to hire somebody new. If I hire someone new, they may not understand the nuances of running my company."

Apple-y's bottom lip jutted forward. "So?" Apple-y knew she sounded like a petulant child, but she was unable to stop.

"So if the company doesn't run smoothly, no money. No money, no presents for Apple-y."

Apple-y's eyes grew wide at his statement. She loved her presents almost as much as she loved the man who brought them to her. "No kill assistant?" she asked, disappointed at his disapproval.

"Not if you still want presents."

"Fine," she sighed. "No kill assistant." So she couldn't rip the woman's face off. *Master said nothing about scarring her.* A huge smile curled back Apple-y's lavishly colored lips. There were so many fun ways to deal with the assistant. The thought almost made her giddy.

"No, Apple-y." Ævar seemed to read the tiger's mind. "No scarring or maiming. The help is off limits. Understand?"

How he know what Apple-y think? It wasn't the solution she wanted, but she would obey her Master's wishes. "Fine. Apple-y...," she began.

Ævar held up his index finger as a reminder she was doing it again. Speaking of herself in—what did Cassius call it? Third person? *Whatever that mean.*

She knew it was a problem, and her propensity for doing such always became worse when she was upset or mad. It wasn't her fault she learned to speak improper English. After all, it wasn't as if she had a normal upbringing. Apple-y had very few memories of her childhood, and the ones that did exist were less than pleasant.

Life had been so difficult then. She had no formal education to speak of. According to her Master, she had to have attended school at some point or else she wouldn't be able to read or do rudimentary math problems. To think about it now, she almost felt that that life belonged to another person on another planet.

She remembered nights so cold her tears froze to her eyelashes. For days, she would go without food. Her hunger became so intense it turned into nausea.

Then there were the men. Short, tall, fat, thin. It didn't matter. Some gave her money, others brought her food, but all would lie to her just to get between her legs. Many were cruel to her, and she lost count of the number who took pleasure in hurting her.

Apple-y closed her eyes, tightly pushing down the thoughts of the last man to hurt her. She could still remember the taste of his blood upon her tongue and hear the crunch and snap of bone and cartilage as she bit into his throat. Her first time to shift had been his last day to live. *Served him right, the bastard.*

A roar of pain broke from Apple-y's body at the memory. She shook uncontrollably, and electricity played along her hands and fingers, forcing claws from her fingertips.

"Let it go," came the command.

Her rational mind knew it was the voice of her Master, but her rational mind wasn't the one in charge at the moment.

"Breathe," Ævar commanded again, but it was too late.

She felt the crisp linen of Ævar's lavender shirt give way to her razor-tipped fingers as they slashed through the material. His flesh caked beneath fishhook nails as Apple-y raked her hands across his shoulders and chest.

The scent of his blood consumed her. Her memories pulled at her, taking her back to that dingy, soulless room with the man who hurt her. It was his blood she was after.

Dipping her head, Apple-y lapped at the warm, sticky substance that flowed down Ævar's chest and abdomen. A loud hiss escaped his lips at the touch of her tongue, spurring her onward, giving her his unspoken permission.

Her head rang from the hastening of her heart, muddling the sounds around her. Male voices surrounded her, she knew that much, but she was unable to make out what they were saying.

Needle-sharp pain penetrated her shoulder, bringing her back for the briefest of moments. Her vision cleared in time to see Cassius standing beside her. Her body became limp. "What you do?" she asked, but she didn't get to hear his answer before falling into a deep sleep.

"I told you she was crazy," Cassius said, lifting her from Ævar's lap and placing her on the nearby sofa. He picked up one of her hands and watched as the claws retracted into her skin.

With haste, Cassius checked Apple-y's pulse rate. He didn't like being this close to the tiger. The medication he had given her was strong, but so was Apple-y's willpower. Good. Her heart was steady and slowing. Maybe he had given her the correct dose after all.

"Don't lecture me, Cassius. I know what I am doing," Ævar said.

Cassius bit the inside of his cheek to keep from blurting out all the things he was thinking. Mostly that Ævar was as crazy as Apple-y for bringing her out of the asylum. Months ago, Ævar decided that Apple-y would succeed where others had failed in killing his brother. Maybe she would, but only if she didn't kill Ævar first.

Maybe he should have just let the Siberian live in her delusion and kill Ævar. So many things would be better if he did, but such wasn't the polar bear's way.

Deep red stains covered what was left of Ævar's shirt, plastering it to his body. The ragged material did little to hide the eight-inch-long gashes covering Ævar's chest and shoulders.

"Obviously." Cassius raised a dark eyebrow.

Ævar pulled the shirt from his body and tossed it into the garbage can. "Do you doubt my decision?"

Cassius watched as Ævar opened the door to his private bath and began to clean the blood from his torso. "When it comes to your brother and that hellcat? No. I don't trust your judgment."

"Careful with your tone, Cassius."

"There is no tone. There is only truth. For whatever reason, you care too little for one and too much for the other. At best, your judgment is clouded." He leaned on the opposite corner of the desk, ever watchful of Ævar's body language.

Cassius wasn't a fool when it came to Ævar and what he was capable of. The shifter didn't like when others questioned his authority, no matter how noble the cause. Ísold was the perfect example of that. Very seldom did Ævar's punishment fit the crime.

"My mistake, old friend. If you would be kind enough to watch over her while I'm gone," Ævar said, opening the window.

A slight glow emanated from Ævar's torso, alerting Cassius to the fact his employer was about to shift and leave him alone with Apple-y, a prospect he didn't find appealing.

"Where are you going?" Cassius asked.

"I must heal before infection from these wounds set in," Ævar answered, all the while the light continuing to expand throughout the length of his body. Each cell filled with energy, separating one from the other, creating a tornado of swirling gold. The light shifted, rearranging in midair, before contracting back into the form of an Arctic wolf. A hint of awe mixed with a hint of jealousy filled Cassius. No matter how many times he changed into his animal form, it would never be quite the spectacle Ævar made. Maybe it was a wolf thing. Then again, Fergus never seemed so flashy, so maybe it was an Ævar thing.

The wolf stared at Cassius, waiting for an answer.

"Yes, I will take care of her, and no, I won't restrain her. That sedative should last another thirty minutes or so. By then she should be back to normal." *Although I'm not too sure what normal is for her.* Luckily Cassius's answer satisfied Ævar, who casually leapt from the window.

Cassius went to Apple-y's side. He didn't like to admit to having any feelings where Apple-y was concerned, but he truly felt sorry for her. Like so many in Ævar's life, Apple-y was expendable, and she wouldn't understand that fact until it was too late.

CHAPTER 12

"Hey, CJ," Ghost chirped. He walked toward her, carrying a bowl and dipping out what looked like cheesecake or maybe ice cream.

CJ glanced up from the computer screen. It amazed her how much Ghost and Mika ate, and neither could have more than one percent body fat. All she had to do was look at a piece of cake, and it would end up on her hips.

"Are you eating again?" she asked.

"Hey, I'm a growing wolf. I need to keep up my strength."

CJ grunted and returned to the computer. She may have only known Ghost for a few months, but it did not take her long to understand that sometimes, where Ghost was concerned, it was best to leave things alone.

Ghost half-leaned half-sat on the desk beside her. "So, what are you doing?"

"Just going through some pictures that Arial emailed me."

CJ noticed a physical straightening of Ghost's posture and demeanor at the mention of Arial's name.

"Pictures of what?" He craned his neck, trying to see the computer monitor.

"She didn't want me to worry about the office. So she sent me some pictures of her and the other staff members. She also wanted me to know they missed me." CJ sighed and pointed to a photo of her ex-staff members holding up a sign reading "We Miss You!" with a big, sad face drawn on it.

Ghost nudged her shoulder. "You okay?"

"A little homesick, I guess. It was really hard to say goodbye to those guys."

"It's hard leaving everyone and everything for a new life."

CJ caught the sadness in Ghost's tone. Mika had told her bits and pieces of how Ghost came to be at Haven with him and the others. Although she found it hard to be away from friends and family, she couldn't imagine being thrust into that situation as a child.

"So, you think any of the ladies back at your office might be interested in dating a shifter?" Ghost wiggled his eyebrows.

Aaaaaaaaand he's back, she thought. "For you? That would be a—no."

"Ouch, that hurts." He mockingly clutched his chest.

"Mm, hmm, I'm sure it does."

"Hey, I'm a good guy."

Ghost was a good guy. He was also "that" guy. On occasion, CJ couldn't help but hum the song *I'm Sexy and I Know It* when he walked by. If he heard her, he never let on. Then again, he probably liked it.

Ghost was the one with the reputation for being perpetually on the catch and release program. Even Mika had a hard time remembering how many women Ghost had dated over the years. There was no way she would allow one of her friends to be one of his catches.

"Heeeelloooo?" Ghost said when she took too long to answer.

"Yes, Ghost. You are a great guy. But you are also a scoundrel when it comes to women."

Ghost opened his mouth for rebuttal, but the look she gave him told him not to bother.

"That one is pretty cute," Ghost said, pointing to a rather attractive brunette on the monitor and taking control of the mouse. "What else you got?"

CJ rolled her eyes. "Don't you have anything better to do?"

"Not really." He continued browsing her photos.

CJ looked at the faces of her friends as they flicked across the screen. She ached with longing to see her old friends. What she wouldn't give for a night of margaritas and chick flicks with Arial. Heck, she would even take a Saturday of mani/pedis and shopping with Bethany Rose.

Now there was a thought. Out of all her friends, Bethany Rose would be the only one she would even imagine could give Ghost a run for his money. Squinting in Ghost's direction, she tried to imagine Ghost and Bethany together. *Nah, it would never work.* She let the idea go.

"You could always invite them to come here," he suggested.

"I suppose I could." She had planned on asking her friends to visit before the wedding, something she almost slipped up and told Ghost.

She and Mika agreed the only logical choice was for Saint to perform their ceremony, and they didn't want to tell Fergus and Ghost until they could tell everyone at the same time. She hoped that whatever had taken Saint away would soon be resolved so her newly formed family would be back together.

"Or we could fly back for a couple of days," Ghost suggested.

"We?"

"Yeah, we. You, Mika...me."

"Nice try, little brother, but no," Mika said from the doorway.

"You can't blame a guy for trying," Ghost said.

"I can if that guy is you." CJ felt Mika's hands rest comfortably on her shoulders.

"Besides," CJ said, "if we went to Florida, I would have to see my mother, and last time I tried to call her, she refused to answer."

Mika kissed the top of her head. "You will work out your difference, Little Star."

"Of course you will. Your mom will come around," Ghost added.

CJ hoped the guys were right. She hated not speaking with her mother. Leave it to Gypsy Lynn to act like the victim. If anyone had the right to ignore someone, it was CJ.

She could hear her mother lamenting to her friends about how her daughter walked away from her career and family to chase after a man.

Wonder if Mom will mention the fact that she lied about my father's death or that she knew who and what Mika was? CJ knew the answer to those questions was a big, fat no.

So the last words CJ said to her mother had something to do with the possibility that her grandchildren might be puppies. Was that really a reason to hold a grudge?

The walls of Haven rocked with a thunderous roar, followed by crashing glass. CJ, Mika, and Ghost looked from one to the other before scrabbling up the stairs toward the commotion.

Rigid as steel, Fergus stood in the middle of the expansive, upstairs hallway. His hands clenched in tight fists at his sides. He completely ignored the claret droplets of blood streaking down the back of his right hand and splashing onto the reflective shards of glass that lay at his feet. From her position, CJ could see his flesh begin to singe in reaction to the silver backing of the mirror. She knew silver was caustic to shifters, but she didn't realize the reaction would be immediate.

CJ had to admit she held a healthy dose of fear where Fergus was concerned. She could see the rage swirl in a windstorm about him, though he refused to even flinch. From the beginning, CJ had sensed the feral part of him, and it was the part she felt certain he was wrestling back into the cage this very moment. No matter how much she feared him, first and foremost, she was the guardian, and as such, it was her duty to care for all of them.

Wait, Mika sent the message to her, gently touching her arm. *Give me a moment.* "Brother, what is wrong?" Mika asked.

"I do not know which angers me more. The lies or the fact Bridget still lives."

"Oh, crap," Ghost whispered.

"Oh, crap indeed," Fergus echoed.

"Man, that was one of my favorite mirrors," Ghost lamented.

Ghost, now isn't a good time to push at Fergus. CJ heard Mika as he scolded Ghost.

Ghost crossed his arms over his chest, pouting. *Well, it was,* Ghost added.

CJ decided it was best to ignore Ghost and Mika to focus on Fergus. *Mika, Fergus is bleeding, He needs my help.*

Patience, Little Star.

"Does Dr. G know?" Ghost asked.

"It was Grey that told me." Fergus flexed his hand. "CJ, would you mind?" He held his hand toward her.

She was shocked at his asking for her help but relieved all the same. "Ghost, can you go get my medical kit? I think I left it in the kitchen."

CJ was beside herself. It didn't matter who this Bridget person was or what she had done, but there was no need for Fergus to break the furnishings. The mirror, like most everything in the manor house, was an antique, and unless Fergus got a rein on his temper, CJ was unsure how much furniture would be left.

Ghost bounded back up the stairs. "Here you go," he said, handing her the white box marked "first aid."

Taking a pair of tweezers from the medicine kit, CJ removed the tiny slivers of glass lodged in Fergus's flesh. She had to give him kudos for his stoicism. Most people would at least acknowledge the pain, but not Fergus. The only way she even knew he was breathing was the feel of his breath ruffling the top of her head as he stared out the huge window behind her.

It occurred to CJ that a little glass in the hand was probably nothing more than an annoyance to Fergus. Mika had told her only a few of the battles and wars Fergus had fought over the years. None knew the true numbers of assignments Theriontrope had sent him on. Even if it had only been one per year, it would mean he had been in at least two hundred fights. No wonder he was so jaded.

A wave of guilt flashed through CJ as she looked up at Fergus. Had he heard what she was saying? With him, she could never be sure. "Why the mirror?" CJ had to ask.

"Because Michael Grey was on the other side," Fergus answered.

"That doesn't make sense. How was Michael on the other side of a mirror?" she asked.

"You see, CJ," Ghost jumped in. "Fergus has a special gift when it comes to mirrors. He can use them like you use a video call."

"Huh?"

"He means Fergus could Skype before it was even invented," Mika added.

"You mean like a webcam?" she asked.

"Exactly," Ghost said.

"But…how?" she asked again.

"Magic," Mika shrugged.

A few short months ago, CJ would have laughed in Mika's face at his statement, but she had come to accept the world of shifters was filled with the unexplained. If they said Fergus used a magic mirror to make a call, who was she to argue?

"We all have different talents," Mika said.

"I'll say." She began bandaging Fergus's hand. "Okay then. Who is Bridget?"

"Saint's fiancé," Ghost said.

"Ex-fiancé," Fergus and Mika said in unison. Both made sure to punctuate the "ex" part.

CJ manipulated Fergus's hand and fingers, checking for any signs of breaks or sprains. She was pretty sure nothing was broken, but she wanted to be sure. "You're kidding. Saint was married?"

"No." All three men answered in unison.

Okay, CJ thought. *Add that to the list of things to ask Mika when we are alone.* "Nothing appears to be broken, and even if it was, you could always shift."

"Thank you." Fergus inclined his head slightly. "Now if you will excuse me."

"Going to New Orleans?" Ghost asked.

"Yes," Fergus answered. "And no, you may not come. No one may come," he directed his statement toward Mika.

"Is there anything I can do?" Mika asked.

"Yes. Could you please place a call to Kellas and make arrangements for my lodging."

"Of course. Is there anything else?"

"No," Fergus said. "Bridget was my responsibility, and against my better judgment, I deferred to Saint as how to handle the situation. That shan't happen again."

Mika placed a reassuring hand on Fergus's shoulder. "We understand. Know we are here if need be."

"Thank you, my brother," Fergus said. "Just as Saint has his dilemmas, so have I mine."

CHAPTER 13

Janet snuggled deeper into the warmth of her bed. She should get up. Soon Eric would be knocking at her door asking for breakfast. She had been able to put him off yesterday with the lure of cinnamon rolls, but there was no way she would do that two days in a row. Besides, she liked the smoky, sweet smell of bacon lingering in the air. It made the apartment feel more like a home.

New Orleans was Janet's home, but a part of her had always longed for a home in the country. She could imagine a large two-story farmhouse with a wraparound porch. It would be the perfect place to have her morning coffee while watching the sun rise over the treetops.

She would also build a spacious greenhouse out back with a meditation space. Inside she would place a set of comfortable chairs and a small table where she would stop and take tea in between her gardening. The only thing that could make her dream complete would be someone to share it with.

Breathing deep, Janet could almost smell the aroma of fresh baked bread wafting underneath her bedroom door. *That smells wonderful,* she thought.

Thank you.

What the…? Janet's eyes flew open at the sound of Saint's voice. Relief morphed to disappointment when she realized his statement was merely her imagination. Not that she actually expected him to be there. It would have been nice if he was. *What am I saying?*

With a huff, Janet threw back the covers. She barely knew the man. *It might be nice to get to know him.* Who was she kidding? When it came to Saint Wolfe, she would most definitely like to get to know him better.

I would like that also. She heard his voice again. *Breakfast is almost complete if you wish to join me.*

Gape-mouthed, she stared at the door. How could he have heard her, let alone answer her? It was a trick of her mind. That was the only logical explanation. She almost giggled at the *harrumph* she imagined coming from him at her last statement.

Opening the door a sliver, Janet peaked down the hallway. The clunk of cabinet doors added to the rhythm of off-key humming that made its way from the kitchen. *Great,* she groaned. The last thing she wanted was for him to see her with smeared mascara, bedhead, and morning breath. She would need to use all the stealth she possessed to sneak past the kitchen and Saint before he had a chance to see the morning Janet.

Taking a fortifying breath, she tiptoed down the hall, silently cursing every floorboard that popped or creaked under her feet. Janet peeked around the doorway. Saint had his back to the door as he tended to something on the stove. *Thank you.* She mouthed the words toward the ceiling and continued on her path. She estimated there was only six more feet between her and her target. *Princess Fiona goes in, and Princess Ryhinni emerges,* she mused, remembering the ogre princess from *Shrek.*

The sound of Saint clearing his throat halted Janet in her tracks. She needn't turn around to know Saint stood behind her.

"Your breakfast will be ready when you are finished," he said. The beauty of his accent touched her in a way she couldn't explain.

"Thank you," she squeaked.

"You are most welcome...princess."

After breakfast, Saint meandered through the aisles of books inside My Spicy Cauldron. He was positive there had to be a method to Janet's filing system, but for the life of him, he couldn't decipher it. At least, she could have arranged them in alphabetical by last name of author.

"I have been meaning to rearrange these and put them in a better order," she said, as she appeared beside him.

"It does seem to be a bit scattered."

Janet's chocolate-colored eyes smiled up at him. "Scattered would be a good word. Confusing might be another."

Saint clasped his hands behind his back, fighting back an overwhelming urge to take her in his arms and kiss her breathless. The thought shocked him. Unlike his younger brother, Saint didn't seek the company of women. Through the years, it was easy for Saint to convince himself that love and family weren't in the stars for him.

Bridget had been his first and last romantic affiliation, and he believed it had been enough—until now. However, now wasn't a good time. He must put some things in order first. Then he could more fully entertain the possibility of a relationship with Janet. For the moment, he would do well to keep his hands to himself.

He could feel uneasiness in Janet as she watched him. Her pulse began to quicken, heating and intensifying the scent of her skin. Out of the corner of his eye, Saint saw movement.

In a rare move of assertion, Saint took her hand in his. The shock on Janet's face soon faded when he placed her palm against the solid wall of his chest. He had no idea what prompted him to do such a thing. It had been a knee-jerk reaction at best and one he hoped he wouldn't come to regret.

Saint fully expected her to jerk away. Instead, Janet stepped closer, allowing her hand to linger upon his breast, just above his heart. Again, he was comforted by the warmth of her hand and astonished by how this slightest of touches stilled the anxiety that rode his soul. *If only this moment would never end.*

"What did you mean by 'my kind'?" he asked.

"My kind?" She seemed confused.

"Yesterday you said 'your kind thinks they are the only ones connected to the spirits or the Universe or the gods.' 'My kind.' To what were you referring?"

Janet glanced about, making sure no one was within earshot. "I mean your kind. Shifters," she whispered, as she looked up at him. "Oh, don't look so surprised. I could tell the moment I saw you."

"Really?" Saint asked, trying not to sound as amused as he felt. "And how is that possible?"

"Shifters have a double aura. One is always golden. It represents the animal in you. The other is normally colored depending upon your mood, thoughts, etc."

To say he was surprised by her statement was, indeed, an understatement. *Double aura?* In all his years, he had never heard such a thing, and he made a mental note to add that to his list of research topics for his return to Haven.

"See. You're doing it again," Janet said. "I can tell you don't believe me. Just like all the other shifters that come here. You ask a question then ridicule me when I tell you what I know to be true." Janet dropped her head in resignation.

"I did nothing of the sort. It is simply, in my experience, a truly psychic human is uncommon," Saint said.

"Uncommon, maybe, but not impossible," Janet said, her tone colored by her frustration. "Okay...let's do this." Janet jumped in before Saint had a chance at rebuttal. "Let me tell you a few things I have picked up about you, Mr. Wolfe, and if after I have finished you disagree with anything I have said, I won't try and sway your opinions. However, if any of my words ring true, then you have to agree that there is a chance, however remote, that humans can indeed be connected, as you like to call it. Is it a deal or are you to prejudice to give me a chance?"

Prejudiced? Saint scoffed. He was the epitome of open-minded. Okay. Maybe epitome was too strong of a word, but he was liberal of thought in many areas and quite progressive for a shifter of his years. Could he help it if a human's ability to tap into the Universe wasn't one of those areas?

Saint found Janet's passion utterly adorable, even if it was completely without merit, and before he could put a rein on his tongue, he agreed to her proposition. "Very well, I accept your offer," Saint answered. "Though I find it hard to believe you can convince me otherwise."

Janet simply smiled and began. "You, Saint Wolfe, are extremely intelligent. You question most everything and everyone. You believe yourself to be an open book, yet you shield your emotions beneath an extremely poised, albeit charming, exterior.

"You freely give your time and advice when asked, yet no one reciprocates, or more to the point, you don't give yourself the latitude to ask.

"You are fiercely loyal, especially where your family is concerned, and you will stop at nothing to help any one of them. Even going so far as to put your own life in danger.

"Your eyes are the most unusual fern green I have ever seen," she said, placing her free hand against his cheek. "They make me want to walk barefoot in the soft mosses of the forest floor. They reflect your pain and your wisdom. You have been hurt more deeply than any seem to know, and you now question the authority you once held in the highest regard.

"You have been touched by death in a way I don't understand. I can feel its coldness deep in your soul, and it is personal. It is the reason you fear little or nothing and the reason you are here. You need to end the perpetual cold."

Saint stood dumbstruck. As much as he hated to admit it, Janet was right. He was fiercely loyal to his family, and that loyalty had hurt him in ways no one could know or understand. But what struck him most was the gentleness with which she spoke and the touch of her hand upon his skin.

An unbidden thought crossed Saint's mind that he could spend the rest of his life just listening to the lilt of her voice and allowing her warmth to soothe him. *A fool's fantasy*, he decided and pushed the thoughts from his mind.

"But," she continued, "I must warn you. If you continue on this quest, searching for the woman you claim you are not searching for, you will be tested. Your loyalties and your will-power will be pushed to their limits. I know you will not want to ask for help, but you must. You are always there for others, and they will be there for you."

Saint had heard the term "lost in someone's eyes," but he had never experienced it. Not until now. As he looked into the mocha depths of Janet's eyes, that was exactly how he felt—lost. Only she existed in this time and this space. The rest of the world be damned.

"Geeze, Mom, get a room!" Eric's voice broke the silence between Saint and Janet, causing them both to jump back.

"I agree with the kid. Get a room." Saint looked past the young man to find his older brother standing there. He heard the small whimper escape Janet's throat before she pushed past everyone and disappeared through the curtains to Princess Ryhinni's reading room.

"What did you do to my mom?" Eric asked, stepping up to Saint.

"Who? Me?" Saint stammered. "I did nothing to your mother."

Though the teenager was quite a bit smaller than Saint, he didn't back down. "Yeah? Then why was she crying?"

"You are the one who blurted out for her to seek shelter," Saint defended.

"To seek shelter? What are you talking about?" Eric asked.

"You said to get a room, which makes very little sense considering you live here."

"Whatever, dude. I know she rented that room to you, but don't think that just because you made us breakfast, you can be my new dad." Eric said, poking Saint in the chest. "Stay away from my mom." Eric stormed up the stairs. The ceiling reverberated with each of Eric's footsteps, culminating in a WHAM.

Saint stared, wide-eyed, at his brother. "What was that all about?"

"You tell me," Fergus said.

"Was I wrong? Is that not what he meant by 'get a room'?"

"You are too literal, you know that?"

Saint's brow knitted together. He did know he took things literally. Ghost had accused him of that quite frequently, but language usage changed too rapidly for him to keep up with every little nuance.

Fergus grinned. "He meant you looked like the Big Bad Wolf about to devour Little Red Riding Hood.

"Preposterous!" Saint exclaimed. "She was merely...."

"Merely what?"

"She was merely telling me my fortune."

Fergus crossed his arms over his chest and leaned against the bookshelf. "Is that what you kids are calling it these days?"

Saint adjusted his vest. "Well, I've never!"

Fergus grinned widely. "Keep looking at Little Red like that and you will."

CHAPTER 14

Embarrassed? Devastated? Ticked-off. Janet sat in Princess Ryhinni's reading room, listening to the silence around her as she stared into her crystal ball. The table vibrated beneath her fingers as she bounced her leg up and down on the hardwood floor. She hoped that concentrating on the orb would show her the best way to deal with Eric.

How could he have embarrassed me like that? Better yet, why had she even felt embarrassed about what she was doing? Could she help it that from his crisply starched collar to his immaculately shined shoes, Aidan Wolfe was the sexiest man, shifter or not, she had ever seen?

So why did that make her so mad? She was mad at everyone and everything. Mad at the sign for hanging above her store. Mad at Eric for embarrassing her. Mad at herself for inviting Saint for tea and then allowing him to rent her spare room. Mad at Saint for accepting the invitation and frustrated with her body for reacting to him the way it did.

Darn my soft heart. She slammed her palm against the table, causing the crystal ball to hop a few spaces.

"Mom!" she heard Eric yell.

Great. What was she going to do with him? There were days it was easy to be a mother. Sometimes her son was the most perfect of the gods' creations. Then there were moments when she wanted to throttle him. "Give me strength," she prayed softly, as she touched the talisman at her throat. Someone needed to; because it was going to take everything she had to keep from grounding him for the next fifteen years of his life.

"Mom!" Eric called again.

"In here," Janet yelled back. It was best if he came to her since her body refused to stop trembling.

Outside the curtain, she heard Eric stomp down the stairs. How was she supposed to explain this to him? Better yet, what was there to explain? Again she reminded herself she hadn't done anything wrong. With a groan, Janet dropped her head on the table.

"Mom? Please don't cry." Janet felt his arm circle about her shoulders in a half-hearted hug.

"I'm fine," Janet answered, and she was, kind of. Even if she wasn't at the moment, she would be. She always was. No matter how complicated her life became, Janet Beesinger always turned out fine.

"Then he must have hypnotized you or something for you to act like that. Right?"

Janet raised her head. "He didn't do anything to me."

"How else do you explain the way you were acting?"

"How was I acting?" Who was she kidding? Two more seconds and she would have thrown caution to the wind and Saint to the ground. That would have put a permanent crease in his prim and proper shorts!

"You know," Eric answered, flipping the hair from his face.

"No, I don't know," Janet said, speaking deliberately.

Eric rose quickly. "Come on, Mom. You guys were about to start making out in the middle of the store."

Janet's body stiffened. "We were not!" All of a sudden, she could hear her grandfather's voice. "The scalded dog always hollers first." She shook her head. She wasn't a scalded dog.

Okay. Maybe she had wondered what it would be like to kiss his perfect lips. What if she did want to kiss Saint? She was a grown woman, and she could kiss whomever she liked. "I think you are exaggerating." She tried to sound innocent, but it wasn't working. "And what if I did find Mr. Wolfe attractive?" she conceded. "I can have a relationship with whomever I want."

"Aw, gross, Mom." Eric groaned. "What did you have to bring up sex for?"

Janet shot to her feet. She needed to head Eric off before he might later say something in front of Saint that she would regret. Luckily, no one, including Saint, was about. A pang of sadness coursed through her at his absence. *It's official. I am losing it,* she thought, trying to shake off her disappointment. "Who said anything about sex?" she whispered. "I am talking about relationships."

"Same thing," Eric said.

"No, they aren't. Sex is a relationship, but it isn't the only relationship between a man and a woman."

"Come on, Mom. Don't say that word."

"Sex?" Janet watched Eric's face contort. "How did I raise you to be a prude?"

Janet knew this day would eventually come. It was one she dreaded and hoped for at the same time. It had been her decision to spend the last fifteen years of her life being a mother. Not wanting to give Child Protective Services any reason to take Eric away, Janet refused to date anyone. Even as Eric became older, she found very little time for a relationship. It had always been the two of them. Finally, it hit her. He was scared of losing her.

"I get it, honey. It's only been the two of us since you were born, but that doesn't mean I wouldn't like to eventually have a man in my life."

She watched in silence as Eric mulled over her words. It would be easier if he wasn't forced into the situation Janet knew was looming over the horizon.

"I'm not saying you can't have a man in your life," Eric finally spoke. "But does it have to be a wolf?" Eric slumped onto the stool behind the counter.

"So he's a shape shifter. You've been around shifters since you were born."

"I know, but if you want to date a shifter, then date Kel."

"Kel and I are just friends. Besides, I will probably never see Saint again."

"What a stupid name."

"Eric Haaken Beesinger! You know, people might think the same about your name."

"At least it's not Saint," he grumped.

Janet began tidying things that were already tidy. She had no idea why he held a dislike for a man he didn't even know, but whatever it was, she needed to figure it out. There was no way she could date Saint if her son didn't like him. *Date Aidan? Where did that come from?* "Eric," she began her voice calm. "Why shouldn't I date him?"

"I don't know." He shrugged.

Most of the time, Janet would listen to her son when he had feelings about people or situations, but this time he was way off the mark. After meeting Saint, she knew no matter how much she may try to stay away from him, this particular wolf was now a permanent part of her life. Getting Eric to understand that fact might not be too easy.

The tiny bell on the shop door jingled as it opened. Both Janet and Eric fell silent as they gawked at the man standing in the shop. Janet tried not to stare, but she couldn't stop.

Dressed from head to foot in crimson, the man looked like an extra from a pirate film. His hair, a mixture of auburn, brown, and blonde, hung loosely about his shoulders. The rose-colored glasses perched on the end of his nose did little to hide the fact his eyes were an unusual shade of violet. But the thing that most stood out about this man was his ears. They were ever so slightly pointed.

In all of her years living in New Orleans, she had seen a lot of unusual people, but this man was different from anyone she had met before. She could tell by his aura and his stance that he wasn't human, yet he wasn't shifter either.

"May I help you?" Janet said, finally finding her voice.

Locking the door behind him, the man turned the "open" sign to "closed" before stepping toward Eric.

Eric moved nearer to his mother.

"Eric, go upstairs." She pushed him towards the doorway.

"The boy has nothing to fear from me. In fact, he is the reason I am here, but, of course, you knew that."

Janet felt Eric's body tremble as he pressed closer to her. "Sir, I don't know who you are or what you are, but I suggest you leave my shop at once before I call the police."

A mirthless smiled bowed the man's lips. "Do you think I fear humans? My kind walked this plane long before your species was brought into existence, and we will be here long after you have destroyed each other."

"What do you want?" Janet demanded.

"Proof." The man stepped closer.

Even as he spoke to her, the man's eyes never left Eric. Panic gripped her. "Run, Eric!" She pushed her son away. "I said "run, Eric!"" she yelled and reached for the phone. Pain shot through her wrist as the creature grabbed her and bent her hand backwards, forcing her to drop the phone.

Eric barely cleared the curtains to Princess Ryhinni's room when he heard his mother cry out in pain.

The man bent close to her ear. "Do you think there is anyplace he can hide that I cannot get to him?" he asked through gritted teeth.

"Who are you, and what do you want with Eric?"

"That is none of your concern."

A loud buzz began to hum from the lights above their heads, as static electricity began to swirl around the room. Both Janet and her captor turned, but he didn't release his grip on her.

Eric stood in the center of the room, his arms down at his sides. Janet eyes grew wide at the sight of him.

"Let go of my mom," Eric demanded.

"Or what?" the man laughed. "A pup such as you can do no harm to me."

Janet could see Eric's aura grow and expand outward, turning from a pure crystalline to a bright gold. It was common for Eric's aura to push outward when he was upset. It had done so since he was a child. She learned the best way to handle these situations was to try to keep him calm, which didn't seem to be an option at this time.

"I told you to let her go."

The florescent lights above their heads roared with a deafening hum. Janet looked up at the one directly above Eric's head, glowing with an unusual yellowish haze, then back to her son. "Eric, I need you to try and calm down." Again she cried out as the man twisted her wrist even further.

"Stop," Eric commanded, and threw up his hands. Without warning, a bolt of lightning shot from each of his palms. The errant electricity hit the man in the chest with enough force to send him flying backwards. Like a ragdoll, he slammed into the bookshelf nearest the door.

The lights above Eric's head exploded, covering him in a phosphorescent shower. Janet covered her head to block out the bright flashes and falling debris. Time stilled as light after light burst throughout the room.

The room fell silent, and Janet counted to ten before opening her eyes. Across from her lay Eric, his body curled into a ball upon the floor, shaking violently. She looked about the room for the stranger, but he was gone. Filled with terror, she crawled her way to her son, ignoring the pain in her hands, as shards of glass dug deep into her palms.

"Eric," she whispered, struggling to pull his convulsing body into her lap. "Honey, open your eyes. Talk to me." She waited the span of a breath and then another. "Come on, Eric. Open your eyes," she begged, and tapped his cheek with her hand. Finally, his eyes fluttered open.

"Mom...." he whispered.

"Don't talk, just listen. Can you get up?"

Eric shook his head.

"Damn," she cursed under her breath. No longer was Eric the little boy she toted on her hip. Even though he was only fifteen, he was already nearing six feet tall and probably outweighed her. It would be impossible for her to get him to his feet without his help. And she couldn't leave him lying there.

Tears pricked Janet's eyes as her mind raced, trying to determine how she could possibly get Eric up the stairs and into his bed.

She could always call 911, but how would she explain what happened? Somehow, Janet didn't think they would understand her son becoming a human lightening rod who shot bolts of electricity through his hands. Heck, she wasn't even sure she believed it, and she was a witness.

Where was her knight-in-shining-armor when she needed him?

Instinctively, Janet reached for Saint. She knew it was probably impossible, but a part of her wondered if she thought hard enough, would he come sweeping back into her shop, his black opera coat swirling about his legs, and save the day?

There was no question in Janet's mind that he had the strength to easily carry Eric since all of his species possessed great physical strength.

"Mommy?" Eric's weak voice broke Janet's train of thought.

He hadn't called her "mommy" since he was a little boy. Her heart clinched at the sound. He seemed so fragile and small and completely unlike his earlier personae. Gently, she stroked the hair from his face. "What, honey?" she asked, but he never answered. He was already asleep.

CHAPTER 15

Lucas scrutinized the portrait hanging above the marble fireplace. Napoleon Bonaparte posed regally, staring out across the expanse of the large room. The painting had always been one of Lucas's favorites, and he remembered with fondness watching the young Napoleon as he sat for the portrait.

At that time, Bonaparte was First Consul of France, and Lucas suggested Jean Auguste Dominique Ingres as the artist to paint the future ruler. A few years later, Ingres would again have the opportunity to paint Bonaparte's portrait, but by then, the young consul would have risen to the office of emperor.

Lucas raised his glass of claret in salute to the exiled emperor before taking a sip. Ah, to go back in time. Actually, he could. However, to tamper with history wouldn't be looked upon favorably by the Sisters of All Life and Knowledge. He had been the recipient of their wrath once before and did not wish to do so again.

The sound of footsteps brought Lucas back from his mental wanderings. He could tell by the thudding stride Bridget had returned, and she was not a woman in a good mood. Then again, when was she ever?

"I take it your journey was unsuccessful?" he asked, as she sat beside him and waited for her wine to be poured.

"That depends on your definition of successful," she answered, taking a sip from the cut crystal goblet.

Lucas glanced at her. A small crease had formed above the bridge of her nose, marring her perfect features, and had he not known better, Lucas would have thought she had been crying.

"Did you get to the boy?"

"Yes," she whispered.

"And?"

"And...I did as you asked. I tried to plant the seeds of doubts in the boy's mind. It remains to be seen if they take root. He is not a typical teenager."

"No, he definitely is not," Lucas said, as he cut the small medallion of beef on his plate.

"I'm through with this."

Lucas quietly placed his knife and fork on the table and leaned back in his chair. Bridget refused to look at him. Instead, she stared into the flame of the candle in front of her. Lucas had had a sneaking suspicion she might find this particular job a bit distasteful, but they had come too far for her to get cold feet now.

"So you finally wish to die?" He knew the answer to his question before he asked it, but he needed to get her attention.

Bridget cut a scathing glance his direction before downing her glass with one gulp.

"Need I remind you it was you who came to me, swearing your allegiance, if only I brought you back from the Underworld?" Lucas asked.

He watched intently as Bridget looked down at the onyx and bronze ring on the index finger of her right hand. "I remember," she whispered.

He never imagined she could still have feelings for the one known as Saint, but obviously he had been mistaken. "I have always told you, if you wish to end our arrangement, return the ring, and your life in the Underworld is yours once again." He extended his hand toward her.

Silently, he waited as Bridget twisted the ring around her finger. When she didn't answer, he took her hand, giving it a reassuring squeeze. "I didn't think so," he said, and returned to his meal.

"I don't want to hurt Saint any more than I already have."

A spiteful laugh broke from his throat. "What? After almost a century, you have developed a conscience? Don't kid yourself, mademoiselle. You love him no more now than you did then. Which, if I remember correctly, was not at all."

He could tell by her silence he had struck a chord within her. Although Bridget had been engaged to the cleric of Delta Pack, she had never loved him. Everyone had known that. Theirs was a marriage arranged from a debt owed to Lucas by her father.

At the time Lucas proposed the arrangement, he had no idea Arturo would actually sell out his own daughter. Then again, money and power were always dominant motivators to both humans and shifters. Lucas was unsure what motivated Monsieur LeCœur more – the offer of immeasurable wealth and free run of New Orleans or the thought of corrupting one of the strongest and purest souls the fates had ever created.

For Lucas, it was the latter. After all, Saint was favored among of the gods of Asgard, and irritating the Aesir had always been great fun for him.

Still, Lucas could see how Bridget had probably developed a fondness for the wolf.

"I just want this over," she said.

"And it shall be, my child. It shall be." Lucas looked up as the door to the hall opened, and Haldane Scarlethand entered the room. Long, slender, and dressed in crimson from head to foot, the elf was easily recognizable.

Haldane glided without a sound across the floor. Mesmerizing purple and violet eyes stared down at Lucas. Elegantly, the elf leaned down and whispered something in his ear. Rising slowly, with a knowing nod, Haldane dismissed himself, retreating as silently as he appeared.

"Well, this is an unexpected surprise," Lucas said as he rose from the table.

"What is?" Bridget asked.

"It seems, my dear, that we are not the only ones keeping secrets." Lucas noted the confused look on Bridget's face. "Don't worry yourself, my child. When you need to know, I'll tell you," he said, placing a fatherly kiss on the top of her head and with an elegant wave of his hand disappeared.

Reaching for the decanter of wine, Bridget poured another glass, downed it with two gulps, and filled the glass again without hesitation. Maybe that's what she needed. Maybe being blind drunk would numb her enough to forget her feelings.

She should have never followed Saint through the streets of New Orleans. She felt his confusion as he searched for her along the busy streets. As far as she could tell, he had not seen her, even though he had looked in her direction more than once.

To most of the world, she was dead, and Lucas had made sure her existence was shielded from the Theriontrope Foundation and Delta Pack.

Once she befriended CJ Carson, she was sure her identity would be discovered. Fortunately for Bridget, CJ's mother forced her into pushing Mika from any physical contact. The last thing Bridget needed was for Mika to see her and alert the others. If the Delta Pack had known she was still alive—correction—if Fergus had known she was alive, he would have stopped at nothing to kill her–again.

Bridget took another sip of wine and continued to stare into the candle flame. *Fire.* That was something she and Saint had in common. Both of their names meant fire, a fact Saint shared with her the first time they met.

When Bridget's father told her she was to marry a member of the illustrious Delta Pack, she laughed in his face. She was sure he was joking, but Arturo LeCœur didn't relent. Bridget was ordered to marry Saint Wolfe.

For goddess's sake, she had never even met the man and was expected to marry him? What was her father thinking? She remembered pleading with her father that if she was to have an arranged marriage, at least allow it to be to Ghost. If the rumors about Ghost were to be believed, a flip of her skirt and he would be putty in her hands.

Arturo would speak of it no longer. There was to be a wedding, and her intended would be Saint. It wasn't until she met him that she came to believe the proposition wasn't a bad one. He was so handsome standing at the foot of the grand staircase waiting on her.

Dressed in black from head to toe, Saint was the epitome of class and sophistication, but it was more than that. There was an air of purity about him that was intoxicating. Finally, she understood what the rumors had always spoken of–Saint was truly favored by the goddess, even if he didn't realize it.

Throughout their courtship, Bridget began to comprehend a soul as pure as his would never accept her or her pack's lifestyle. The statement "every man has his price" didn't apply where Saint was concerned. He was too vetted in his beliefs and philosophies. Not to mention, he loved humans too much. He would never treat them like the inferior cattle they were.

An image of the human known as Princess Ryhinni sprang into

Bridget's mind. All shifters in New Orleans and the surrounding parishes knew of the psychic and her son.

Princess, my French ass!

Hidden in the shadows, Bridget watched the interchange between Janet and Saint. She had seen the way the human looked at Saint and, in return, the way he looked at the human. Not even after they announced their engagement had he looked at Bridget with such longing in his eyes. If it weren't for the kid and Fergus showing up…. Bridget slammed her fist against the table. She refused to let her thoughts go there.

Although she was against Loki's plan where Saint was concerned, she was less enthused with the thought of him bonding with a human. Bridget hissed out an angry breath.

It had been a long time since she had hunted for her food. Glancing over her shoulder, she listened for any signs of Loki. Silence. He never told her she couldn't hunt humans. If he found out, he would only scold her and reprimand her for being a bad wolf.

Bridget thought of Princess Ryhinni again. Janet's willingness to help shifters left her an easy target. Wouldn't that be a wonderful gift for Saint? One of his precious humans a feast for his ex-love?

A fiendish smile crossed Bridget's face, but it faded as quickly as it emerged. Both the psychic and her son were under the protection of Kellas Scott.

Bridget had no idea how old or powerful Kellas actually was. She only knew when Loki spoke of the ancient Celt; it was with an almost reverent esteem. That was enough to tell Bridget to stay away from the princess, but New Orleans was a big city. The Quarter would be filled with quick takeout, but what would be the fun in that? And thanks to cell phones and ur_vids.com, someone would probably upload a video of her getting a snack on Bourbon Street. *Stupid internet.*

Strains of *Hungry Like the Wolf* broke the silence. Fishing her phone from the top of her boot, she checked the caller ID before answering. "CJ," she groaned. Talk about the last person she wanted to talk to right now.

"Hey, CJ," Bridget chirped, sounding more accommodating than she felt. "How's Montana?"

"It's great," CJ answered. "You ready to come out for a visit?"

Over my dead body, Bridget thought. Heading out to Montana for a reunion with Saint and the other members of his pack was exactly what she wanted to do.

"Bethany Rose, you there?" CJ asked.

Bridget cringed. By the gods, how she hated that name, but Loki insisted on it.

"Yeah, I'm just thinking about your question. I don't think I can get there anytime soon."

"Well, I need you to check your calendar and find a good time."

"Any particular reason why?"

"Well, yeah. I need my friends here for my wedding."

Gut-punched. That was the only way Bridget could describe the aching in her stomach. Even if she wanted to attend CJ's wedding, she couldn't. To step one foot on to Haven's soil would be signing her death warrant.

Bridget snorted. What would CJ do when she discovered one of her best friends worked as a spy for the enemy, a spy whose history included the Delta Pack and its cleric. No matter how Bridget examined the situation, it did not turn out well.

"I'm sorry, CJ. I don't think I can make it."

"What do you mean you can't make it? A date hasn't been set yet. That's why I am calling you."

Now is the best time to end this, Bridget thought. Even though she didn't care for most humans, Bridget had grown quite fond of this one, similar to how one feels about a beloved pet.

"I don't like Mika." She heard the quick intake of CJ's breath.

"You don't even know Mika," CJ protested.

"It doesn't matter. He took you away from everyone and everything you knew. That isn't love, CJ that is selfish manipulation."

"You sound like my mother."

"Well, maybe your mother is right."

"You do realize you are agreeing with my mother, right?"

"Look, Charlie Jean, if you want to throw your life away that is your business. However, I will have no part of it."

CHAPTER 16

"So, little brother," Fergus said, as he walked in step with Saint. "Where are we off to?"

Saint raised an eyebrow. "We are off to nowhere. You are returning to Haven, and I will continue…." Saint stopped in midstride, turning back in the direction of My Spicy Cauldron. "Odd."

"What is it?" Fergus asked.

"I'm not quite sure. For a moment, I thought I heard Janet's voice."

"Janet? Is that the woman you are so enamored with?"

"I'm not enamored with her." But even as the words fell from his lips, Saint knew it was a lie. Goddess, help him. He was enamored with her, but she wasn't the reason he was here.

Are you so sure? The voice inside him asked, and Saint quickly slammed the door on that thought.

"I am sure. I am here for one reason and one reason only," he said, resuming his walk. Saint glanced at the few people they passed on the street. He could only imagine what they were thinking by the stares that he and Fergus were getting. "It would have been much easier for me to blend in if you hadn't shown up," Saint groused.

"Yeah, like a guy wearing a two-piece suit and full-length opera coat in ninety-degree weather blends right in."

"I blend in better than someone who looks like a bouncer in a biker bar."

"You know, if you weren't in such a foul temperament, you might realize the absurdity of your statement."

Saint stopped in midstride. "Absurdity?"

"Yes, absurdity. Need I remind you of where we are?"

Saint had to concede his brother was right. Anywhere else, Fergus might look out of place, but in New Orleans, a man in black denim, biker boots, and leather bracers fit right in.

"Be that as it may, I'm not in a foul temperament," Saint said.

Saint had no idea where he was going. After the confrontation between him and Eric, he figured removing himself from Janet's shop was the best course of action. Not that he wanted to. He could hear Janet's muffled breathing as she fought back her tears. His first instinct had been to go to her, to comfort her. However, Fergus's hand on his arm told him it was best to leave things be.

Saint stopped beneath a small bit of shade. "Why are you here, brother?"

Fergus pretended to watch a group of women as they sashayed passed them on the street. If Ghost had been there, he would have changed directions to follow them. Luckily, Fergus wasn't of a mind to do so.

Any trace of gentleness vanished from Fergus's face. Fergus could never be accused of being a soft touch, but where his family was concerned, he could be a bit more lenient. Not a lot, but maybe a little around the edges. Still, the look on Fergus's face reminded Saint of when he was a child.

With the death of their parents, it became Fergus's responsibility be both mother and father to Saint, as well as chief disciplinarian. Whenever Fergus would have to punish Saint, a pained expression crossed his face, just as it did now.

"It's about Bridget," Fergus said.

Saint's stiffened at the mention of her name. He wasn't in the mood for one of Fergus's diatribes about his ex-fiancé. "Please, let it go." Saint plodded onward.

"How can I? Since returning from the Underworld, you skulk about the house in silence, and all of a sudden you wish to return to New Orleans. You haven't set foot in Louisiana since that night."

"I don't skulk."

Fergus adjusted the strap of his duffle bag across his shoulder. "You skulk. Ask anyone. Even Ghost noticed you're acting differently."

"Ghost is more astute than you give him credit for."

"Don't change the subject, Aodhàn."

"How can I change the subject when I no idea what this conversation is about?"

"This conversation is about Bridget and the fact that she is very much alive, and according to Kellas Scott, she has been seen here in New Orleans. Saint, are you even listening to me?"

Saint held up his hand for silence. Positioning his head to better hear what was behind him, Saint concentrated, blocking out all sounds except those coming from the direction of My Spicy Cauldron. *Saint, I need you.* Janet's voice was little more than a whisper inside his head. Seeing no time for explanations, Saint began running back the way they had come.

"Didn't you hear what I said?" Fergus asked, catching up with his brother.

Saint didn't break stride. "Yes, I heard you, but I really don't have time to talk about it right now."

Within minutes, Saint arrived at the door of My Spicy Cauldron. Trying the door, he found it unlocked. The overwhelming scent of singed dust and ozone filled Saint's nostrils. A thin film of dust and debris covered the entire contents of the shop. Scattered books and broken glass littered the floor. Janet's once pristine store now lay in shambles.

"We're closed," Janet said, causing Saint's head to snap in her direction.

Saint ran to the mother and child. He had no idea how something this devastating could take place, but he would do what he could to help. "Let me have him," Saint said, and without any hesitation lifted Eric's limp body from the floor.

Janet scrambled to her feet. "Help me get him to his room," she pleaded.

Silently, Saint followed Janet through the curtains of Princess Ryhinni's reading room, into the back of the store, and up the staircase. He didn't speak as he placed Eric into his bed and watched as Janet doted over her son.

He saw the anguish in Janet's face as she tucked the covers around Eric. Janet's love for her son triggered something hidden in the corner of Saint's psyche. He wondered what it would have been like to have a mother whose main concern was the wellbeing of her children. Not that he missed his mother, since it was hard to miss something he never had.

"Can you please go down and lock the shop?" Janet asked, looking to Fergus. Saint thought it rather odd. However, Janet seemed to be in shock and probably had no idea who she was actually speaking to. Fergus merely nodded his head and went to do as she asked.

Warily, Saint watched Janet. Her breathing was rapid but shallow, and he wondered if she was on the verge of going into shock.

"Have you called for medical help?" Saint asked.

Janet stroked Eric's face. "No," she answered. "I only called you."

Saint swallowed. For Janet to reach for him so easily was unexpected. "I see." He tugged at the bottom of his vest. "Would you like for us to call someone?

"I don't know what I would tell them."

The despair in Janet's voice tore at the fabric of his soul. He couldn't stand idly by and do nothing. CJ would come if he called her. Eric was not a shifter, but she could still help.

"You could help him," Janet said. "I know you are a healer. I saw it when I read you."

"Well, yes. I do have some skill in that arena, but...."

Janet placed her hand on his, sending gooseflesh streaking up his arm.

"Saint?"

His name was the only plea he needed. Saint covered her hand with his. "Of course, my princess, I will do anything you ask of me."

A weak smile found its way to Janet's eyes, melting Saint's heart all the more. Motioning for her to sit, Saint removed his opera coat. "Would you mind?" he asked, handing the coat to Janet.

Saint fought against his instincts. A part of him, a rather large part, longed to cradle Janet close to his chest and tell her everything would be fine, that he would fix whatever was wrong with Eric and help to put her life back to normal. There was no way he could promise that. He also didn't want their first embrace to be in a moment of desperation.

Dipping into his vest pocket, Saint retrieved a long, silver chain with a medallion on the end. Given to him before the turn of the nineteenth century, the pendant was blessed by a Druidic priest at the dawning of the summer solstice. Celtic carvings covered both sides of the disc, and in the center of the filigreed disc sat a dark green stone. For Saint, the pendant served as a tool of both divination and protection.

Turning his thoughts inward, Saint asked the goddess for vision and guidance in the healing of Eric. He held the medallion above Eric's body and, using it like a CAT scan, moved it along the central line of Eric's body. For Saint, the world melted away. He focused on the sound of Eric's breathing, and he vaguely recognized Fergus's aura as his brother entered the room.

In his mind's eye, Saint caught glimpses of what happened earlier. He envisioned the boy standing in the center of the shop. Electricity surged into every cell and atom of Eric's body. A vibration began in the center of Saint's solar plexus. The feeling was similar to what he felt before shifting, though not exactly. Heat radiated from the back of his head, washing over him like a waterfall, and with a loud whoosh, the sensation was gone. Saint's knees buckled from the release of energy, and he felt the strength of his brother's hands steadying him.

I am fine, brother, Saint sent the message to Fergus.

No. You're not.

Saint glanced in Fergus's direction.

With reluctance, Fergus released his grasp. *Very well, I will trust you know what you are doing.*

Centering himself, Saint again focused on the medallion as he placed it above each of Eric's seven main energy centers or chakras. The directional spin of the pendant could be very telling. If it spun clockwise, that chakra was open, if it spun counter clockwise, the chakra was closed, and if it remained still, the chakra was blocked.

Slowly, the pendant began spinning in a clockwise motion, but before Saint realized what was happening, the silver chain of the pendant became a whirling dervish in his hand. No matter how many times he stilled the trinket, within seconds it would resume its gyrations.

Taking the fob between his palms, Saint closed his eyes and said a prayer of thanks to the goddess before placing the pendant back in his pocket.

"Well?" Janet asked, inching toward the edge of her seat. "Is he okay?"

"Your son will be fine. He merely needs to rest." Unable to look at Janet, Saint took his coat and exited into the hallway.

The muscles in front of Saint's ears ached. It wasn't until he needed to speak that he realized how tightly he had clamped down on his jaw. Saint assumed the reason he clinched his jaw was to counter the stress being placed on his body and the intense accelerating of his heartbeat.

Never before had he felt anything as intense as the energy coursing through Eric's body. He could still feel the vibrations in his hands and arms.

Saint dropped his head. He needed proper time to process all he had felt and seen. Eric was merely a boy, yet he possessed a higher vibrational energy than most of the shifters Saint knew and definitely more power than any human. How was it even possible for Eric to discharge that much power and live?

Saint came to the only logical conclusion possible. Eric wasn't fully human, but he wasn't a shifter either. *Which left*....

The rattle of the door knob alerted him to Janet's presence. "Saint?"

Her voice seemed so fragile to his ears. He didn't wish to be rude, yet speaking with her wasn't what he wanted to do either. If he wanted, he could melt through the floor, but he had no idea where he would land. Plus, Fergus didn't rear him to be discourteous to women, so running wasn't an option.

"Aidan, please." She touched the hollow between his shoulder blades. "What is wrong? Why did you leave?" Janet stepped in front of him.

Saint focused his attention on a spot near the top of the doorframe. It was easier than looking into her eyes.

"Why won't you look at me?"

How could he shut her out when she needed him so? *She needed him?* Saint's thoughts came to a screeching halt. Did she need him? Probably not, but maybe? *For the love of Odin! When did I become so wishy-washy?*

With apprehension, Saint did as she asked. The fear and sadness he found there were enough to make him weep.

"Why are you leaving?" she asked.

Saint clasped his wrists behind his back, being cognizant not to rock back on his heels. Now wasn't a good time to adopt any of Ghost's bad habits. Then again, what *would* Ghost do?

What am I thinking? Ghost would be the last of his brothers he would wish to emulate. That being said, Ghost was the best when it came to shading the truth to suit his own needs.

"I need time to think," he answered and walked past her.

"Wait," she said, and cried out in pain when she accidentally hit the banister with her hand.

With preternatural speed, Saint grabbed her hand. "Let me see," he said.

Turning her palms upward, Saint could see the numerous cuts Janet had sustained when she crawled across the floor. Small flecks of frosted glass embedded in her hands sparkled in the light. Saint hissed, swearing eloquently in a language few had heard before.

"Do you have a first aid kit?" he asked.

"Bathroom. Under the sink," she whispered.

Saint steered Janet toward the kitchen and helped her to sit before fetching the supplies he required.

"I need to get back to Eric," she said, trying to get up.

"You need to let me help you," he said, placing her hands palms up on the table. "My brother can watch after him a bit longer," he said, sending the message to Fergus at the same time.

I don't like this, Fergus returned. *Do you have any idea what you're getting into here?*

Saint detected apprehension in Janet at the mention of his brother. "Despite his appearance, Fergus is actually rather good with children. We have two younger brothers, and he practically raised them both," Saint said, as he tended to her wounds. He hadn't a clue what he was doing when it came to this woman—he simply accepted his need to do so.

Saint? Fergus called to him.

In truth, no, I do not, Saint answered.

How did you know something had happened?

Saint thought for a moment. He didn't want to answer Fergus's question. He could almost hear the doubt jostling about in his brother's mind. *She called to me, and I answered,* Saint said, being careful not to cause Janet any further pain.

Since you don't carry a cell phone, I would be interested in knowing how she spoke with you.

In the same manner as we are speaking now, Saint said.

Are you serious?

Quite. It was obvious to Saint that Fergus lacked enthusiasm at his answer. He could almost feel his brother's "humph" from the other room. *And before you ask, no, I have never found telepathy with humans particularly easy.*

Why her? Why now?

I cannot answer that. I only know it happened. Now, please. Watch after her son while I tend to her wounds.

I am not convinced any further involvement with this woman is such a good idea, Fergus advised.

Saint had to agree. He wasn't sure it was such a good idea either, and yet it seemed he had no other choice. *Please, brother, as a favor to me.*

Fergus released a long, slow breath. *As you wish, but as soon as you are finished, we leave. Agreed?*

Saint neither agreed nor disagreed. He chose not to answer. If he wanted, he could push the boundaries of Janet's subconscious and wander through her mind for answers, but Saint didn't feel it was the proper thing to do. Not if he was to build any type of relationship with her.

The wheels in Saint's mind slammed to a screeching halt. *Relationship? What am I thinking?* Fergus was right. He should just tend to Janet's cuts and walk away. It would be for the best, and that was what he intended to do.

Saint shook his head, trying to remove the thought. *Relationship indeed!* With the glass removed, he began to dress her wounds.

"Saint?" Janet whispered.

"Hmm?"

"What won't you tell me about Eric?"

Saint turned her hands over in his, examining his proficiency in bandaging. "First, you must answer a question for me."

All color drained from Janet's face at Saint's comment, yet he could tell she tried put up a strong front. He half expected her to say no, and that was definitely her right to do so. In fact, he wanted her to say no. It would be much easier for him to keep his speculations to himself than to have his assumptions confirmed since he wasn't sure he could process the truth.

"Okay," she conceded. "What do you want to know?"

Undeniably, something in Janet's demeanor caused him to take a mental step back. His next question would probably ruin any whatever relationship he could have with this woman. He could see the springy arms of the robot from *Lost in Space* flailing about as he tried to caution everyone of impending danger. "Warning, Will Robinson. Warning. Proceed with caution!" *Why did I ever watch that show with Ghost?*

"There is no easy way to ask this."

Janet placed her hands in her lap. "Then just ask."

"Very well. Who is Eric's father?"

CHAPTER 17

A cold wave of anger shot from the top of Janet's head to the soles of her feet. Should she have slapped him for being so bold? What was she supposed to do? Even if she lied to him, he would eventually find out the truth.

I should kick him and his brother out on their tails, she thought. No matter how cute Saint's tail was. How dare he! Who did he think he was to question who or what her son was? Should she be indignant and walk away?

That is no way to start a relationship, her spirit guide, Edgar, piped in.

Stop it, Edgar. Not now, she shot back and prayed Saint couldn't hear what was going on inside her head.

"I don't know," she answered with a sigh. She could tell Saint didn't believe her. "I know you don't believe me, but I really don't know."

"You're not the boy's mother?"

"Yes. No. I mean yes."

Saint pinched the bridge of his nose. "You either are or you aren't. Which is it?"

Janet curled her lips between her teeth, trying not to answer. Eric was her son and hers alone. She had been mother, father, and complete family to him. It didn't matter who his father was. He was her son.

It is time, Edgar said. *The time to hide no longer.*

"No," she whispered. "I can't."

"Can't or won't?" Saint asked.

Her guide spoke up again. *There can be no lies between you. Let your life be what it is meant to be.*

"You're not going to leave me alone until I tell him, are you?" She glanced to the ceiling and saw Saint do the same.

You know the answer to that.

"Geeze, you are such a noodge."

"Excuse me? I merely asked a simple question."

"Not you," Janet snapped. "Edgar, my spirit guide."

"Your spirit guide?"

Janet stared blankly at Saint. Here was a man that could change from human to animal at will, and he was questioning her about a spirit guide? The nerve. It would be useless to bring up that fact right at the moment. Obviously being able to get guidance from the other side was something Mr. Wolfe didn't understand.

She couldn't stand there forever. She needed to say something before her spirit guide whacked her in the back of the head if Saint walked away. Mustering the courage, Janet opened her mouth to speak.

"Hey, Janet, you up there?" A gruff voice called out.

Janet breathed a sigh of relief and thanked Thor for saving her from having to answer Saint's question. "I'm up here, Kel," she called.

As soon as Kel reached the top of the stairs, Janet threw herself into his arms. Kel was Janet's dearest and oldest friend. He had been in her life since her move back to New Orleans and was one of the few that had been with her every step of the way with Eric. In fact, he was probably the closest thing to a father Eric had.

Tears streamed down Janet's face, as she began to sob

uncontrollably. Today had been more than she bargained for, and try as she might, she could not stop the steady river of tears and gasps that flowed from her. She felt her feet leave the floor as Kel lifted her in his powerful arms.

She should have fought him and made him put her down, but she was so tired, and Kel's compassion overwhelmed her. She sensed her body being gently placed on her bed. Without opening her eyes, she reached for her pillow and buried her face in the cool fabric as wave after wave of tears overtook her.

Janet tried to shut out all thought from her head but couldn't. She could still see Eric standing in the middle of her bookstore. Light radiating from his body as lightning zinged from his hands. *Lightning! How was that even possible?* When he collapsed, she was positive he was dead. How could anyone survive what her son had gone through?

Yet he lay in the room next to her, being watched over by a shape shifter that scared the snot out of her. At least she thought they were still there. Who knew? She should have told them to leave. Then again, seeing Kel carrying her into the bedroom may have been enough to run Saint off. He was probably in his room right now packing. The thought brought another wave of tears. This was too much, just too much.

Saint's leaving was for the best, really. *This way I don't have to look him in the face or say goodbye. Yes*, she reasoned. *This is best.* But if it was for the best, then why did her heart feel like someone stomped on it?

Janet felt the bed shift under the weight of Kel's massive frame. She should have known he would want to talk about what had happened downstairs and why two strange men were standing in her hallway. He always wanted to talk things out.

Typically, she would oblige, but not this time. She didn't have the mental stamina to pacify Kel's need to ask a million and one questions. At the moment all she wanted was to lie in a little ball, cuddle her pillow, and cry.

A feeling of tranquility came over her as she listened to Kel's deep, rhythmic breaths. She didn't remember ever hearing Kel make that sound before. It was less of an exhale and more of a vibration. The best way she could describe it was a purr. Whatever it was, it was comforting.

"Okay, darlin'," he drawled, "from the looks of things downstairs, I have a pretty good idea what happened, but I need to know why it happened."

Darn it. Just when she was about to go to sleep, he had to start talking. Janet pressed her eyes closed. She didn't want to think about what happened downstairs or about the guy with the pointy ears. Pulling the pillow over her face, she attempted to melt into the mattress. Maybe if she stayed in that position, Kel would take the hint and walk away.

"I'm going to find out eventually, so you might as well tell me."

He was right. He would find out, so she could either go ahead and talk about it now or talk about it later. Later would be better.

"Okay," Kel said. "I need to go take care of the guys in the hall. Then we'll talk. You just lie here and get some rest."

With a sniff, Janet pulled her weary body into a seated position. As much as she didn't want to discuss the events downstairs, she knew it would be best to do it now while everything was fresh in her mind. She twisted the end of her blouse in nervous frustration. "He had pointy ears," she said, trying to gauge Kel's reaction. There wasn't one.

"What else?" he asked.

"And violet eyes."

"Human?"

Janet shook her head. "I don't think so, but he definitely wasn't a shifter," she answered before Kel had a chance to ask.

"Mmm hmm," Kel grunted. "What about his clothes? How was he dressed?"

"He looked like an extra from a movie. Tricolored hair, deep red suit...." Kel's right eye twitched. The expression in his gold-green eyes brought her description to a halt. "You know who that was, don't you?"

Kel pulled an afghan from nearby and placed it over Janet's legs. "It is possible," he answered. "Did he say anything to you?"

Acid churned in the pit of Janet's stomach. "What aren't you telling me?"

Kel placed a stern hand on her leg. "Did he say anything to you or Eric?"

"Yes. He said he came for Eric and proof." Again, tears pricked the back of her eyes at the memory of the man's fingers wrapped around her wrist. She automatically checked for a bruise on her wrist.

"I'll take care of downstairs."

"Don't hurt them."

Kel peered down at her, the angle accentuating his stature. "Who?"

"Saint and his brother."

Kel stoked his beard. "Have they done anything that would warrant my hurting them?"

"No," she answered.

"Then there is nothing to worry about."

Janet grabbed the tail of his black Harley-Davidson t-shirt. "They are coming for him, aren't they?" Her voice trembled as she asked.

Kel shook his head. "Nah. You got nothing to worry about. Now get some rest, Cher." With a soft click of the door handle, Kel was gone.

Get some rest. That was easy for him to say. He wasn't the one whose kid blew up the place. Groaning, Janet hugged the pillow against her face, but no matter how much she tried, she couldn't get the image out of her mind. And what about Saint? It was obvious he found something when he was assessing Eric. Why else would he ask who the child's father was?

What did it matter? Eric was hers, no one else's. *It does matter*, she thought. She could still hear Saint's question ringing in her ears. If she told him the truth, would he even believe her? More to the point, she would have to admit to everyone, including herself, Eric was adopted.

Only one person knew the identity of Eric's biological parents, and that was Kel. In fact, he was the one who facilitated the adoption.

She had known Kel for a year or so when he approached her about adopting an infant. She was apprehensive about the idea. She had no family to speak of, only a core group of friends who could possibly help when she needed them. Janet also worried about the baby's birth parents changing their minds and attempting to take him or her away.

Kel assured her that neither the mother nor the father would ask for the child's return. So far, he was right. The only information he ever gave to Janet about Eric's parents was that the mother was human and the father was not. Janet just always assumed the father was a shifter, a suspicion Kel never denied. Then again, he never confirmed it either.

In light of recent events, the time may have come to keep the secret no longer. A shifter may have many non-human abilities, but as far as Janet knew, shooting electricity wasn't one of them.

CHAPTER 18

The Wolfe brothers stood in the hallway and gawked at the massive man as he took Janet into her bedroom and shut the door.

Saint felt the pressure of Fergus's strong hand as it clamped down on his shoulder. "Well, my brother. It appears the time has come for us to take our leave."

Saint refused to move. "You may leave if you wish. In fact, I wish that you would. I, however, am staying here."

"Look, Saint, I'm all for casting out old demons, but this is...."

"Is what?"

Fergus combed a large hand through his auburn hair. "Honestly, I don't know, but let the big guy take care of it. Looks like the two of them are real cozy." He nudged his chin toward the door.

"It's not like that," Saint defended.

"It certainly looks like that," Fergus argued.

"Looks are often deceiving, my brother."

"Right, and soon swine will take to the air," Fergus grumped.

"Could you not simply say 'when pigs fly'? Even I say 'when pigs fly'. Really, Fergus...."

The sound of an opening door stopped Saint from any further

retort to what was probably one of the most asinine statements his brother had ever made. Kel emerged from Janet's room, shutting the door softly behind him.

In less than three strides, Kel came to stand before the brothers. Jet black hair jutted upward in short spikes, adding another inch to his already impressive height of near seven feet. Saint had to admit that Kel's hair definitely complemented the same color goatee that covered his rapier chin.

The three men regarded each other, and Saint found it rather unsettling. Seldom did that happen, and it only served to fuel his agitation.

Kel drew in a deep breath and, in one swift movement, swept both Fergus and Saint into a giant bear-hug. "Ha, ha!" he bellowed. "I thought I caught a whiff of wolf when I walked in."

"Kellas, you're choking us," Saint coughed out.

"You always were a bit soft," Kel said, dropping both Saint and Fergus to the ground.

Saint adjusted the cuffs of his shirt. "I resent that statement."

"Ah...wolf, you know I'm just ribbing ya," Kel teased. "I know you can hold your own."

Fergus rubbed his whisker-stubbled chin. "What are you doing here?"

"I live here, in case you have forgotten," Kel answered.

"You live...here?" Fergus asked.

"With Janet and the boy? Nah. I still have that little place down in the Garden District. You remember it. By the way," he said, peeking over his shoulder, "call me Kel. I'll explain later. Let's take this downstairs."

Glass crunched underfoot as Saint and the others walked across the old plank floor.

"What happened here?" Fergus asked, clearing away the dust and debris from the counter.

"I'm not sure." Lifting his head, Saint sniffed the air. The unmistakable scent of ozone mixed with the garlic odor of phosphorus permeated his senses, but there was the hint of something else lingering in the air. Saint searched his memory for the answer. "Kel, have you any idea what happened here?"

"I have an idea," Kel answered.

"And?" Fergus prodded.

Kel slid into the spot that Fergus had already cleared. "I'd rather not say."

"Then what can you tell us or, should I say, what will you tell us?" Saint questioned.

"Looks like there's a mess to clean up," Kel answered.

This wasn't the first time Saint and the other members of Delta Pack had dealings with Kellas Scott. The cat had been in and out of their lives many times over the years. Though not officially a part of the Pack, he was definitely an ally and one whose particular skill set had been called upon many times.

Releasing a deliberate breath, Saint turned from the others. His life was changing. He could feel it. Normally, he allowed the ebb and flow of the Universe to take him where it willed, but with the events of the past few months, Saint began to question the logic of his choice.

All he wanted was to find a nice, quiet place to sit and think. Was that too much to ask? That had been his mission earlier before his ruminations were brought to a halt by Fergus and Ghost or before he met the woman upstairs and now Kellas Scott was somehow in the picture.

What more would the goddess and the sisters throw his way? He was almost afraid to ask and too tired to play one of Kellas's guessing games.

"Very well," Saint replied. "I know you will tell us in your own sweet time." He sucked in a sharp breath as his right hand made contact with the back of his left. Saint examined the spot on his hand. "I suppose we need to find lodging and a pharmacy." For a small bite, it itched like hell.

"What happened?" Fergus asked, as he craned his neck trying to get a better look. "It looks like a bite of some kind."

"I suppose it was a mosquito," Saint answered. He thought of the odd windstorm that had encircled him earlier.

Fergus commented over Saint's shoulder. "Maybe you should pop back to Haven and have the guardian take a look at it.

The site of the wound had puffed and turned an angry red color. Still, the thought of his returning to Haven was out of the question. He had thought his quick shift last night would have healed such a small wound. Then again, he thought the same with the discomfort around his heart.

With a hasty tug, Saint pulled the cuff of his shirt down over the offending spot. *Out of sight, out of mind.*

"I am perfectly capable of tending to my own wounds, Fergus."

"Of course you are, brother."

"Thank you for your concern." Saint said. "Now that you have delivered your message, are you ready to return to Haven?" Saint hoped his change of topic would be enough to deter any further conversation about his hand. He appreciated how Fergus still tried to protect him after all these years, but at the moment, there was much more to deal with than a little bug bite.

"Very well," Fergus said. "Arrangements have already been made for us to stay with Kellas." Fergus brought his orange gaze to rest on Kel.

Saint ignored Fergus's statement. He didn't want to get into a lengthy conversation about where he would or would not be spending the night.

"So," Kel began. "What brings the Wolfe brothers to my fair city?"

And there it was, subject changed, and once again Kel hadn't answer Saint's question. There was no need for him or Fergus to probe any further. Kel had said all he was going to say on the subject.

Fergus was the first to answer. "My brother is here chasing ghosts."

Kel let loose a hearty laugh that shook the room. "Ghost! Where is that boy? Why I haven't seen him since...." Kel looked to Saint and then quickly cast his gaze to the floor.

"You can say it." Saint turned his back to Kel and Fergus. "You haven't seen Ghost or any of us since the week of the wedding."

"The almost wedding," Fergus added. "Thank the gods."

"You needn't remind me of what a fool I was," Saint despaired.

"Bridget fooled us all, my friend," Kel said.

Saint shook his head. "Not all of us." He dared not look at this brother. "But I should have seen through her disguise."

"Men are all fools where the fairer sex is concerned," Kel sympathized.

Again, Saint looked toward the ceiling and Janet. Was Kel in love with her? And what of Eric? Could he be Kel's son? Is that why he was so tight-lipped about everything?

The thought caused more unrest in Saint than he was willing to admit. As much as he hated it, Saint knew the best thing to do would be to go right to the source and simply ask, but in truth, questioning Kellas Scott was never simple. The large man had an irritating propensity for evading the truth.

"Spit it out, wolf." Kel's voice boomed through the silence.

"Very well. What is your relationship to Janet and the boy?"

Kel crossed his arms over his broad chest, reminding Saint of his older brother. Actually, a lot about Kel reminded him of Fergus. "And please," Saint added, "spare me your normal, diversionary tactics."

It didn't matter how long Kel took, this was one answer Saint was willing to wait for. With ease, his mind wandered up the staircase, down the hall, and into Janet's bedroom. He could feel her move restlessly as she slept.

"Why are you so interested in Janet?" Kel asked. A small twitch jerked at the corner of his mouth.

Saint wagged his finger. "Ah, ah. No diversion."

"If you are asking if my interest in Janet is more than platonic, the answer is no. We're just friends. I like her kid. He reminds me a lot of Ghost when he was a pup."

"May Odin save us from another," Fergus grumbled under his breath.

"Ah, Ghost's a good kid. You don't give him enough credit," Kel said, slapping Fergus on the back and pushing him forward by about two foot.

Saint felt a great relief at Kel's words, both about Ghost and Janet. It wasn't his place to question Kel's relationship with Janet, but as long as Kel said they were only friends, he would sort out the rest later.

Kel's large, black boots thudded against the dusty, wooden floor as he slid from the counter.

"Well, guess I need to get this place cleaned up."

"How may we assist?" Saint asked.

"Don't worry. I got it." Kel smiled. "Just get behind me."

Saint wanted to question Kel's sanity, but he did what was asked.

It was hard for Saint to see from his position, yet he could feel Kel drawing large amounts of energy from the room. He was accustomed to the vacuum inside of a wormhole, and this felt no different. The air round them chilled as Kel rubbed his massive hands together as if warming them. Kel twisted his hands, cupping them, shaping the errant energy into a bright blue ball of light.

"Watch and learn, boys," Kel teased and, with the ease of a big league pitcher, sent the ball of light flying from his hands.

Faster and faster, the sphere wound its way about the room. No matter how much he tried, Saint was unable to keep watch on the light as it zipped its way across the room. The sphere swooped down to the floor, picked up the shards of broken glass, and returned them to the light fixtures. Books leapt back onto the shelves as pictures righted themselves upon the wall, returning everything to its proper position.

With a loud whistle, the ball dove over Fergus and Saint's heads, forcing them to duck. Holding up his hand, Kel summoned the light back to him, and with one thunderous clap, the ball disappeared.

When he was positive the ball of energy was gone, Saint returned to an upright position. He looked around the shop in awe. Every item was perfectly in place, down to the opened day planner on the counter.

Fergus raked a hand across his face. "How did you...?"

A wide grin covered Kel's face. "Would you believe magic?"

"I know of no such magic," Saint said.

"Well, now you do." Kel rummaged in his front jean pocket. "Here," he said, tossing a set of keys to Fergus. "You know the house."

"What about you?" Saint asked.

"Don't worry about me, wolf. I know my way home."

CHAPTER 19

Kel checked over his shoulder, insuring he wasn't being followed down the alleyway. Too much was going on in his city. He never thought he would see Bridget again. He had heard she was alive but had not given it another thought until Fergus called him.

"Shit," he cursed and kicked a pebble with the rounded toe of his boots. Just as he told Fergus and Saint, he had a suspicion about what happened in Janet's shop, and although he tried not to, Kel couldn't help but fear the worst.

As Kel watched Eric grow, he understood it was only a matter of time before the boy would come into his powers. He didn't however, expect it to happen so soon. If Janet's description was correct, then the Blatt-Elfen also knew. The question was who was the elf working for and why were they so concerned with Eric.

Extending his arms, Kel embraced the sunlight and wind. He tilted his face skyward and basked in the warmth of the sun caressing his skin. What he wouldn't give to be stretched out in the hammock nestled in the trees behind his house, but first he had something to take care of.

Kel drew an Odal, the runic symbol for Odin, above his head. "All Father, we must speak," he said to the clouds. "I need your counsel and your wisdom."

The clouds churned above him, turning from puffy white to heavy gray. Lightning streaked across the sky, and wind howled down the alley, forming a mini–tornado heading straight toward Kel. The cat didn't flinch as the funnel-cloud swept him into its grasp. He'd never been a fan of this mode of travel, and no matter how hard he tried, he always landed dizzy and disoriented.

As quickly as the storm began, it dissipated, depositing Kel at the edge of the rainbow bridge that connected the world of the gods to the world of man. A firm hand tightened around Kel's bicep as he teetered slightly. As always, Heimdallr was there to steady him.

"Thank you, old friend," Kel said, once he felt confident he could stand on his own.

"One would think after all these eons, you would become accustomed to that," said Heimdallr. He was the sentinel over Bifrost and Asgard. It was his job to warn the gods of the beginning of Ragnarock. The whitest of the gods, Heimdallr stood near the same height as Kel.

Reflections of the tricolor bridge bounced off the watchman's golden smile. "Here, this will help," he said, thrusting a goblet of mead toward Kel.

Not one to turn down an offering from one of the gods, Kel accepted the glass, and the sweet, honeyed wine bubbled on Kel's tongue. Wiping his mouth with the back of his hand, he thanked Heimdallr for his hospitality.

"The All Father is expecting you," the pale man said

"That all-knowing thing really comes in handy."

Heimdallr nodded. "True. It also helps when transport is provided." He stepped aside, giving Kel full view of the solid white horse that seemed to materialize before his eyes. The horse stood no less than nineteen hands. A bridle of deep crimson leather decorated in gold cradled the horse's head, its straps resting on the beast's broad shoulders. For a saddle, only a blanket the same deep color as the bridle lay across the horse's back.

"What? No Corvette?" Kel said, taking the reins in hand.

"That is blasphemy in the presence of such a fine animal," Heimdallr said.

With a loud grunt Kel flung himself onto the horse's back.

"No need to guide her," Heimdallr said, smoothing his hand along the animal's withers. "Simply tell her where to go."

The horse's ears turned in Kel's direction, awaiting his instructions. "You're kidding."

"I could, but in this, I don't."

Kel nudged the horse on its sides. "To Odin." The horse turned a large brown eye in Kel's direction. She needn't be able to speak for him to know she was thinking – *excuse me? You want what?"*

"To the All Father," Kel tried again. Still the horse didn't move. "You know, a little help here would be nice," Kel said. He didn't intend for his tone to sound as sarcastic as it did, but if Heimdallr knew how to get the beast to move, he should have helped.

Heimdallr raised his hand. "To Valhalla!" He commanded, smacking the animal on her haunches. The horse reared upward, forcing Kel to tighten the pressure of his legs about her sides. The horse took this as a signal to bolt. Kel could hear Heimdallr's laughter echoing across the bridge. He needn't look behind him to know the god was doubled over in laughter.

It took mere moments for the mare to come to a screeching halt outside the gates of Valhalla. "What ho?" A voice called from above. "Who goes there?"

"Kellas Köttr. The All Father is expecting me," Kel called back. With a loud creak, the ancient gate, Valgrind, began to open, allowing him passage into the home of Odin and his kin. Valhalla was the most incredible structure he had ever seen. The stone and wood walls extended far beyond anyone's ability to see. Once inside, Kel would be faced with an intricate labyrinth of halls, suites, and rooms. Fortunately for him, the All Father's suite was in the main building.

Dismounting, Kel turned the horse over to the waiting servant and entered into Odin's hall, where many a once-fallen warrior now enjoyed the hospitality of the Valkyries. Kel hoped when his time came, he too would be swept into the arms of a Rhinemaiden and deposited here among his comrades.

A smile crossed Kel's face as an elderly man, dressed in a dusty blue cloak and drooping hat, shuffled in his direction. "All Father," Kel said, as the man stopped before him.

Raising his head, the man peered from beneath the wide brim of his hat. "How could you be sure it was I" Odin asked, a fleck of amusement dancing in his one good eye.

"Your staff," Kel answered. "It was doing little to steady your steps."

A look of bemusement covered Odin's face. "I use it more for rhythm than anything else," he said, removing his hat and cloak, handing them to a maiden that happened to walk by. "Now, Köttr, what is so urgent?"

Kel dropped his voice to a whisper. "We may have a slight problem."

"Walk with me," Odin said.

Odin rested his hand upon the hilt of his sword. "I take it you come about the boy."

"I do," Kel answered.

"You say there is a problem?"

"Not yet, but one is coming."

"Why worry before it is time?" The All Father asked.

Kel rubbed the back of his neck. "His powers are already manifesting."

Odin grunted. It was a sign the All Father was thinking, and Kel figured it was best not to disturb him.

The All Father led Kel the length of the meeting hall. Stepping out into the waning daylight, Kel could make out fires dotting the countryside. Off in the distance fiddle and drums could be heard. Snippets of conversations found their way to his ears. Most were tales of great feats on the battlefield, and a few were of the families they left behind, something old warriors, alive or dead, seem to have in common. It was a site he never expected to see again.

Kel enjoyed the creature comforts his home had provided over the years, but something about the scene before him made him nostalgic. He couldn't help but wonder how many of his old comrades might be among the encampments before him.

"I see. Who else knows of this?" Odin asked.

"Only his mother."

Odin nodded. "She is his mother. It is only natural she would discover this."

Kel hesitated. He wondered whether or not he should mention the Wolfe brothers, but surely the All Father knew they were involved . The Blatt-Elfen was a different story.

"There is one other that knows. A Blatt-Elfen was in Janet's store today." Kel said.

"A Leaf-Elf? That is unusual. Rarely do they go where the humans can see them, and they can be particularly nasty." Odin said.

"I can't be certain, but I believe it is Scarlethand."

Odin stroked his long, white beard, humming a tune only he knew. To Kel's ears, it sounded more random than melodic.

"Scarlethand, you say?"

"I believe so. Janet's description fit him perfectly."

"You must move them."

Kel blinked, unsure he heard Odin correctly. "Move them? If Scarlethand found them once, he could find them again. Wouldn't it be better to remove the elf altogether?"

Odin's laughter surprised Kel. "Have you ever battled a Blatt-Elfen?"

Kel wondered how he was supposed to remember every battle or opponent he had met in his life. There had been too many wars, too many skirmishes, too many adversaries. There had to be a Blatt-Elfen in the mix somewhere.

"The fact you can't remember tells me you have not."

"And why is that?"

"Very few who walk away from such a fight, the ones who do remember. The time for battles will come. For now, protect the boy and his mother."

Kel started to speak, but before he could utter another syllable, he was swept back in the whirlwind and deposited into the alley where his journey had begun.

CHAPTER 20

Tucked behind an ivy-covered wall, Kel's two-story Victorian house was an oasis on such a warm day. Saint found Kel's ability to remain in the same home since the 1890s rather impressive. It wasn't an easy task for a shifter but living in New Orleans helped.

A bronze statue of Thor watched over the entrance of the home. Its reflection showed in gilded mirror which hung on the opposite wall. Kellas's home was a juxtaposition of ancient and modern styles. The combination of symmetry and mysticism were the perfect combination for Kellas Scott.

Saint sat on the screened-in veranda, his head leaned back against the rattan of the old strap rocker. His opera coat and vest lay folded in the chair beside him. The hypnotic creak, creak, creak of the rockers against the porch floor lulled him into a light slumber.

Saint had thought long and hard about staying at the store while Janet slept, but he needed to process what happened while working on Eric. He had never seen his medallion act in such a manner.

It had been nearly eighty years since Saint had spent time in his beloved city. Though other members of his pack had come and gone quite frequently, he could never bring himself to do so. The spectral memories of his past were too numerous and too painful for him to face.

Once upon a time, Saint had hoped to settle in New Orleans, to leave behind the others, and start his own pack with Bridget and the children they would have. As Saint drifted from consciousness, he thought of his once adored Bridget.

In the late 1900s, Delta Pack traveled to New Orleans at the request of the Foundation. The alpha from a well-known and extremely connected French family was in need of escort while staying in the city. Arturo LeCœur was very wealthy, and the governor hoped for someone with Arturo's wealth to settle in New Orleans.

Little did the people of New Orleans realize the city was largely built by shape shifters. To this day, humans still believed the city's nickname, the Crescent City, came from the curvature of the river, but Saint knew the truth.

The name was actually a throwback to its shifter roots and one of the symbols used by the Theriontrope Foundation to denote those welcoming to shifters. The symbol was a crescent moon. Calling New Orleans the Crescent City was, and still is, equivalent to placing a big welcome sign above the city saying "shifters come on down!"

When Arturo came to the city, he brought not only his wife but also his daughter and quite a large number of his pack. Somehow, the job fell to Saint to watch over Bridget during her stay.

At first, Saint balked at the idea, insisting it was a job better suited to Ghost, but Arturo wouldn't hear of such a thing. Saint had to be Bridget's guard. The patriarch trusted no other with his daughter.

Bridget's beauty was without question. Her black eyes captivated him, and much to Saint's chagrin, he fell for Bridget the moment she descended the staircase at the New Orleans Opera House. She loved books and opera and simply sitting for hours listening to the world as it jostled by.

All the things Saint found so dear, Bridget did also. She was more than he had hoped for, and he considered himself blessed.

But something about their relationship never quite fit. Saint's gut warned she was wrong for him — *if only I had heeded my inner voice.*

No matter what Fergus thought, Bridget was long dead, and Saint was here to say his final goodbye. Something he should have done years ago but never felt able to do until now. Now, he had made his pact with the beautiful queen of the Underworld.

A dog barked in the distance, rousting him slightly. With little effort, Saint slipped back into the dark corners of his thoughts. Thoughts of his family mingled with memories of New Orleans and Bridget before finding their way to Janet Beesinger.

How many people had he met in his two-hundred years of existence? Easily thousands. Yet none made him feel the way she did. So how could such a brief meeting with one person mean so much?

Janet had been correct in her assessment of him and death. He did know death in a way no one could understand nor would they want to.

"A life for a life," Hel had told him. "That is the price."

A life for a life. Saint found it difficult to admit to his reluctance at accepting the terms Hel set forth. After all, it wasn't simply any life for CJ's. It was his. He was a healer, not a bringer of pain. So how could he deny Mika of his true-mate or a life of happiness? Saint would never forgive himself if he did.

So his deal with Hel was struck. When the time came, Saint would join her in the Underworld in trade for CJ's soul being returned to her body.

Saint could almost feel the icy touch of Hel as she pressed her lips against his, bestowing upon him the true kiss of death. She took a small part of him with her as they parted, leaving in its place the unbearable pressure he felt now.

How he wished she had taken him in that moment instead of sending him back to his normal life. Normal? When was anything about his life normal?

His whole life had been spent in service to the goddess and doing what was best for his pack and others, and this is how Freyja returns his loyalty—with an eternity in Hell.

Saint pushed away his anger. There was no need to dwell on what was to be; he could only deal with what was.

Again, he replayed Janet's words over in his mind, hoping to find a happier thought. A sly smile quirked the corner of his mouth, and somewhere inside, he felt a sense of pride in Janet and her connection to the Universe.

She told him he was fiercely loyal to his family and he was. He would stop at nothing to protect them. But who was there to protect him? Who was there to share his life, to help ease the incessant loneliness?

Now that Mika had found his true mate, how much longer would it be before the others found theirs? Probably not long. Saint could feel a shift in the Universe and within their pack. It was only a matter of time until Fergus and Ghost found their true-mates. Once that happened, once he was sure there was someone to take care of his brothers, Saint would take his leave of this world.

Please don't be so sad.

Peace settled over Saint. *Funny.* He almost thought he heard Janet's voice. He still didn't understand how he had been able to hear her before breakfast. It could only have been due to their close proximity. However, now they were miles away, so that theory didn't hold up unless she had somehow opened a telepathic link between them during his reading.

It was a plausible explanation for their initial link, but it wouldn't explain their link. It wouldn't explain her ability to sense his emotions. That involved a much deeper connection, an impossible, if not irrational, idea.

Aidan?

He liked it when she called him that. Her voice was a balm to his raw nerves. No one other than Fergus ever called him by his given name, and Fergus's voice was anything but gentle or soothing.

Aidan, where did you go? I woke and you were gone.

Saint almost laughed. This had to be a dream. Why else would she seem upset at his absence? Of course, this was a dream. There was no other explanation.

Aidan, are you there?

Yes, I am here, he answered. Why not? It was a dream. He might as well play along.

Saint had an image of Janet in his mind. She sat behind the counter of her shop, her chin resting upon her hand as she played with a strand of hair, continuously twisting it around her finger.

You decided not to rent the room?

Yes, I thought it for the best, considering everything.

You mean considering Eric, she said.

Saint didn't know what to say. Eric was one of the reasons he left her apartment, but not the only one. It was obvious the subject of Eric's father was sensitive for Janet and, whatever her secret, Saint wouldn't push. He had his own issues to attend, but before their relationship could go any further, he would have to know the truth.

Will I ever see you again?

Saint gripped the arms of the chair. He hadn't expected that question. Of course, she would see him again. Should he play it cool as Ghost would say and make no promises? Or should he walk away and suppress the thought and feelings that swirled in him? He found both ideas to be unacceptable. *If you wish to see me, then you shall,* he answered.

Are you serious? She sounded flustered. *I mean okay. Really?*

He could even imagine a crimson blush coloring her cheeks in embarrassment at her straightforwardness. Was it wrong for him to find her discomfort adorable?

When the time is right, we shall see each other again. I have matters that must be tended to, but as soon as I can, I will find a way to you.

Saint felt her hesitation in believing his statement. *I don't make promises I don't intend to keep.* He tried to allay the doubts in her mind.

But you didn't promise. You simply said we would see each other again.

Saint never said he would do something and then reneged on his word. Didn't she understand the promise was implied? *Very well, I promise I will see you again.*

He felt the warmth of her smile at his statement, and for the briefest of moments, Saint felt that warmth permeate his soul and thought to himself, *what a wonderful dream.*

CHAPTER 21

"Where is Saint?" Fergus asked, as he walked into the kitchen of Kel's house.

Kel reminded Fergus of a mad scientist in the kitchen. Bottles of spices and marinades littered nearly every inch of counter space. If Fergus's memory served correctly, he knew Kel was an extraordinary cook, maybe not as good as Saint, but if the aromas were any indication, things would turn out just as he imagined.

"He said something about going to Mass," Kel answered, breaking eggs into a bowl. "Thought I might whip up some dinner. I'm getting a bit hungry. What about you?"

"Starved." Fergus answered, even though his mind was elsewhere in search of Saint.

I assure you, I'm fine. Saint spoke to Fergus through their common channel. *It has been so long since I have attended Mass. I will call if need be.*

I have never understood your attachment to human religions, Fergus said.

I know, my dear brother, and you never shall.

Maybe I should go with you.

And to what end? So I can listen to you harrumph through the whole of the Mass? Thank you for your offer, but I believe I shall pass.

Saint was right. Fergus would be uncomfortable during the service. However, he wasn't some melancholic female prone to bouts of sighing and definitely not harrumphing. Fergus could sense his brother's amusement at his irritation.

No one could ever accuse you of being a melancholic female, Fergus. A curmudgeon, maybe.

Who calls me that? Ghost? Does Ghost call me a curmudgeon?

Ghost has said nothing, my brother. Now if you will excuse me, I have arrived at the cathedral.

I do not have a good feeling about this, Saint.

All will be well. Know I will call for you if need be. With that, Saint ended their conversation.

Fergus went to the refrigerator. "I will take that beer now."

"Help yourself." Kel poured the eggs into a hot pan and swirled them about. "Fergus, I may have a bit of a problem, and it's one you and Haven may have to help with."

Fergus twirled the bottle cap through his fingers in the same fashion magicians roll a coin through theirs. His thoughts homed in on a time he stood side by side with Kel on the battlefield. The general populace had no idea how involved shifters were in the world of human politics or how many wars they had fought in to protect both humans and shifters alike. Fergus did since he had been involved in most of them.

"The great Kellas Scott is in need of my service? Are you not the one who swore many times a cat needed no one but himself to depend on?"

"This is serious, Fergus."

"I am being serious. I may not have Saint's know-it-all memory, but I do remember that."

"You're never going to let that go, are you?"

Without looking, Fergus flipped the bottle cap across the room. He felt satisfaction at the rustle of plastic telling him the cap found its target. "My decision to offer you a place within the pack was not done lightly."

"Nor was my decision to decline your offer, but it was something I felt I had to do," Kel said, placing a rather large hunk of meat in a skillet. "Look, Fergus, are you going to help me or not?"

"Of course I will." Fergus finally conceded. "What do you need?"

Kel wiped his hands on a towel and threw it over his shoulder. "I ask for asylum for a friend."

"A friend?" Fergus asked, leaning back. "Can your friend not ask?"

"No." Kel sat the finished plate of steak and eggs before Fergus.

"And why not?"

"Two reasons, really."

"The first one?"

"The first is because my friend is a human," Kel said.

Fergus chewed slowly as he mulled over Kel's statement. He could say no, but ultimately it was the guardian's decision, not his. Fergus crossed his arms over his chest. "And the second?"

"The second is the poor kid has no idea how much trouble is about to come her way."

CHAPTER 22

With reverence and respect, Saint entered St. Louis Cathedral. Dipping his hand in the font, he bowed and crossed himself before taking a seat on one of the well-worn pews. His long fingers caressed the dark, lacquered wood of the bench. The coolness was oddly comforting, as the wood glided effortlessly beneath his fingertips.

Saint always found it sad his kind had no centralized church to speak of. As the years went by, it seemed fewer of his kind understood their connection to the goddess. He enjoyed the formality and ceremony of the Catholic Church, even if he didn't agree with its theology, and it made him sad that in the world of shifters, there was no firm belief system and no ritual.

He breathed deeply, taking in the scents of frankincense, myrrh, and roses that permeated the wood from the centuries of incense being carried throughout the cathedral. The fragrance brought back so many memories. So much time had passed and yet, in some ways, not enough.

Others began to file into the cathedral. Some people milled about, speaking to old friends. Others went straight to the spots Saint knew they had probably sat in for years. Most were silent. Like him, they were reflecting on their lives. Then again, they could have been deciding where they were going for lunch.

Out of his peripheral vision, Saint caught a glimpse of a petite woman taking a seat behind him. From seemingly nowhere, a cold breeze rushed across his neck and down his spine. *Odd.* He looked about to see if perhaps he sat beneath an air vent. The words on the archway above his head caught his attention. Releasing a sigh, he whispered the phrase aloud, taking pleasure in the way the Latin felt upon his tongue. "*Sanctus Dominus Deus Sabaoth,*" he whispered, reading the words he found there.

"Holy Lord of Host."

Saint was immobilized by the sound of the female voice behind him. It may have been more than half a century since he had spoken to her, but Bridget's voice was forever ingrained in his memory.

A tiny hand slid around his shoulder. "Please don't turn around, *mon ami,*" she said.

The wound on the back of his hand began to itch, and he clasped both of them tightly in his lap. "As you wish."

He caught the scent of vanilla as she leaned in closer. It stunned him that she still wore the scent.

"You don't seem surprised to see me," she said.

"In truth, I am not. I am, however, surprised you have elected to speak with me." Saint sat rigid, his head down, his vision transfixed to a spot on the floor.

"You must be careful," she whispered. "There are forces at play here that you don't understand."

Saint didn't acknowledge Bridget's statement. Instead, he chose to think of the contrast between the warm southern lilt of Janet's accent compared to the cold, haughtiness of Bridget's. "Please do not be offended, but due to our past history, surely you can understand my hesitation at trusting the slightest word that falls from your lips."

The warmth of Bridget's breath passed by his ear. "I know you will never forgive me for what transpired between us…."

An uncharacteristic chortle escaped Saint at her words. *Forgive?* Forgiveness had been easy. With his eidetic memory, forgetting had been impossible. Often his dreams had been haunted with reminisces of the evening before their wedding, the evening the truth about the LeCœur family was revealed. Sometimes he wished her family had succeeded in killing him.

Saint pinched the bridge of his nose. How he had longed to see her again, to hear her voice, or to catch the slightest glimpse of her. Now she sat mere inches from him, but the moment was less than fulfilling. What had he expected? It wasn't that he wanted another relationship with her. He knew that would be impossible.

No matter what lay between them, Saint had felt guilt for the way Bridget's life turned out. He alone knew why Bridget was in Germany when World War II erupted. She had gone there to fulfill one of Saint's dreams for her—to be an opera singer.

Had it not been for Bridget's mother, Saint would have never known she could sing. What mother wouldn't be proud that her daughter took voice lessons from one of the greatest vocal teachers of all time, Francesco Lamperti. Saint was amazed at the revelation. He had many talents. However none of them was musical, and no matter what Ghost said, howling in the moonlight wasn't the same as truly singing.

After much coaxing from him and her family, Bridget had sung for him. Her voice flowed with the ease of silk sliding across skin, carrying with it such emotion and beauty he could do no less than weep. How she could waste such a wonderful gift and not pursue a career on the stage were astonishing to him. When asked, Bridget shrugged. The only reason she could give was her insecurity in being good enough.

Then and there, Saint had vowed to take his betrothed to Europe after they were wed. There he would serve as her impresario. The opera world would be richer with her in it.

If only he had known the allegory in the first aria she sang for him. He could almost hear Bridget singing once again.

"Cara sposa, amante cara, dove sei? Deh, ritorna a' pianti miei?" he whispered. *My dear betrothed, my dear one, where are you? Come back to my tears!* How sad Handel was no longer one of his favorite composers.

The creaking of the seat behind reminded him he wasn't alone. He took in a cleansing breath. It was done. He had returned to New Orleans to say goodbye to Bridget's memory and put his own burdens to rest.

Again, I ask, are you so sure? The voice of the Universe caught him off guard.

Of course, I'm sure, he answered back. Even to Saint, the statement sounded shaky. Bridget had to be the reason he was here. What else could there be?

What else, indeed. Had he heard correctly? Had the Universe just mocked him?

Enough, he demanded. He was done with the Universe's games. Saint rose to leave but stopped when Bridget reached for him. The warmth of her hand upon his held him in place. Saint studied the petite fingers wrapped tightly around his wrist. The engagement ring he had given her a century ago still rested upon her hand.

"I beg you, *mon amour*, put aside your hatred and listen to me."

"You gave up the right to call me that the night you and your family tried to end my life." He could feel her gaze searching his face for any signs of emotion from him. "I see you still wear my ring." His words were almost an accusation.

Quickly she pulled her hand away and cradled it close to her chest.

"*Oui*. It is beautiful, and I have always loved it," she answered.

"Obviously more so than you did me, but if it eases your heart to know, I forgave you long ago." Without another word, Saint worked his way past the remaining members of the congregation and onto the steps outside the cathedral.

Exhaustion overtook him as the weight of a hundred lifetimes pressed down upon his chest, denying him of breath. Cradling his left arm with his right, Saint stumbled onto Chartress Street. Droplets of perspiration beaded across his lip and brow from his battle with the nausea that roiled in his stomach. *This cannot be happening.*

He needed help. Reaching out, he grasped for the person nearest him.

Fergus! He called to his brother as he fell against the hard stone. *Brother, help me.*

Voices shouted above him, calling out for 911 and the police. He had always known this day would come. Death is an inevitability of every life, even that of a shifter. In his mind, Saint somehow imagined his passing as more heroic. He chuckled at the thought of him as a hero, then laughed all the harder at himself for laughing as he lay dying.

Warmth and calmness surrounded him. He closed his eyes, giving into the beauty of dusky lilac illumination that surrounded him. He had had a good life. If Janet was correct in her reading, then everything leading up to this point was as it should be.

Janet. Princess Ryhinni. There was something about the woman that made him want to get to know her better, and he had intended to do so. *Too bad the opportunity will never come to fruition.*

"Hello, sweet wolf." Hel's thick, Nordic accent oozed between the cobweb-filled spaces inside Saint's head.

The faint sound of rustling fabric surrounded him as cool satin glided across the back of his hand. Opening his eyes, Saint realized he still lay in the street outside St. Louis Cathedral. Like a scene from one of the B movies Ghost loved so much, the strangers around him were frozen statues amidst chaos. The only thing missing was the cheesy music.

An icy wind wafted over his face, bringing with it the scent of lavender, a fragrance he had come to associate with the goddess Hel. Saint's dread was now confirmed. The goddess had come to gather the balance of their debt. Gentle fingers brushed along his forehead and jawline, forcing gooseflesh to erupt along his shoulders.

He followed the slender line of her arm upwards and across her bare shoulder. An aura of lilac pulsed around her, making it difficult to tell where the material of her gown ended and her flesh began. Flecks of amethyst jewels danced throughout her hair. The queen was lilac stardust against the dimming autumn sky.

Saint found it strangely curious Hel would pick his favorite color to wear as she appeared to him now. *Could she have worn it to impress me?* The thought was ludicrous at best. What need would Hel have to impress anyone, let alone one such as he? *Still, it is my favorite color. Oh my, I am beginning to think like Ghost.*

"Rise, Wolf," she commanded.

Without question, he obeyed. How interesting, he thought. It was an odd sensation to stand outside one's own body and nothing like looking in a mirror.

Gingerly, he picked his way through the paralyzed crowd. "You can stop time?" Saint asked, looking at their contorted faces.

"Not exactly," Hel answered. "However, I can slow my surroundings to the point all living creatures appear to freeze. One of the benefits of being me," she said, taking his arm.

Hel's ever present coldness seeped through the layers of his clothing, chilling the exact spot she touched. The sensation was one he assumed would eventually become tolerable since he now belonged to her.

"To what end?" Saint asked.

"Excuse me?"

"What purpose could altering time have?"

"If the need arises, I can use it to remove someone from harm's way. Quite contrary to what some may have you believe, I am not innately evil or cruel."

Saint placed his hand on hers where it rested in the crook of his arm. "I have no doubt that you possess great compassion. You could not preside over your realm if you did not."

Hel ducked her head as she appeared to blush at his words. "You appear worried, dear Saint." Gracefully, she stepped around a woman who pointed in the direction of his body.

"Not worried, my queen, merely perplexed."

"About?"

"I assumed I would have a bit more time with my family. I have very little in the way of possessions, but I'd hoped to have a chance to set a few of my affairs in order and to spend a bit more time with my family.

Hel led him down the street. Stopping near a Tarot reader, she peered in contemplation over the diviner's shoulder. Saint watched as Hel removed the Four of Cups from the spread and replaced it with the Knave.

Hel raised pale eyebrows. "Do you think the woman is going to listen?" she asked. "Humans seldom do."

If it was possible, Saint found the queen of the Underworld to be even more melancholy than before. Her aura, although a lovely shade of purple, neither danced nor expanded to include him the way it did when last they met.

"Her majesty appears unhappy," Saint said. "Would you care to discuss whatever troubles you. I am a rather good listener." He led her to a nearby park bench, motioning her to sit.

"Oh, my dear wolf," she began, taking his hand in hers.

Saint's heart quickened at Hel's words. Never had he met another that intimidated and enthralled him the way she did.

"Do you remember our arrangement?" she asked.

"I do." He stiffened. "And I'm ready to take my place."

"So gallant," she smiled weakly. "In truth, I am weary of being alone. To have you join me would be a comfort. However, you have made the fulfillment of our contract difficult."

"Pardon?"

"I am not a fool, Saint, so do not treat me as such."

"I would never think to do so, but I don't understand what I could have possibly done."

Hel pulled away, giving him a respite from her frigid touch.

"I suppose I cannot blame you," she said. "The fates have always had a way of casting a stone in the pool.

"The fates?" Saint questioned. "What do the sisters have to do with us?"

"So wise, yet so naïve. Do not believe for a moment your life is completely your own. The Sisters of All Life and Knowledge control you and the guardians you love so much. In the end, they control us all.

Saint moved away, placing his hands behind his back. Was it possible? Could there be nothing within his control? *Preposterous*.

"Don't misunderstand my words. We all have free will, but no matter our choices or our destination, the sisters have a way of turning everything to fit their agenda."

Saint pondered the queen's words. If every turn of his life was as it should be, how much belonged to him and how much belonged to the

He glanced back at Hel. With his photographic memory, he could recall every line and angle of the goddess's face. Yet his memory failed to do justice to her otherworldly beauty. Again, he searched the recesses of his mind for an ode or poem that would describe her beauty, and again he was left lacking.

Maybe he could learn to have feelings for her. The queen was well versed, witty, and intelligent—all the qualities Saint hoped for in a companion. Somehow, he could learn to endure her touch.

Much like the human mannequins surrounding his lifeless body, Hel became motionless, and although Saint had not thought it possible, she seemed bereft.

"I should be hurt by your reticence," she said. "But in truth, I am touched you would ever consider caring for one such as I."

Saint felt a twinge of guilt. He had forgotten Hel's ability to hear his thoughts even when he didn't want her to. Wait. He had forgotten? Impossible. He never forgot anything.

"Your majesty…."

The goddess held up her hand for his silence. "*Nok*," she said.

Saint was unfamiliar with the language, but he understood the sentiment behind it. *Stop. Enough.*

Hel continued. "The terms of our agreement were simple. *Your* soul, sweet wolf, for that of the guardian, correct?"

"Correct," he answered, daring not to look in her eyes for fear she would see his sorrow. "I assumed that is why you are here."

"I may be a monster in the eyes of many, but none can call me a thief. I will not take what is not mine."

Saint tilted his head. This conversation was almost as painful as some he had had with Ghost. "A thief, majesty?"

"You truly are unaware of the situation."

"Forgive me, Goddess, but I have no idea what you area talking about."

"The woman from the bookstore. How do you feel about her?"

Hel posed an excellent question. How did he feel about her? Janet had come into his life less than twenty-four hours ago. Yet, he must confess he did find her...curious. However, curiosity wasn't an emotion. "Feel? I have no answer for that."

"Do you love her?"

Love? He was fond of her, but love? Even if Saint did have an answer to Hel's question, he didn't feel the need to share. "Forgive me my candor," he said, "but I do not see where that is any of your concern."

Lightning flashed in Hel's cornflower blue eyes. The flesh on the right side of her face became translucent, melting like candlewax off hot embers.

Most men would cower in fear at the spectacle before them. Instead, Saint found it utterly fascinating. Mesmerized by the display, he watched her skeletal claw point in his direction.

"The moment you met her, could you not feel the silver threads of your lives being drawn together? Binding you? Becoming one strand?" Spittle flowed from her exposed maw. "The fates have bound you. Your lives are now one. As long as you live, so does she."

"And if I die?"

"So does she." The words whistled through teeth and bone.

Saint's legs buckled beneath him, forcing him to lean against a nearby bench. Just when he thought he had a handle on his life, the fates changed the rules. "But Janet is human. How? Why?"

"One does not question the sisters. Those who do pay a heavy toll."

"Truly, I knew nothing about this."

Hel seemed to be contemplating his words. He didn't want to think about what would happen if she didn't accept his explanation.

"I believe you," she said, her beauty returning as her anger subsided. "However, your ignorance of the situation does not negate your promise to me. When your time comes, you will take your place at my side. As for your human?" Hel shrugged "I make no promises."

Saint opened his mouth to speak but stopped. What argument could he make? He did promise Hel that he would return to Helheim as her companion. At the time, it was the only logical thing for him to do to insure the guardian and shifters as a whole survived. He never expected to find a mate, especially one that was human, but now....

"Excuse me, your majesty. Am I to understand the fates have chosen a mate for me and that her life is now tied to mine?" Hel nodded. "Is that true with everyone?"

"Sometimes yes. Sometimes no."

"Then it is possible the same holds true for Mika and his mate. So long as one lives, the other lives also." Well, there was one problem solved.

"The time grows late," she said, coming to his side, feathering thin fingers across his brow. "Return now, my beautiful wolf. Your life in the physical realm awaits."

CHAPTER 23

"Mom, you okay?"

Janet heard the click, click, click of the wooden rings that held the curtain to Princess Ryhinni's reading room. She pushed the hair from his forehead to get a better look at Eric's eyes. For the life of her, she had no idea why he insisted on letting his hair continually cover his face.

"Ah, Mom," he groaned and pulled away, checking the store to make sure no one saw her fussing over him. "Stop."

She pulled her son into a big bear hug, squeezing him with all her strength. She hated to admit it, but sometimes she did hug him in public solely to irritate him.

"People might see." He tried to push away.

"The last customer left a few minutes ago, and I was just about to close up," she said. "Can you lock the door?" she asked, relinquishing her hold. Janet cried out as stabbing pain shot through her left shoulder and down her arm.

"Mom!"

Janet slumped forward. Her head spun, forcing her to grab the edge of the counter. As soon as she shut her eyes, Janet was bombarded by scenes of Jackson Square. She stood outside the doors of St. Louis

Cathedral, and she watched as people greeted each other while passing through the massive, black doorway.

Murmurs and gasps rose from the throng as the people parted, allowing a man to pass. Clad in black from head to toe, he staggered from the doorway. His long coat swirled about his legs as he collapsed in the street.

"Aidan!" she yelled out, and she again stood in her store. "We've got to go." She scrambled, grabbing her keys from the counter and pushing Eric from behind.

"Where're we going?" he asked over his shoulder.

"Church. Now move."

Running wasn't something Janet did. Ever. But Saint needed her. *Dang it.* She could have driven, but why? It would be faster to run, or walk really fast in her case. She had always meant to start a workout regimen, but she never did. *When this is over,* she promised herself.

She heard Eric's footfalls come in line with her own. There would be explaining to do, and she would as soon as she could speak, but at the moment, it took all her concentration to keep going.

Her lungs burned and her side ached. Still she pressed harder. *Just a few more steps.*

Turning the corner, she noted the crowd gathered in a circle outside the cathedral. They stood nearby, pointing at the figure on the ground and mumbling. She prayed her premonition was wrong, but the moment she caught a glimpse of the high-glossed shoes and black trousers, she knew her prayers had been in vain.

"Aidan," she yelled, grabbing the person closest to her and clawing her way through the mass of people. Janet fell to her knees beside the lifeless body of Saint.

She tapped his cheek. "Aidan," she pleaded "Please, Aidan, don't do this. What happened?" she demanded to the people around them. Her question was met with blank stares and shrugs.

The air thinned and cooled as the crowd moved back. Paramedics pushing a stretcher made their way toward her. "Move, people. Let us through." She heard the gruff, masculine voice of the man on her left. He was the thinner of the pair, with a long face and receding hairline that probably started thinning in high school. "Let us through, ma'am. We need to get him some air," he said.

Thank the gods. Someone called 911. Janet watched as the emergency techs check Saint's vitals. "He's breathing, but nonresponsive," the squattier of the two men said. "Possible stroke."

"A stroke? But he's too young to have a stroke," Janet said. In all honesty, Janet had no idea how old Saint was, but considering what he was, the possibility of a stroke seemed astronomical. They had to be wrong.

"Do you know this man?" The emergency tech directed the question to Janet.

"No...yes...well, kind of." Janet shook her head.

"Name?"

"Janet Beesinger."

The guy with the thinning blond hair said, pointing at Saint, "His name."

Janet rubbed the spot between her eyes. *Really, there is a brain inside my head, mister.* "Saint," she answered. "Saint Wolfe." Janet tried not to pay attention to the strange looks the techs gave each other. So his name was Saint, big deal. This was the south. There were all kinds of strange names floating around down here.

"And up." She heard the gruff voice again as they lifted Saint into the ambulance.

Without asking, Janet started to climb into the back with Saint, only to be held back.

"Sorry, ma'am, you're not family. You can't go," the squatty guy said and slammed the door.

"But where are you taking him?" Janet asked, trailing behind the driver.

"Oschner Medical," he said. "Contact his family if you know them."

As the ambulance pulled away, so did the crowd. Janet stood alone as everyone returned to their work or whatever. She looked behind her expecting to see Eric standing nearby. Fear rose in her throat when she realized he was nowhere to be seen. Janet had been so lost in her worry over Saint, she had almost forgotten he had gone with her.

"Wait." Janet closed her eyes. Blocking out the sights and sounds of the French Quarter, she cast a psychic net, searching for her son. In her mind's eye, she walked the path back to My Spicy Cauldron, trying to pick up any trace of Eric and found nothing.

"Eric!" she yelled, searching each face that walked by. "Eric!" She spun in a circle, then again. *No, no, no, no, no.* There was no way this was happening. The scene before her twisted off kilter as Janet's breaths came in small gasps. She needed to sit down, but there was nowhere close enough, and walking didn't feel like an option.

Janet blinked and then blinked again as Kel's form came into view. She had no idea how he always knew she was in trouble, but he did.

"Easy now," he said, taking her by the arm. "What's going on?"

"This is all so crazy. I...I...knew something was wrong. I could feel it. So we ran down here, and Saint was on the ground...and the paramedics came and took him...and now Eric is gone...and I don't know what to do...." Janet tried to make her explanation coherent, but she was sure it came out sounding like gibberish.

"The boy was with you?"

"Yes. He was right here." She pointed to the ground.

"Okay. Okay," Kel tried to sooth her. "He probably just went to Café Du Mond for some beignets. Come on," he said, taking her by the hand.

"He's not there," she said with more calm than she felt.

"You can't be sure."

Janet stared up at Kel. How dare he question her? How many years had he known her and Eric? Call it mother's intuition, call it psychic ability. The name didn't matter. She knew.

"Don't, Kel. I am hanging on by a thread here. I don't need you to start doubting me now. Eric!" She whipped around to find Fergus standing behind her. She hadn't seen him appear but was pretty sure he had come with Kel.

Grief ripped at the very core of Janet's being, overwhelming her, draining her body of its energy, and crumpling her to the ground where only minutes before Saint had lain. *I'm not this strong,* she thought. *I can't lose two men that I love at the same time.* Love two men? Of course, she loved her son, but Saint? They had met only hours ago, yet in her heart she knew. It didn't matter to her what he was because she knew who he was. She had gazed into the depths of his soul and fell in love with the beauty she found there.

What did matter at the moment was Eric. He had to be her main focus and concern.

From somewhere in the distance, she heard Kel's voice. She had no idea whether he called the police or ordered pizza, but she knew it was he that lifted her from the earth. "Come on, darlin'. Let's get you off the ground."

Without so much as a whimper, Janet permitted him to escort her to a nearby bench.

"I can't do this, Kel," she whispered, falling into the seat. "Eric is my whole life. I can't lose him. Not now."

"You haven't lost him. The police are on their way. We will find him."

Kel's words may have sounded positive, but Janet sensed his reticence. He too feared Eric had been taken.

"You swore me no one would ever come for him," she whispered.

Kel shook his head. "They didn't."

"What if they changed their minds? What if they decided they wanted him back?"

"I'm sure that isn't the case."

"You don't know," Janet snapped. "Eric is getting close to becoming a man. Maybe his father decided it was time he took over."

"I promise you, Janet. That didn't happen."

"What makes you so sure?"

Kel took her by the hand, forcing her to look into his eyes. "Because," he said, "if his father wanted him back, I would have been told, but the time has come for you and Eric to leave this place."

"I can't talk about this right now," she said, her voice escalating to a fevered pitch. "Eric!"

"Now or later, makes no difference. The decision has been made."

What was he saying? She couldn't leave New Orleans. This was her and Eric's home. No matter who or what came after them, she would always have Kel to protect her. Unless she had a nervous breakdown from all the stress she was under, then he could take Eric wherever he wanted.

*   *   *

The fine hairs at the nape of Fergus's neck stood at attention, alerting him to the presence of another of his kind in the area. Scanning the crowd, he caught sight of Bridget doing her best to weave in and out of the throng of people milling around the square.

Fergus needed little time to assess the situation. Grey had already given him the go ahead to do what must be done. He heard Kel call after him, and so did Bridget

Don't do it, Fergus thought. *Don't run. Damn.* "Why do they always have to run?" He muttered and gave chase as Bridget took off. Fergus hated running on two legs. What he wouldn't give to be able to shift into a wolf at this moment.

Bridget ran across Decatur Street and along the side of Jax Brewery with Fergus fast on her heels. Fergus slowed his pace to a sprint. He knew the area fairly well. Once she made it across the parking lot and the railroad tracks, there was no place for her to go. He would literally have her with her back against the wall.

He stalked Bridget. There was satisfaction in watching her scramble, searching for a way out. *Caught like a rat in a trap*, he thought, as he approached her, grinning. "Are you ready to die and stay dead this time?"

Bridget spun on her heels, forcing her back up against the roughhewn bricks of the levy. "You would actually kill me?" she asked.

"You really have to ask me that?" Fergus adjust the snaps on his bracers.

She placed her hands flat against the wall. "I suppose I do."

Fergus narrowed his eyes. Bridget was up to something. He could tell. Why else would she expose her midsection to him? It was too easy of a target. "Why couldn't you stay dead?" he asked.

"What? And miss out on all this fun?" She smirked, inserting her hands into the back pockets of her jeans and shrugged. "You know, your brother has forgiven me. Why can't you?"

"Simple," Fergus said. "I'm not as understanding as my brother."

"*C'est vrai.*" Bridget said, using the French words for "that's true." "Let us wait no longer. If you are to avenge your brother, then do so."

The palms of Fergus's hands itched with the desire to do just that. He took a mental inventory of the weapons he had hidden on his body and which would be the most effective.

Letting Bridget go was the last thing he wanted to do, but he couldn't risk killing her in such an exposed area. All he needed was for someone to capture this on video, and getting arrested for Bridget's death wasn't on his to-do list. By the goddess, how he hated technology.

"As much as I would love to oblige you, I must put it off for another day." He refused to move as Bridget sashayed past him. She was going to leave, and there was little he could do about it.

*   *   *

"Mom! Mom!"

Janet twirled around, seeing Eric charging toward her. She didn't know whether to hug him, shake him, or ground him. In the mood she was in, it could be all three.

She pulled her son into her arms. Janet didn't care how much her public display embarrassed Eric. She was going to hug the stuffing out of him, then shake him, then ground him. *Yep, good thing I have a plan.* "Where have you been?" she asked, doing her best to contain her emotions.

"Listen," Eric gulped for air. "The ambulance driver was the guy from the shop. You know the strange guy with the ears and the red suit?"

"Did you get her?" Kel asked, as Fergus approached the group.

"Now isn't the time," he said. "Where did they take Saint? I need to get him back to Haven."

"Oschner Medical," Janet said.

"We need to get him before he is seen by a physician." Fergus

204

directed his statement to Kel.

"Agreed," Kel said. "He needs the guardian, not a human hospital."

It never occurred to Janet Saint would need special attention. The fact he was a shifter never entered her mind, but what if Eric said was right? If the ambulance was being driven by an elf, then it was a reasonable conclusion Saint wasn't being taken to the hospital, but if not there, then where? Janet did her best to avoid Fergus's fiery gaze. In his agitated state, she didn't want to be the one to tell him his brother was taken by elves. *Elves.* Even she had a hard time accepting it.

"I don't think Saint was taken to a hospital." Kel spoke up.

Janet sucked in her breath. *Okay, so Kel's gonna be the one. Better him than me.*

"I saw the ambulance," Fergus said. "Where else would he go?"

"An elf took him." Kel grimaced.

"Which ones? The ones at the North Pole or the ones that make cookies?"

"You're being ridiculous," Janet said, before she had a chance to censor her mouth. *Dang it! Where is that damn gatekeeper when I need him?* A knot formed in the pit of Janet's stomach as the full weight of his gaze fell upon her. She could almost see Fergus's muscles coil and tighten, a serpent prepared to strike without warning.

"Madame," Fergus said. "I have been accused of many things in my life. However, none can accuse me of being ridiculous."

Now there was a statement she could believe.

"Be serious," Kel said.

"You are the one talking about elves, and you are telling me to be serious."

"This is serious, Fergus. Elves are after Eric and have Saint. We need to get to Haven, and we need to make a plan," Kel said.

"You go to Haven. I'm going after Saint."

From the look on Fergus's face, Janet was quite sure he had no idea which direction he needed to go

Fergus pointed toward Eric. "You," he said. "You saw which way they went."

Eric jumped. "What?" his voice cracking between octaves in surprise. "Me?"

"Yes, you. Which way did they take him?"

"They…erm…."

"Speak up, boy," Fergus commanded.

Eric raised a shaky hand. "Left down Decatur."

"Then so shall I." Fergus moved in that direction.

"Don't be an ass," Kel said.

"You dare question my actions?" Fergus asked.

Janet leapt into protection mode, pushing Eric behind her as Fergus grabbed Kel by the collar of his t-shirt.

Kel held up his hands in resignation. "Never, old friend, but don't allow your love for your brother to cloud your judgment."

"My judgment is not clouded."

"Well, it's certainly not clear either," Janet said. From the corner of her eye, she caught a glimpse of Kel flinching at her comment.

Fergus's implacable resolve never wavered as he addressed Janet. "Excuse me?"

Janet huffed in frustration. Fergus was an act-first-ask-questions-later kind of guy, but Janet's gut told her this wasn't the best time for such an approach. "Did you stop for a second to think this could be a trap? They take Saint, knowing you would come after him, and then they take you or possibly even kill you." With more bravery than she felt, Janet placed a hand on Fergus's arm. It was an odd sensation to touch the smooth, worn leather of his archer's bracers instead of flesh. *Who wears those things in this day and age?* "You don't want that, do you?"

Fergus cocked his head to the left, and for a moment, Janet wondered if he even heard what she said.

"I apologize, old friend," Fergus said, as he released Kel's collar. "I only wish to do what is best for Saint."

"Understandable," Kel said, repositioning his shirt. "I don't know why the leaf elves took him or what they want with Eric, but you and I both know they aren't working alone."

"None of this is making any sense," Fergus said. "The elves haven't been seen or heard of in years. What could they possibly want with your son?"

Janet looked to Kel, her eyes pleading for help. He was the only one who could remotely answer that question.

"What aren't you telling me?" Fergus asked, looking suspiciously at Kel.

"We need to go. This discussion must be held until somewhere more private," Kel said.

"Very well," Fergus said. "What do you suggest?"

Janet held her breath. In her heart, she knew what Kel's answer would be.

Everyone must go to Haven.

CHAPTER 24

The piercing noise of the ambulance siren made its way into Saint's subconscious and into his dreams. He found it unusual that his dream was varying shades of sepia since normally they were in color. Looking down, he realized he stood on the edge of the cliff, high above the scene of the battle. The pop and bangs of bullets echoed off the rock formations in an almost deafening roar.

Cries of "incoming" filled the air, and Saint dropped to the ground, covering his head. The yells were replaced by the deep drone of B-17 flying fortresses that flew overhead, their fighter escorts close at hand. The ground shook beneath him, knocking him from side to side as the missiles exploded.

"Aidan?" Janet's gentle drawl rousted him from his slumber. "Aidan, wake up."

Saint couldn't help but smile at the sight of Janet's face floating above him, his heart swelling with love at the sight of her. *Could any woman be more beautiful?*

"Come on, sleepyhead," she said, "busy day ahead."

"I would rather lie here and look at you," he said, reaching for her, but she slipped away.

"No time for that now, Mr. Wolfe. We have lots to do this morning."

Saint groaned and covered his eyes with his forearm. His entire body ached with exhaustion. The only thing he wanted to do was sleep for a hundred years. Jarring pain knocked the breath from his body, forcing his eyes to open. A pair of green eyes stared down at him from the small, round face of a little girl.

The child could have been no more than three or four with a crown of flaming red curls. Squeals of laughter sliced the air as masculine hands lifted her.

"Leave uncle alone. He needs his beauty rest." Fergus smiled down at him and, with a wink, took the little girl away.

A strange feeling came over Saint at the sight of Fergus with the child. He was delighted by the fact his brother was now a father. However, he couldn't curb his own disappointment that Evie wasn't his. *Evie? Yes. That seemed fitting for the child.*

There was motion beneath him, rushing him backwards. He tried to reach out and grab hold of anything that could slow down the momentum, but his body refused to move. It was if he was being restrained, but at least there were no more sirens.

A band of pressure encircled his head, making it difficult to focus since his brain seemed a swollen mass of mush. With a groan, he opened his eyes and awoke to a blurry, white world. He could sense more than see the man that sat beside him.

"Where am I?" he asked.

The man beside him yelled to the driver. Saint was sure he should know the language, but the pain in his head kept him from accessing it. Not quite Gaelic and not quite Norse, the language was a strange admixture of the two. Yet he was positive he had heard it before.

Removing his hat, the man allowed a long silver-white braid to fall over his right shoulder. Pale light shimmered like fairy dust about the man's face, transforming his pug-like nose and thick features into ones more angular and defined.

"I believe you forgot something," Saint said, looking at the man's orange-yellow eyes. "Your ears, they should be pointed, should they not? You are, after all, an elf."

A strange smile tugged at the corner of the elf's lips. "That is something I have always found refreshing with you, Saint. You never waste time with small talk."

Saint squinted. He thought the elf looked familiar. He had met but a few in his life, but that was years ago. Still, this particular elf seemed to know him. *Why can't I remember?*

"I suppose I shouldn't be too surprised you don't recognize me. After all, I was but a youth the last time we met."

The elf reached across Saint's body, tightening the straps that held him to the stretcher. Dark green ink marred the pale, almost translucent skin on the underside of the elf's wrist. Saint recognized the five-pointed leaf and vine scrollwork that were the hallmark of the leaf elf.

"Calamus?" Saint asked.

His question sparked a twinkle in the elf's eyes, and Saint's recognition gave the elf unspoken permission to allow the tattoo on his face to manifest. Starting above his left eye, the design snaked its way along the contours of the elf's face and disappeared inside the collar of his moss green coat.

"We were told you were dead," Saint said.

"Propaganda started by the Esura after our defeat in the battle of the seven kingdoms."

"Why would you allow such a thing?"

Anger flashed in the elf's eyes. Saint was unsure if Calamus's anger was due to his remembrance of the battle or of Saint's questioning.

"I truly wish you had not recognized me."

"And why is that?" Saint asked.

"Because now I must do this," Calamus said before landing a right hook to Saint's chin.

CHAPTER 25

Janet heard the muffled sounds of Kel and Fergus's voices as they spoke in the other room. Occasionally, she would hear her name or Eric's name or Saint's. It frustrated Janet to know other people were making decisions about the lives of her and her son. It didn't help that she was still upset at Eric for disappearing. Although it was for a good cause, he should've told her before he left. Once she and he were safe at Haven, Janet would have to have a discussion with him.

"Can you just stay with us?" Janet asked as Kel walked into her room.

"I could, but with the onset of Eric's ability, Haven is the best place for him."

Janet pursed her lips. It was an unwitting habit she had that meant she didn't trust what he said.

"But this is his home," she protested. "What better place for him? Besides, what if he zaps someone again? what if he zaps Fergus?"

Kel snickered. "Everyone would applaud."

"Not funny."

Kel sobered. "Seriously, that is why Haven is best."

"What about school? I can't just take him away from his friends."

"Friends are overrated, and there is homeschooling. The kid could have no better teachers than Saint and Fergus."

Janet gasped. "Fergus? What on earth could Fergus teach him?"

"How to fish. How to hunt."

Janet cut her eyes at Kel. "Really? Fishing and hunting?"

"On second thought, maybe Eric just needs Saint as a teacher."

Her heart sank at the mention of Saint's name. "Is there any word?"

"No. Fergus has called everyone he knows, including the head of Theriontrope, and Haven, in case he showed up there."

"Do you think he'll find him?"

"Fergus loves his brother, and he will do nothing short of moving heaven and earth to find Saint."

Janet closed her eyes and shut out the world. There was no way she could think about all of this now. She didn't want to. She had a business to run and appointments to keep. How was she supposed to do that when she was halfway across the country?

There was always the telephone. Spirit energy could always find her whether she was physically in the room with a client or not. As far as Eric's education was concerned, Janet was reminded she had also been taught outside the traditional setting. She still wondered who her grandmother bribed so she would be allowed to be homeschooled.

With a deep breath and shaky resolve, Janet finished packing for her trip to Haven. She had no idea what to expect as far as weather. She assumed it would be cold, but New Orleans cold and Montana cold were two different types of cold.

With a harrumph of disgust, she threw items in the bag. She had no idea what to take and wasn't sure if it mattered. None of her clothes appealed to her, and she wished for the time and resources to buy a whole new wardrobe. Saint was a man of dignity and polish. The last thing he needed was a woman who looked a frump.

You could wear a potato sack and he would still find you attractive, Edgar said.

Not now, Edgar, she pleaded. *There is no way you can possibly know what Saint thinks.*

I know men and human nature.

Maybe you do, but Saint is...is....

Different, Edgar filled in the blank.

Yes. Different.

Even so, he is still a man. And as such...

Janet had heard more than enough. Mentally, she placed her hands in her ears and started singing, "la, la, la, connect the dots." It wasn't the most mature thing to do, but that was her signal to Edgar their conversation was over.

"Oh well," she mumbled. Closing the suitcase, she made her way to the living room where Kel waited. "I suppose I'm ready," she said, placing the last of her belongings at her feet.

CHAPTER 26

Ghost stood outside the door to Saint's bedroom. He missed his brother and friend. Saint, Fergus, and Mika were the only family her could fully remember having. Sure, there were things he remembered about his biological family. He recalled the color of his mother's eyes and the way she sang to him while rocking him to sleep, but the memories were fading like a photo in the sun.

How many hours had he spent with Saint, studying not only reading and writing, but also science, math, and history. Even if Ghost had attended public school, none would have taught him near as much as Saint.

Placing his hand on the doorknob, Ghost gave it a turn, only to find the door locked. *That's odd*, he thought. Saint never locked his door. He supposed it was possible the maid had secured the room, but even that didn't seem right.

With a loud crack and boom, the earth quaked, rattling all the windows in the main house of Haven. Instinctively, Ghost covered his head and got as low to the ground as possible. He didn't remember ever experiencing earthquakes at Haven before, but he supposed it was possible.

When the rumblings ceased, Ghost fled down the stairs and out onto the balcony where he joined Mika and CJ. The two looked as confused as he felt.

"Do you mind explaining what that was?" Ghost said.

Mika pointed to the far left corner of the woods. Where once stood acres of old-growth pines was a blank space. It looked as if someone had clear-cut roughly five acres.

"Get changed," Mika said, unbuttoning his shirt and laying it across the concrete railing. "We need to go see what's going on."

"Aye, aye, captain," Ghost said as he began to unbutton his jeans. He noticed CJ had turned her back to him. He thought by now she would be accustomed to their changing in front of her.

"We'll be back soon," Mika said, kissing CJ on the forehead.

Standing back, Ghost stretched out his arms and called forth his animal form. Golden light surrounded him as the molecules of his body expanded and shifted into an Arctic wolf. By the time he was finished, Mika had already gotten a head start.

Soon Ghost joined Mika, and the two raced toward the source of the disturbance. Small tremors required them to adjust their footing in midstride. Dead branches snapped and fell all around them. It reminded Ghost of one of his least favorite games—dodge ball. He never liked the dodging part, and he definitely didn't like the getting hit by the ball part. Yep, he hated that game.

He and Mika paused, observing the barren soil where a forest once stood. The strange thing was there were no signs of the trees being logged. No stumps, no wood chips, not even a leaf lay on the ground. Ghost could liken it only to a bomb exploding, but even a bomb would have left shrapnel.

What happened to the trees? They were just here, I mean, like an hour ago.

I don't know, Mika answered, sniffing close to the soil.

Ghost wasn't sure what Mika thought he might find, but he guessed they had to try. *Anything?*

No.

Do you remember when we brought back CJ and you asked what happened to your room? Ghost asked.

I do, Mika said, examining one of the remaining trees.

And do you remember Saint told us how Haven started changing, preparing for you to bring CJ back?

I do.

Do you think it could be doing that now?

Mika halted. *Why would Haven be changing now? There is nothing going on other than....*

Saint, they said in unison. As fast as possible, the pair raced back to the main house. Clearing the edge of the gardens they saw Fergus and a small entourage move up the balcony stairs and into the house.

CHAPTER 27

Saint's throat filled with dust, and he choked down the urge to cough. He could hear soft footfalls and murmurs. Wherever he was, he was not alone.

His eyes blinked open to a sideways world. Cold from the stone floor beneath him crept through his clothing and latched onto his skin. He found the sensation oddly comforting. It reminded him of the hours he spent kneeling in prayer on the sandstone floor of the priory.

When he was younger, Saint questioned how to handle the mixture of his animal and human natures. How could he live by the rules of man when he was not wholly a man? In the same turn, how could he live by the rules that governed wolves when he was not completely a wolf?

His angst sent him on a quest around the world, looking for answers. Eventually, he aligned himself with the Dominican friars. Maybe it was their commitment to study, or maybe it was their nickname, *Domini canes*. Saint always found the play on the name Dominican clever and appropriate since it meant the Hounds of the Lord. Both seemed fitting for one such as he, and he relished his time of study, prayer, and contemplation.

But as time went on, Saint came to realize that most all religions are similar, although most people would argue that fact. He learned to embrace the wolf residing within and returned to Haven to work alongside his brother as an enforcer for Theriontrope. He may have left the Black Friars behind, but because of them, he would always be known as Saint.

Saint longed to rub his eyes, but his arms felt heavy against the floor. He tugged at them, only to discover his wrists were bound together.

Brothers? he called along his pack's common telepathic link. *Fergus? Are you there?*

There was no answer from the rest of his pack. Saint flipped through the Rolodex in his brain. He could remember only two instances when he was unable to reach his brothers. One was in the years Fergus had been held captive. The other had been only a few months ago when he and Mika took their trip into the Underworld. Once on the other side, the pack's telepathy short-circuited, making communication between the pack members impossible.

Opening his animal senses to the world around him, Saint discerned the presence of three others. None of them vibrated with the energy of a shifter or human. Two were elven, and he assumed one of those was Calamus. The third was definitely masculine, yet unlike any he had sensed before.

"You can open your eyes, monk," the non-elf said.

As Ghost would say, "Busted."

"I no longer consider myself to be a monk," Saint said, opening his eyes as requested. "To do so would give the impression I reside in a monastery, which I do not."

"I don't know. Four men living in seclusion sounds rather like a monastery to me. But what do I know?" the stranger said, as he pushed his long frame away from the table where he leaned.

With a nod of his head, the man gave an unspoken order. A flash of green entered Saint's peripheral vision, as strong hands grabbed him from behind and lifted him into a nearby chair. He could tell by the feel of the energy around him, Calamus was his handler.

"Going to the highest bidder these days?" Saint asked the elf, as he adjusted the straps that held Saint's hands in place.

"An elf has to do something to relieve the tedium," Calamus said.

"Obviously." Saint refused to give into the uneasiness in the pit of his gut.

"Normally, I wouldn't feel the need to introduce myself," said the man Saint didn't know. "However, for you I will make an exception. Lucas Darkwater," he said with a slight bow of his head.

Saint tried to place the man's accent. He was positive Lucas wasn't Danish, although the vowel sounds were similar. "I take it I should know of you?" Saint asked.

Lucas laughed at his question. "What about Loki? Is that a name you are familiar with?"

"Loki?" Saint stilled. "That is impossible. Loki was...is...."

"A myth? A fable? Have you not already learned that we do exist? That is the problem with your species. You have lost your faith."

In Saint's estimation, there was nothing remotely godlike about the man who called himself Loki. In fact, he looked rather mundane for a god in his precisely creased slacks and cotton shirt. Then again, shifters looked human. Saint's head began to ache. He despised incongruity.

"Let me help you put this into perspective. Do you not pray to Freyja ad nauseam on a daily basis?"

"I think ad nauseam is a bit of an exaggeration, but I understand that's your opinion."

"Would you do that if you did not believe her to exist?"

Again, Saint retreated into the world inside his head. He tried to call out to his brothers. Only darkness and emptiness returned.

"Did you notice the bindings about your wrist?" Loki asked.

Saint twisted his wrists, examining the straps that bound him. The rope was made of something other than nylon or hemp. Lifting the rope to his face, Saint inhaled deeply. *Horsehair.*

"'Why horsehair?' you may ask. Simple. It comes from the mane of Sleippner, and I am positive you know his significance," Loki said.

"Sleippner is Odin's eight-legged horse. And if the myths are to be believed, he is one of your children."

"Your bindings are the reason you can't reach your pack or shift into a wolf. In essence, that rope makes you human." Loki moved toward to Saint, bending close enough for him to feel the god's breath upon his neck.

Loki whispered into his ear. "Even your precious goddess can't hear your pleas. Think for me, monk, what is my job?"

"I was unaware the gods required employment," Saint said.

A hearty laugh from Loki echoed throughout the old building, breaking the oppressive silence. "I was warned about your bluntness."

Saint tilted his head. "I find nothing amusing in my statement. I purely stated a fact."

"So you did," Loki said, curbing his amusement. "I will rephrase my question. What am I best known for?"

"Chaos," Saint answered flatly.

"That's right, chaos." Loki removed the fastener from Saint's dark auburn hair and handed it to Calamus.

Saint's skin crawled at the feel of the god's fingertips as they brushed the flesh beneath the tab collar of his shirt. Tiny bumps erupted across his skin when, in one swift movement, Loki ripped the shirt from Saint's body.

"What is your greatest fear, monk?"

Focusing on his breath, Saint fought the urge to jerk away from Loki, who pushed the shifter's hair to one side of his neck. "Death does not scare me."

A smirk twisted Loki's lips. "Of course it doesn't. You have kissed death and found her enchanting, did you not?" Loki stood fully behind him now. Even if Saint turned his head to either side, he couldn't see where the god had gone.

Screwing his eyes tightly shut at the mention of the goddess Hel, Saint tried to push the memory of her beautiful, pale face from his mind. "Interesting choice for a wolf, isn't it?" Loki asked, tracing the outline of the griffin tattooed between Saint's shoulders.

Involuntarily, his shoulders contracted at Loki's touch. "Would you believe I did it on a dare?"

"There are worse things than death, Saint. Besides, Freyja loves you too much for me to bring her wrath upon me for killing you, and I can see why," he said, trailing his fingers across Saint's shoulders.

A second set of footsteps entered the room. They were lighter than those of Loki's. Whispers hissed behind him, and Saint struggled to hear what was being said. The language was ancient and unfamiliar to him, although he picked out a slight trace of Gaelic.

Glancing around, he noted bits of broken glass on the floor, apparently from the blank patches in the colored glass above his head. The fresco in the ceiling was faded, but Saint was able to make out the Virgin Mary surrounded by angels, her hands outstretched toward the infant Jesus. There was irony in Loki's choice of stronghold. Where else would one bring an ex-Dominican then an abandoned church dedicated to the Virgin Mary?

"Now, where were we?" Loki sat upon the altar across from Saint. "Ah, yes. Your fear. We both know there is something you prize above all else. Even more than you prize your family."

"I have lived too long and seen too much for fear to affect me."

"Are you really so sure?"

Saint didn't answer. He had already answered the god. If Loki chose not to listen, what more could he do?

"Very well, then." Loki returned, looking behind Saint. "You may proceed." Loki's steely gaze held little in the way of compassion or ambivalence.

Cold metal pressed against the base of his neck, forcing a hiss from Saint's lips as the sharp barbs penetrated his flesh. Strong arms pulled Saint into a standing position, sending pins and needles coursing through his legs. A push from behind caused him to stumble before he found his footing.

"Calamus, there is no need to be rude," Loki scolded the elf. "Saint won't give you any problem, will you?"

Saint bowed his head in acknowledgement. "Could you at least remove my bonds?"

"Soon enough," Loki answered absently. "Tell me, monk. What is it like to remember everyone and everything that you have seen or heard?"

Saint shrugged. "I have no point of reference for such a question since I know no other way."

"Have you ever wondered what it would be like if you lost such a gift? If you could no longer remember your brothers or Haven or even how to feed yourself?"

Something in the inflection of Loki's tone forced Saint to halt his breath. The mark left behind by the barbs began to itch along with the one on his hand.

"Once you are secured in your room, I will have Haldane remove your bonds. You will remain my guest for a day. After that, you may go home."

Saint followed the god's gesture toward a small cell that seemed to appear automatically. Why had he not noticed that before?

"And before you get any ideas, I will tell you the bars were constructed in Svartalfheim, courtesy of the dark elves. So trying to escape would be useless."

"I would never think of it." Saint said.

"Not even a little walking through walls? Yes, I do know about that."

Saint wanted to ask Loki how he could know such a thing. As far as he knew, only his pack was privy to that information. Not even Michael Grey knew of Saint's ability. "You have my word. I shall not attempt escape, but I must ask what was in the injection?"

"It is my own special strain of rabies."

Rabies? What an odd choice. "Rabies is treatable," Saint said.

"Normally, yes, but this one was designed specifically for you, using your exact RNA sequence to aid in the mutation."

Saint was dumbstruck. If left untreated, the rabies virus would attack his central nervous system. Even if he could shift and try to heal, the fact the virus was constructed specifically for him would make it almost impossible to heal through vaccines.

"How is that possible?"

"All I needed was a bit of your blood, which I was able to attain with a little help." Loki motioned toward Saint's hands.

The Blatt-Elfen, Saint thought, as he remembered the peculiar funnel of leaves that moved about him that left the scratch on his hand. Leaf elves were named due to their ability to transform themselves into whirling masses of leaves. It was one trait that made them particularly lethal in battle.

"You must stay here overnight, and then you will be taken home. I can't take the chance you will heal yourself, so here you must stay. Now, as they say, I must jet."

"Wait." Saint stepped toward him, only to be restrained about his arms. "At least let me contact my brother."

Loki spun the air with his hand. "Request denied. I'm sure no explanation is needed."

Saint closed his eyes, trying to shut out the fear clawing at his heart. If not treated, he would lose his memory and his intellect. In the end, he would go completely mad.

"You see, dear priest, for you there is something worse than death."

CHAPTER 28

Janet was still queasy from the trip to Haven. Unlike her son, she didn't find transportation through a wormhole "sick." Sickening, maybe. Upon arrival, she met Mika and CJ, members of Saint's pack. Fergus explained to her that CJ was Mika's mate, but more importantly, she was the guardian.

Since childhood, Janet had heard of the guardians of Haven. There were very few multi-generational helpers who hadn't heard of the connection between shifters and the guardians.

A rush of heat inflamed her face. As a teenager, she fantasized about guardian. She had never seen pictures of Haven, but she could imagine living there and working with the shifters. Of course, the Haven inside her mind had no comparison to the real manor she saw before her now.

Not that she had seen much of it other than her and Eric's room. She wondered where her son had gotten off to. The last she saw of him, he was tagging after Kel and Fergus.

"Just use the intercom if you need anything," CJ told Janet before depositing her in the library.

Pulling a fleece throw from a nearby chair, Janet wrapped it about her shoulders and tucked her legs beneath her, collapsing on the nearest sofa she could find. *I really should've brought warmer clothes. Geeze,* she thought rubbing her hands together.

Sighing, she closed her eyes. All Janet needed was for her son to be safe and to know that Saint was alive. She had overheard Fergus and Kel speaking with the others. It seemed no matter how much Fergus tried, he couldn't contact Saint. She could tell it was hard for Fergus to keep a rein on his temper. No matter how gruff he appeared, Janet sensed he was actually a man who cared deeply for his family although he had the warmth of an alligator.

"Well, hello, nurse."

Janet looked up to see a rather attractive man watching her. Had she not known better, Janet would have thought… never mind. She was obviously too tired to think straight. "You must be Ghost," she said, trying not to stare at his eyes. *Such an unusual color.*

"Guilty," he said, a broad smile covering his face. "And you are?" He stepped into the room.

"I'm Janet Bessinger. My son, Eric, and I will be staying here for a while."

"You're not a shifter?"

Janet bit down on her bottom lip. It never occurred to her anyone would question whether or not she was a human. "No, I'm a regular human."

"And an attractive one at that," he said.

Janet didn't know whether to be flattered or not. Something about his swagger told her that his compliment was just part of his modus operandi.

"Hold on. Beesinger? Any relation to Fortis Beesinger?"

"You know of my great-grandfather?"

"Sure. Anytime we lost Saint, we could always find him at Fortis's apothecary. In fact, that was the first place we took Saint after the attack."

"Ghost!" Fergus's voice boomed from where he stood in the doorway, shaking Janet to the core. "That subject is *not* open for discussion."

"Okay, big dog. Whatever you say," Ghost said, with a roll of his eyes.

Fergus's looks reminded Janet of Saint. There could be no doubt in anyone's mind the two were brothers. The only differences she could find were in the brothers' eyes and personality. *Earth and fire,* she thought. That would be the best way to describe them.

"Forgive him," Fergus said. "Ghost is, well, Ghost."

"He's fine," Janet said.

"Yes, I am." Ghost said.

Janet couldn't help but smile. "Would you like to sit?" She scooted toward the end of the leather sofa.

"No, thank you," Fergus said.

"Any word on Saint? Can you reach him?" She pointed to her head, hoping Fergus would understand her sign language for telepathy.

"Nothing."

Janet wished she could do something to relieve Fergus's anxiety, but that would be impossible. She could tell he was the type of man that wouldn't listen.

She wanted to ask what was next. Had he and Kel come up with a plan? It occur to Janet that if Fergus did have a plan, he wouldn't be wasting time with her. Before she could work up the nerve to ask, Eric entered the library and plopped down beside her, trying to take her blanket. With a huff, she adjusted her position. *Some things will never change.*

"Can we go home now?" Eric asked, looking up at her beneath

almost invisible lashes.

She stroked back the hair from his forehead. "Not for a few days."

"Because of the elf?"

"I'm afraid so." Janet glanced up as Kel and the others entered the room.

Eric slumped down. "What am I gonna do stuck here in the middle of nowhere?"

"You'll just have to make do, honey," she said.

"Ghost," Kel called to Ghost before he had time to slink out of the room.

"Yeah?"

"Why don't you and Eric go play *World of Warcraft* or something?"

"What? Why me?"

"Because you excel at it, my brother," Fergus said.

Janet could tell a lot about a family or group by watching the interplay of each person's energy and auras. She couldn't quite put her finger on it, but there was more to the story where Fergus and Ghost were concerned. Their auras were similar. It was a trait she often sensed in parents and children, but she knew that wasn't the case here. Then again, she had never been around a complete pack before.

"Uh, okay, come on, dude," Ghost said. "Let's see what you got."

CHAPTER 29

Saint lay upon the hard mattress of the cot in his cell. He likened it to sleeping on a pile of hay, and he realized that although his bed back at Haven was plain, at least it was comfortable.

Haven. He thought of his home and of his brothers.

Fergus had been right. He never should've left. The realization that soon Fergus would be alone and their clan would completely disappear weighed on Saint's mind. A part of him held out hope that one day he would find someone and fall in love, but he never found the time. There were always missions to complete and riddles to solve.

So far he felt little difference from the injection other than the continual itching, much like the site on the back of his hand. What could he do about it now? Nothing. Thanks to the cages construction, he couldn't escape. The only thing left for him to do was to lie in his cell and wait for the disease to take over his body and mind.

Bridget's accent lilted through the bars of his cage. Sitting up on the cot, he saw her. She glanced his way, then at the floor, as she spoke with the elven guard. Surely, that was not a flicker of remorse he saw in her eyes.

He watched the burgundy-clad elf nod before leaving the room. As usual, Bridget got her way. The heels of her boots reverberated throughout the abandoned sanctuary as she neared.

"Saint?"

Saint lay back down. She could say nothing to him that would change anything. From the beginning, Fergus had warned him Bridget LeCœur was nothing but trouble. How right he had been. There were probably more occasions he should've listened to his big brother, but this had been the most important.

"You can't ignore me forever."

He could hear the petulance in her voice. It was sad, really, that the years had done little to change her. Saint once found her childishness endearing. One pout of her bottom lip or batting of her dark eyelashes and he would do anything for her. *So different than Janet,* he thought.

He had only spent a few minutes with Janet, yet Saint could tell she would never resort to immature tricks to get her way. She was someone who would give of herself freely, not take from others.

"Please, *mon cœur.* Do not treat me so unkind."

"It is not that I treat you unkind. It is that I treat you with indifference."

"If I said I was sorry, would you believe me?"

Saint almost laughed at her statement. *Bridget, sorry? Highly unlikely.* He moved to stand before her. Her dark round eyes peered up at him, and again, Saint could not help but think of her as childlike. So little about her had changed over the years. Of course, her hair and dress were different, but that seemed to be all.

"How are you feeling?" she asked.

"Is that why you came? To ask about my wellbeing?"

Bridget gripped the bars of Saint's cell and placed her forehead against the crossbar. "Dearest love," she whispered.

"I do not believe I was ever your love," he said.

"What happened between us was unfortunate," she said.

"Unfortunate? Which part?" he asked.

"Pardon?"

"You said what happened between us was unfortunate. I wish to know which part you found so unfortunate." Saint clasped his hands behind his back. "Was your being caught in a lie unfortunate? Was it unfortunate I chose to aid humans instead of dining upon them? Was it unfortunate that your family did not succeed in killing me, but mine succeeded in killing yours?"

"I cannot take back what happened."

"Nor can I," he said, as he stepped nearer. Had he not known better, he would've thought there were tears in her eyes. "What do you truly want? It is obvious you are in league with Loki. How else could you come to be here?" He crossed his arms over his chest, and he couldn't help but wonder how Fergus could stand such an uncomfortable position. However, Saint had to admit it was better than being bound.

"I came to warn you, to try and stop anything else from happening to you." She stretched her hand through the bar, only to have him step out of her reach.

"It seems your warning has come a bit too late," Saint said. "My lot, as they say, has been cast."

"There must be something I can do, some concession I make."

Saint thought for a moment. Should he dare ask the question? After all, wasn't it the reason he came on this infernal quest, one that would see the loss of his mind and eventually his life? It was ironic to think that, in the end, Bridget would have her way. His death would be on her hands.

How many times had he questioned Bridget's love for him? How many times had he thought "if only"?

Your life is as it should be. Saint remembered Janet's words.

It was hard to accept that everything he had been through in his two-hundred-plus years was as it should be. Was it right that he should give his heart away to Bridget? Was it right that he should give his soul to the queen of the Underworld? It was right that the fates chose this point in his life to show him his true-mate? *His true-mate?* Now he understood why so many had cursed the fates throughout history.

"No, there is nothing I need other than a shirt," he said.

Bridget dipped her head to look at him through a fringe of black lashes. Her habit was to do so just before asking for a favor, though in his position, Saint couldn't wager a guess as to what she could possibly want.

"I have no right to ask you this," she began.

This should be interesting.

Bridget looked nervously over her shoulder. "I need to ask for asylum."

"Pardon? *You* wish for asylum?"

"*Oui*, but not for me, for my son."

Bridget's words were a sucker punch to the gut. A son? Bridget had a child? "You want me to take your son to Haven?"

"He was taken from me at birth. I thought he was adopted, but the day I discovered that was a lie, I vowed to find him, and I finally have."

Saint couldn't look at her. It hurt too much to know that the woman he once loved, that he thought was his mate, had a child by another. A child she was too selfish to keep.

"I could say no," he said.

"I know, but.... Saint, the Alliance has him."

The Alliance was a shifter's hell on earth, a torture chamber of experimentation and violence.

A wave of exhaustion washed over Saint. For Bridget to allow such a fate to befall her own flesh and blood was inconceivable. *Dear Freyja, I am a patient and understanding man, but this is too much.*

"Please, Saint. I can't allow him to be tortured and killed by humans."

"Why not? Is that not precisely what you did to humans? They were all someone's son or daughter, yet that never hampered you or your pack," Saint said.

"That is different."

"How?"

"Humans are inferior creatures." Bridget spat at the ground.

Astounding. He had hoped if Bridget was alive, she would have changed, not because he cared for her, but because if she could change, then maybe his intuition hadn't been wrong.

"And yet, those inferior beings have your son. I suppose you wish for Delta Pack to rescue him?"

"I have a way to get him out and to Haven. I just need you to say you will help."

Damn. The Alliance was a sworn enemy of shifters. The pack had already destroyed more of its facilities than he cared to count. It mattered little who the boy's mother was. There was no way he could allow any to be held by those vermin.

Saint stepped closer, wrapping his hands around the bars of his cell. "I will help," he said, "but know this: my decision to comply with your wishes has nothing to do with our past."

Bridget laid her forehead against his fingers. "Thank you, thank you, thank you," she whispered and kissed his hand. "You are a good man, Saint Wolfe. I can think of no one better to entrust Mingon to.

CHAPTER 30

Saint tried to make sense of the mess that had become his life. He regretted very little about his life, but at this moment, his biggest regret was coming to New Orleans. He may love the city, but the city didn't love him.

It was hard for him to understand how things had come this far. He believed Hel when she said it wasn't his time, which she wouldn't take an innocent. But only a few hours ago, Loki signed Saint's death warrant and that of Janet's. It was possible he could find another to take his place in his agreement with Hel, yet he still didn't know if that would release him from his bond. Hel was a goddess after all, and he didn't believe she would be inclined to barter in this particular situation.

What have I done to displease you? he asked Freyja. *I have been a loyal servant. I have done everything ever asked of me, and this is how you repay me? By giving me a designer strain of rabies and having me agree to take on the son of my ex-fiancé? Let us not forget I finally find my true-mate and I am relatively sure her son hates me.*

Even through all the battles and wars he served in, never once had Saint taken a life, though there had been ample opportunity to do so. He sought only to do good, and what was right, so that when he finally did die, he would spend his eternity in paradise, not Helhiem. Flinging his arm over his eyes, Saint blocked out the ethereal fresco above. It reminded him too much of the goddess and how she had abandoned him.

He needed sleep.

Rattling keys woke Saint from a fitful slumber. The image of Calamus came into view as the elf opened the door. "Breakfast," he said.

With a groan, Saint swung his feet to the floor. Every movement of his body sent dull, throbbing pain racing along every nerve. It was a feeling he was unfamiliar with. He had experienced aches or pains before, but as a shifter his body had a way of healing when transforming from one form to another. It would be easy to blame his discomfort on poor sleeping arrangements, but he knew better.

"I'm curious," Saint said. "The tattoo above your eye...."

Calamus faced Saint. His hair was down this morning, partially covering the tribal-like design in question.

"It is the mark of the queen's guard," Calamus said, referring to Andromeda the Fifth, queen of the elves.

"I am aware of its meaning. What I don't understand is how you came to have one, since the position and honor are reserved for Vollblut Blatt-Elfen or pure-blood."

Calamus slammed the tray down, causing the rickety table to sway from the force of the blow. "My loyalty and my ability outweigh my pedigree."

"I'm glad to see things turned out well for you." Saint smoothed the back his hair and adjusted his vest. It was a rather odd feeling to go without a shirt, but considering Loki had destroyed it, he didn't have a choice.

"With no thanks to my father," Calamus said.

"With all due respect, we all thought you were dead."

The elf straightened. "Will there be anything else?"

"No," Saint said. He had wished to learn more about the elf.

Where he had been. Why he felt the need to hide from his father.

Calamus bowed slightly before exiting the cell. "You will be released soon and taken back to Haven."

Haven? He didn't wish to go to Haven. He needed to go to Janet. There was no denying his feelings for her. Fury flashed over him. For once, just once, couldn't he have what he wanted instead of what everyone else wanted? A tremor began in Saint's hands as he thought of confronting Calamus.

Scenarios of attacking the elf flooded Saint's mind. If he could somehow overpower the elf and switch places, then he could go wherever he wished. Even to the moon. What does it matter if the moon was 328,900 miles from Earth, had no atmosphere, and had extreme temperatures. The point was he could go and no one could stop him.

What was he thinking? Saint rubbed his eyes. He had to ground himself and bring his thoughts back to the here and now. Metal clanged against metal as Calamus locked him once more in his cell.

"Since you require nothing further."

"Actually," Saint said rising. "Is there a message you wish for me to relay to your father?"

Calamus seemed perplexed by the question. In Saint's estimation, the question was rather simple. A yes or no answer was all that was needed. Unless the answer was yes, which would then need elaboration.

"Tell my father, Darkness will visit him soon."

CHAPTER 31

Janet lifted her face to the cold, gentle wind of autumn. She had decided to take her afternoon tea on the balcony so she could watch Eric practice archery with Ghost and Mika. She appreciated how the two had taken an interest in Eric in such a short period of time. Maybe she had been wrong not to date and not to have male role models in his life other than Kel.

She had to smile at the seriousness with which Eric took instruction. He seemed genuinely interested in what the shifters had to say, and from what she could tell, he was doing very well. It seemed fitting that they would be practicing with bows and arrows, considering how much Haven reminded her of a castle. All the rooms were huge and ornately decorated.

It was hard for her to admit it, but she had sneaked inside Saint's bedroom. She wasn't proud of the fact. However, it was the only way she had to be close to him. His room was rather sparse with minimalistic furnishing. There were no paintings or photos of any kind, just a rather large statue of some goddess.

She had almost laughed as she opened his closet and found about twenty sets of the same black and white outfit she had last seen him in. She would have been surprised if she found a Hawaiian shirt. Now that would have been funny. Picking up the sleeve of his coat, Janet inhaled his scent. Never before had she thought someone could smell of harmony and love and comfort. It was odd think about, but Saint had the aroma of home.

Janet had held her breath when she heard footsteps wander the hallway, stopping outside Saint's door. What would have happened had she was caught? That would have depended upon who caught her. If it had been CJ then not so much. If it had been Fergus, she might not make it to see Eric's next birthday.

When she had been sure the coast was clear, Janet tiptoed down the stairs and pretended as if nothing happened.

Try as she might, Janet was unable to stop worrying about Saint. It had been almost twenty-four hours, and there was still no word of Saint or his abductors. Eric still insisted it was the elf from the store, but since he was the only one to see it, no one could say for sure.

To be on the safe side, Kel returned to New Orleans to, as he had said, "poke around." As far as anyone could tell, Kel's poking around hadn't helped anything. In truth, Janet thought it was a way for him to get away from Fergus.

"Good grief. Can things get any more complicated?"

"That tends to happen when you fall for a shifter."

Engrossed in her own thoughts, Janet hadn't heard CJ approaching.

"Here," CJ said, offering her a steaming mug of cocoa. "Not sure how you feel about chocolate, but it's one of my favorites."

Janet knew there was a reason she had taken an instant liking to this woman. "That is just what I needed. Thank you," Janet said, her hands soaking in the warmth of the cup. She wanted to ignore CJ's comment about being in love with a shifter. Janet was pretty sure she hadn't given away anything that would reveal her feelings where Saint was concerned.

"He's doing really well," CJ said, nodding toward Eric.

Janet gave a weak smile. "Yes, he is. I'm amazed at how patient Mika and Ghost are with him. It has been a long time since I've seen him laugh and kid around like that."

"Ghost has a tendency to bring it out in people."

"Ghost hides a great deal that way," Janet said, without thinking. "Sorry, I didn't mean...."

CJ took a seat beside her. "It's okay. I'm not surprised you picked up on that. You probably picked up on a lot of things where he was concerned."

Janet found CJ's comment odd. She never discussed her abilities with anyone at Haven As far as she knew, Saint was the only one privy to that information.

CJ kept her eyes on the archery lesson as she spoke. "You won't remember, but I met you years ago. A group of friends and I were on spring break and went to New Orleans. We walked around Jackson Square, and you were doing readings. I stood there for the longest, trying to work up my nerve. Finally, you looked at me and said—"

"You're not crazy. The voice inside your head is only our protector," Janet said.

CJ nodded. "That's right, and you were right," she said, waving to Mika. "That voice protects me always."

Janet could see the love between CJ and Mika and for a moment felt a jealousy she didn't know she had. It wasn't that she wanted Mika. She wanted a man to love her the way Mika obviously did CJ.

"His was the voice?" Janet asked.

"Yes."

"Was it hard getting used to it? Being married to a shifter?"

"We're not married. Yet," CJ answered. "When the time is right, we will be."

Janet nodded her head and mumbled. When Spirit wanted to get a message through, it will get a message through, no matter where or when. Once the message is received, it was up to Janet whether or not to say something about it. She despised blurting things out for fear people would think she was trying to read their minds, which she couldn't do, but even if she could, she wouldn't. That was a strict violation of her personal code, and most of the time, her guides didn't volunteer any information unless asked. But that wasn't always the case. Sometimes, like now, they chimed in with little tidbits of information. It was up to her whether or not to tell anyone.

It was just she and CJ. What did she have to lose? "Will the wedding be before or after the baby is born?"

Janet cringed when CJ snorted hot chocolate into her nose. *Great. She didn't know.* "I'm sorry, CJ. I...I thought you knew," Janet said. "I knew I shouldn't have said anything."

"No, no, no." CJ placed her hand on Janet's arm. "I have wondered, but I have been too scared to take the test. I didn't want to be disappointed."

Janet chuckled. "Take the test. You won't be disappointed."

CJ continued to prattle on, but Janet didn't hear. Gooseflesh raced up her spine, her attention on the other side of the terrace. She realized one particular spot appeared blurred when everything else looked normal, and she wondered if she needed to see an eye doctor. Blinking continuously, Janet tried to clear her vision, but nothing helped.

She yelped as two men stepped out of thin air and onto the patio, one supporting the weight of the other, who was obviously out cold. The man being carried was short with dark complexion and hair, the other Janet knew on sight. "Saint," Janet cried out, alerting everyone to his return.

Before she knew what was happening, Mika, Ghost, and CJ were at Saint's side, fussing over him and relieving him of his passenger. CJ barked out orders to "get the boy down to the medical wing" and led Mika and Ghost into the house.

Janet's heart pounded against to her ribcage at the sight of Saint. This was the first time she had seen him in any state other than perfect. With his hair falling in his face and dust covering his clothes, Janet still found Saint Wolfe to be the most handsome man—ever. She wanted to go to him, to run her hands over his body and see for a fact that he truly stood mere feet away.

Run to him, her heart said. *Run to him and let him know how you feel.*

I can't. I couldn't take his rejection, she argued.

You can and you should.

What if.... Janet didn't get to finish her thought before Fergus was there, embracing his brother and whisking him into the house.

CHAPTER 32

Every joint in Saint's body ached, although he tried not to show it. Removing his wrinkled opera coat, he placed it across the back of the chair. "Stop hovering, Fergus," he said, finding it hard to maneuver with his brother so close by. "Take care of the boy."

"You are my concern, not the boy."

"I am fine." Saint said, moving to the nearest chair.

"No!" He heard CJ from across the room. "On the table." She pointed to an open examination table opposite her, giving Saint the look.

"I simply need to rest."

"You need to do as I say. Now take off your shirt and sit."

Saint held out his arms. "As you can see, I am not wearing a shirt."

CJ glanced up at him and then back to the young man laid out before her. "Then take off your vest and sit down."

Saint did as she asked. Removing his vest, he placed it on top of his coat and slid onto the exam table. "She's become quite bossy, hasn't she?"

"I like a woman with sass." Kel spoke up from behind him. Saint didn't remember seeing Kel when he first arrived, but there was no telling where he had been hiding.

"Me too," Ghost said.

"Getting picky in your old age?" Kel teased.

"Hey, I have standards," Ghost said.

"Yeah, breathing."

"Told you." Saint heard Mika whisper to CJ.

"Everyone stop," Fergus commanded.

"Let them be. It's fine, brother." Saint said

Fergus crossed his arms over his chest. "Ghost needs to show respect."

"Ghost needs to be Ghost, and you would do well to realize that." Saint could feel his ire rising. He only wanted to be left alone, to have a shower and be with Janet.

To say that he had been surprised to see Janet sitting on the veranda was an understatement. She was the last person he expected to see at his home, but she was the first he thought of when he was released. Had it not been for his promise to Bridget, he would have gone to New Orleans. It was fortunate he didn't, and it made him wonder if somehow Calamus knew Janet would be there.

Saint paid special attention as CJ worked on her patient. Mingon's wounds were more extensive than Saint had thought. Actually, he didn't know what to expect. When Bridget asked him to help her son, he assumed him to be a boy, not a young man on the verge of gaining his shifting abilities.

The sound of ripping fabric filled the air as CJ cut and tore Mingon's shirt from his body.

"How is he?" Saint asked.

"He is pretty banged up. His side is bruised. Could be a cracked rib. I won't be sure until I take some x-rays."

Saint wondered if there was a way to keep Mingon's identity away from the others. He could possibly buy a little time, but when the truth came out, Fergus wouldn't be happy with the deception whether he found out now or later.

"Do you know him?" Fergus asked.

"Not personally," Saint said. "I do know his name is Mingon, and he is Bridget's son." Saint could feel all eyes as they turned to look at him. *Oh, why can't I be better at lying?*

"Whoa." Ghost was the first to break the silence.

"Indeed," Saint said.

Fergus laid a hand on Saint's shoulder. "I believe I misheard you. Did you say 'Bridget's son?'"

"I did." From his periphery, Saint could see Kel move his body between Fergus and Mingon.

"You are my brother, and as such rarely do I question your decisions, but are you mad?"

Saint wanted to laugh. Soon he would be but now wasn't the time to bring that up.

Fergus looked to Kel. "Did you know about this?" he asked, pointing a finger in Kel's face.

Kel's body seemed to expand, becoming larger than normal, a feat Saint knew was impossible, and he dismissed it as a trick of an exhausted imagination and fatigue.

"No, I did not," Kel said with added emphasis on the "not."

Fergus snarled, stepping into Kel's space. "I find it interesting you happened to pop back in when Saint shows up with that cur."

Kel leaned forward, refusing to give an inch. "Back down, wolf." Kel's voice morphed into a low growl.

The leather of Fergus's bracers creaked as he readied himself for battle. "And if I don't?"

Saint pinched the bridge of his nose and scrunched his eyes closed.

The fighting all the time was too much. If Fergus wasn't battling Ghost, he was battling Kel. Maybe helping Bridget wasn't the best idea he had, but he couldn't stop himself. And contrary to what everyone probably thought, his decision wasn't based on his feeling, or lack thereof, for Bridget.

He also understood Kel was the only one who could take on Fergus in hand-to-hand combat and be a survivor. He was too tired to keep interceding where his brother was concerned, but if someone didn't step in soon, he would have to.

The scent of peaches and hyacinths found its way to Saint, reminding him of his true-mate. His mind calmed, and he began to breathe again.

"Stop it this instant!"

Saint looked up in time to see Janet wedge her body between Fergus and Kel. Her head bent backwards to give her a better view of the men towering above her. She had the look of a woman not to be tampered with. *How long has she been standing there?*

"Long enough," Janet said, answering the question only she could hear. "I want you to look what you are doing to your brother." She placed her hands on her hips. "I said 'look at him.'" She sounded like a mother scolding a child.

Fergus grumped but did as she asked. The hard lines of his face softening to remorse as he looked at Saint.

Janet poked the center of Fergus's chest. "He doesn't need you standing there peeing on everyone to prove you're the big dog," she said, making air quotes around the last two words. "You're part of this too," she said to Kel.

"What'd I do?" he asked

"You were there." Janet took a deep breath. "I don't know who Bridget is, and frankly, I don't give a tinker's damn, but this poor kid needs your help, and Saint," she stopped and took his hand in hers, "he needs to get cleaned up and rest. Whatever questions or grudges you have can wait."

Saint was humbled by Janet's show of affection. He remembered most every day of his life, and this was the first time anyone had come to his defense. Without forethought, he pulled Janet's hand to his lips, placing a tender kiss on the back of her fingers.

"Thank you, my princess," Saint said.

"You're welcome," she said.

Saint became fascinated by the crimson blush that covered Janet's throat. *How adorable. I've embarrassed her*, he thought.

"What the heck?" CJ asked.

"It is called a hand-kiss," Saint said. "It is considered respectful way to greet a lady. The practice originated in Spanish courts of the 17th and 18th centuries and also the Polish-Lithuanian Commonwealth...."

"Not that." CJ cut off his explanation. "This."

CJ stepped back so the others could see Mingon's arm. Branded into his upper arm was the Greek letter omega with a "W" centered inside it.

Saint felt Janet squeeze his hand as she looked at the red-raw burn. "Is that a brand?"

"I'm afraid it is," CJ said. "And from the look of the rest of him, I don't think he did it willingly."

Saint slipped from the table to get a closer look. He felt nauseous. It was unfathomable that Bridget would allow such a fate to befall her progeny. In her defense, she did say he was taken at birth, but when Bridget told him her son was with the Alliance, he never imagined he would be marked for the ring.

"The Alliance," Fergus said.

Saint nodded. "Yes. This is the reason I agreed to help."

"What's the Alliance?" Janet asked.

"It's a shifter death camp," Kel said. "Shifters are captured for experimentation. Some are forced into blood sport. Bastards."

"The 'W' stands for wolf. The omega stands for the weakest," Saint said.

"So what are you saying?" CJ asked.

"I'm saying this boy was used as bait."

"What kind of mother would let that happen to her child?" Janet asked.

"One like Bridget LeCœur," Fergus said.

Saint could sense Janet's anxiety. "Is that where you were? How did you get away? Did you have to fight?" Her questions came in a rushing breath.

After centuries of loneliness, he finally had someone to share his life with, if only for a short while. Tremors began in his knees, spreading upward into his thighs. Pulling away from Janet, he groped to find his way back to the table, only to be caught by Fergus as he crumpled to the floor.

CHAPTER 33

Ævar's laughter subsided when Cassius entered his office. Although he and Cassius had been friends for more than thirty years, it was hard for Ævar to fully trust the man. It wasn't always that way. In the beginning, Ævar had every confidence in Cassius. There wasn't a plan or scheme of Ævar's that the polar bear wasn't a part of.

Had it not been for Ísold, Cassius would have never become a part of Ævar's life. "Friend he be or foe he make, his first offer you must take." Ísold's words would forever be embedded in his mind. Too bad she didn't warn him of Cassius's betrayal, but to do that, she would have told of her own treachery. How she talked Cassius into aiding her in the escape of Fergus Wolfe, he would never know.

Ævar never admitted to the knowledge of their deceit. Instead he locked Ísold far away and vowed to keep Cassius close. However, that didn't mean he had to tell Cassius everything.

"I apologize for disturbing you," Cassius said as he moved further into the room. "Apple-y." He nodded at the woman balanced on the arm of Ævar's chair.

Ævar didn't need to look in her direction to see the sneer of contempt on her face; he could feel it. *Why can these two not get along?* Ævar wondered.

"No apology needed, old friend," Ævar said. "Apple-y and I were merely making plans for a small trip."

"Apple-y love trips," she said, sliding her arm across Ævar's shoulder.

"Apple-y, Cassius and I need a moment to speak in private." Ævar pulled her arm from around his neck and placed a light kiss on the back of her hand.

"But, master," she whined.

Inwardly, Ævar cringed at the sound. He hated when she whined. Who was he kidding? He would rather have a screwdriver plunged into his ear than to hear anyone make that wretched sound.

"There is no need for her to leave," Cassius said.

"No. She needs to start packing for our trip." He looked solidly into her golden eyes, giving Apple-y a mental push to leave.

"Apple-y leave," she huffed, "but she no like."

"I promise I will make it up to you." Ævar allowed his hand to slide along the curve of her hip. He learned long ago how to entice Apple-y to do as he asked. Like most cats, she wanted to be stroked in the right places and given a treat.

Leaning his chair backwards, Ævar folded his hands across his lap and waited for the door to close.

"Please." He motioned toward Cassius's favorite chair. "Take a seat."

"What I have to say won't take long."

"Very well. Speak."

"It is your mother," Cassius began.

Closing his eyes, Ævar released a long, slow breath. Of course it was his mother. Nearly three days had passed without seeing her, but Ævar assumed it was due to Apple-y's presence in their home. What was it with women and pouting? You would think after a hundred years or more, they would have grown out of the habit.

"What now? Wait," Ævar said. "Let me guess. She fired another housekeeper, or maybe she has broken all the dishes again. No matter. Both can be easily replaced."

"It is neither of those things."

"Well then, what has she done?"

Cassius clasped his hands in front of his body, causing the material of his jacket to bunch slightly and reminding Ævar exactly how large the man was.

"Kenna is refusing to answer the door to her chambers," Cassius said. "And according to your housekeeper, your mother has neither requested nor accepted any nourishment for the past three days."

Ævar waved his hand in dismissal. "She has probably taken to her bed again. How many times has she feigned illness and refused to eat? Give her time. She will come around."

"This isn't that."

"Of course it is," Ævar scoffed. "You and I both know she has these episodes every six to eight months, and when she doesn't get her way, she gives up and things return to normal."

It was a pattern Ævar knew all too well. Kenna would refuse to eat or maybe quit speaking to Ævar as a rebellion against his banishment of Ísold.

"Believe what you will," Cassius said. "But she has taken to her bed and is asking for you."

Ævar picked up the watch lying on his desk and glanced at the time. Not that time actually mattered to him. His calendar was free except for taking Apple-y shopping for her assignment.

Maybe it would be best for him to handle the situation. Kenna was his mother, after all. The day he took her into his home, she became his burden, not Cassius's.

"Thank you, Cassius. I will see to Kenna."

"Is there anything else?"

"Not at the moment," Ævar said as he moved toward the door. "However, don't go far. We have a few things to discuss."

"As you wish," Cassius said, eyeing the sofa. "I will be here when you return."

Shaking his head, Ævar closed the door to his office. He wouldn't be gone five seconds before Cassius would be stretched out on the sofa, napping. *How could one person sleep so much?*

Ignoring his assistant, Ævar punched the call button on the elevator and reminded himself what a brilliant idea it had been to renovate the top floor of this office building, turning it into their home. It helped having everything under one roof.

Sara Comington, Ævar's housekeeper, met him outside his mother's door. She seemed so tiny and frail, as if she would collapse, unable to withstand the pull of gravity. But Ævar knew appearances could be deceptive, and so it was with Sara.

She was one of the strongest in his pack and could take down the most aggressive and ambitious of the young.

"I'm sorry to disturb you, sir, but I fear I had no choice," she said.

Ævar placed a reassuring hand on her arm. "It's fine, Sara. I understand how difficult my mother can be."

Grabbing Ævar's hand, Sara pulled his attention to her grey eyes. "Sir, before you go in, I must warn you...your mother appears different."

"In what way?"

Sara's face crinkled. "She looks faded, Sir."

Ævar stiffened. Faded wasn't a good term to use in describing a shifter. He had never personally met a shifter that faded, but he knew it meant the shifter had lost the will to live. In doing so, a shifter would send his essence back into the Universe, bit by bit, until there was nothing left of the body.

"I appreciate your concern, Sara, but I am sure that isn't the case. You may leave us. I will call if you're needed."

"Of course, sir," she said with a slight bow.

Ævar waited until Sara had disappeared before knocking. "Mother," he called. "Mother, it's me, open the door." No sounds came from within the room.

Ævar took a deep breath, pulling a tight leash on his emotions. He didn't have time for one of his mother's tantrums. He had enough problems dealing with Apple-y's impatience. There was still much to plan where his brother was concerned. He couldn't just send Apple-y into Haven. He was pretty sure Fergus wouldn't recognize her, but it wasn't a chance he was willing to take.

"Mother, I won't ask again. Open this door." *Three. Two. One.* Ævar counted in his head before forcing his way into the room. His heart almost stopped at the sight of Kenna facedown on the floor, her long hair obscuring her face.

Rushing to her side, Ævar fell to his knees. "Mama." He hadn't used that word for his mother in years, and it felt strange upon his lips. Pushing the hair back from her face and tapping her face, he called to her

Joan Hazel

again. "Mama, wake up." It seemed an eternity before she opened her eyes, and he was taken aback by their dusty appearance.

She looks faded. Sara's words played over in his mind.

"Ævar," Kenna whispered.

"Don't speak," he said, scooping her from the floor and placing her on the bed. "I'll call for the doctor." He reached for the phone clipped at his waist.

"No." She placed a shaking hand on his. "There is no need. A physician will do no good." Her voice creaked from disuse.

"I don't care what you say. I am calling the doctor."

Her eyes pleaded with him. "Ævar, it is time. I have lived long enough. It is time you let me go."

"What do you mean, let you go?"

Kenna patted the side of the bed, motioning for him to sit with her. "Mother, I don't have time to sit and chat."

"Of course you don't. You never do." She turned her face from him.

"I have a business to run."

"And a family to destroy," she sniffed.

Ævar's jaw tightened. *So we were back to this.* "It wasn't my fault that your daughter decided to defy me. She had to be punished."

"It doesn't matter anymore. Nothing matters anymore," she sighed.

"You will not fade."

A snort of disdain rose from Kenna. "That isn't your decision. I have nothing left to live for. Your father gone. Your brother gone. Your sister gone, and once I am gone, no one will be left to stand in your way."

Ævar hung his head. Why couldn't she appreciate what he had given her instead of thinking only of the things he had taken away? His feeling for Kenna may not have been as deep as a child's should be, but he

254

couldn't allow her to waste away. But he could think of only one thing that would stop her.

"Fine, Mother, you win."

"I don't understand," she said.

"I know this is a ploy to get Ísold back. I just never thought you would go so far as to kill yourself to get it done."

Kenna shakily pulled her body to a seated position. "What are you saying?"

"I am lifting Ísold's exile. Soon you shall have the reunion you seek."

CHAPTER 34

Janet sat across the room watching CJ and Mika as they tended to Saint, who she noticed was awake and rather fussy. Somehow she knew he wouldn't be a good patient.

She tried not to stare at his bare torso, and she wondered if she could talk him into leaving his shirt off and cooking for her. *As long as it is not bacon, I will oblige.* Janet sucked in a sharp breath. She had forgotten about the Saint's ability to hear her thoughts.

I didn't mean to, Saint said. *I won't exploit our connection any further.*

Feeling his energy disengage with her was an odd sensation. It was like someone removing a warm blanket, leaving her exposed to the cool night air. It was also one she didn't care for. *Saint! Saint, come back!*

Though she couldn't hear it, Janet was sure Saint was laughing at her.

Yes?

Okay, you can stay, but just like with my spirit guides, there's got to be boundaries. Okay? My head is busy enough. I don't need any more people, alive or dead, bumping around up there.

That time she was positive he smiled at her comment. He may have thought she was joking, but she was serious. He had no idea what it was like to have three or four voices carrying on a conversation at the same time.

Saint coughed. N*oooo. I would never know what that felt like.*

Mr. Wolfe, was that sarcasm? she asked.

Possibly.

"Hmph," Janet grunted and blushed when Mika and CJ simultaneously glanced in her direction. Maybe she needed to concentrate on something other than Saint and his biceps. *Amazing what that man kept hidden under all those layers of clothes!*

Awww. She heard before she felt him close the door on their conversation. Who would have thought the stoic man she first met might actually have a sense of humor.

Janet heard Mingon mumbling in his sleep. It had been nearly an hour since his and Saint's arrival, and the boy hadn't opened his eyes once. Janet didn't know whether or not he had been drugged, or if he was so worn out, he had no choice but to sleep.

Janet's heart went out the young man. His human aura was muddy and pulled as tight as possible against his body. It made sense considering everything he'd probably gone through in his short life. He was untrusting and needed to protect himself.

Stroking back the hair from his face, she thought of Eric. What if she hadn't taken him in? Would he have ended up like Mingon, a child no one wanted and made to fight or worse, just to stay alive?

She still hadn't been given a good reason why the elves would be after her son. In her heart, she knew Kel knew more than he was willing to tell her. Sometimes he frustrated her badly. Didn't she deserve to know at least *what* her son's parents were if not *who?* Were they alive? Were they a threat?

Alarms sounded inside her. What if Eric's father was an elf? He didn't have pointy ears, but neither did Saint until he shifted into wolf form. Poor Saint. She had been so rude to him when he asked about Eric's father. He didn't know she wasn't his biological mother.

There can be no secrets, her spirit guide reminded her.

I know. But now isn't a good time.

Time cannot be good or bad. It can only be.

She hated when her guide was so matter-of-fact. She also hated that he would keep nudging her until she did it. *Fine,* she huffed. "Saint, there's something I need to tell you."

Janet shrieked in fear as Mingon swung from the table and grabbed her around the waist. With one arm, he clutched her close to his body. His other hand held her around the throat. Talon-like nails grew from his fingertips, pressing into her neck near the carotid artery.

"Let her go!" Saint growled, pushing Mika and CJ away and jumping from the table.

"No," Mingon said. "Not until you let me go."

Mika took a step forward. "There's no one holding you," he said.

Janet scuffled backwards as Mignon forced them back, pushing the examination table against the wall. "You lie!" Mignon said. "You always lie. You say I can go, then you sic the dogs on me. Well, I won't do it anymore. I won't."

Janet could feel Mingon's pain and fear. In her mind's eye, she received flashes of running as hard and fast as her legs would carry her. Her lungs ached. Pain shot through her right leg as the bullet entered her thigh. She fell at the edge of a lake. Looking into the water, she saw not her reflection, but that of Mingon.

"You poor thing," she whispered.

"You know nothing about me, lady," he said, applying more pressure to her throat.

Within a span of seconds, Saint crossed the room. Janet sucked in air as Mingon's grip released. Coughing, she stumbled forward. She looked back to see Saint pinning the young man to the table. A flash of light revealed the blade of the scalpel Saint held inches from Mingon's throat.

Saint's body heaved with each breath. "You will never, ever lay another hand on her. Do you understand?"

Mingon's eyes widened in terror. Janet knew he didn't mean to hurt her. He was only lashing out in fear. Maybe if she could talk to him, get him to understand no one was there to hurt him.

Saint must have been inside her mind, for he turned on her at the moment, snarling and drooling. His eyes had the look of a wild animal instead of the compassionate being she knew him to be. A part of Janet knew she should be afraid, but this was her Saint. If anyone was going to reach him, it had to be her.

Holding her hands palm out, she moved toward him. "Saint? Saint, I need you put the scalpel down and let him go."

"He hurt you," Saint said.

"No. No, he didn't. See, I'm fine." She tilted her head upward, exposing her neck. There was no way for her to know if she was indeed fine. For Mingon's sake, she hoped there weren't any marks on her.

Mingon wiggled, taking Saint's attention away from Janet. *Crap.* Mingon's look pleaded with her to get the crazy man away. All she could do was give him her best mom stare in hopes he understood not to flinch a muscle.

Aidan, she opened the link between them. *Aidan, please. I beg you. Let him go.* Saint's distress filled her mind. Somewhere beneath the anger, there was disappointment and fear. *He is scared. The same as you are."*

No one, Saint said. *No one knows how I feel.*

I do. Don't you remember in my store when I told you I sensed the pain and cold in you? Let me help you, my love. Let me help you ease that cold.

Saint's rigid posture eased. A howl tore from his throat as he fell to his knees. His gut-wrenching cry ripped at the very core of Janet's being. With trepidation, Janet went to him. She placed her hands on his shoulders to steady herself when he wrapped his arms about her waist, like a man clinging to a life preserver. Saint buried his face against her body. Begging for her forgiveness, he finally released the tears she was sure he had held captive forever.

CHAPTER 35

Peeking through the crack in the library door, Janet tried to pick up any bit of information she could. Fergus had called a family meeting that included everyone except her, Eric, Saint, and Mingon. Kel was even in there. According to Fergus, it was a debriefing, although she had no idea what he meant by that.

Janet had gone through all of Saint's tea blends, picking one she thought he might like, but he turned it down. He was now resting in his own bed after a shower and a sedative. The fact he didn't argue about taking the medication and refused tea seemed a source of worry to everyone.

Eric came to her side, placing an arm around her shoulder. *See, he can be a good kid,* Janet told herself.

"I thought you were playing video games," she said, looking up at Eric, and she wondered if he had a growth spurt overnight.

"I was, but I got bored. Not as much fun without Ghost."

A tiny smile found its way to Janet's lips. With a nod of her head, she motioned Eric away from the door. She felt guilty enough for trying to eavesdrop. She didn't need Fergus to come storming out of the room and run into her.

The pair found a spot near a set of French doors leading out to the veranda. "You like it here?" Janet asked. As typical, Eric shrugged. "You like hanging around Ghost and Mika?"

"They're okay, I guess," he answered.

Oh, how she wished she didn't have to have this conversation, but Eric was old enough, and with his powers coming on, Janet didn't see where she had another choice.

Princess? Are you all right? Saint's sleepy voice brushed across her mind.

I'm fine, Aidan.

I like when you call me that, he said and slowly faded away.

"Eric...."

"Uh oh," he groaned.

"No uh oh. But we do need to talk."

"Mom...."

"Eric, please. Sit down. I have to talk to you about this before I lose my nerve." Eric did as she directed, taking a seat. *Yay, for once he didn't argue.* Janet felt that was a small coup.

Taking a seat beside him, she leaned in close. "We've never discussed your father. Well, only briefly when you thought it was Kel." If Eric had been a dog, his ears would have perked up. *Great, I'm thinking of my kid as an animal. Anyway....*

"I've never talked about him because...because I have no idea who he is." The disappointment on Eric's face was almost more than she could take.

"What do you mean, you don't know my dad?"

"No. I never met him."

"So I was one of those in-vitro babies?"

You could have knocked Janet over with a feather. That was the last thing she thought Eric would say, and although she didn't want to lie to the kid, it was her way out. *Thor forgive me.*

"Yes," she said, trying not to sound too anxious. "I really wanted a child, and I didn't want to wait until I found the right person, so...I got artificial insemination." Janet watched the emotions playing across Eric's face. There was no telling how Eric was going to handle the information. *Thor help me. He hasn't run away, so that's a good sign.*

"What about the, you know." He opened his hands exposing the palms. "Did you know about that?"

"No. How could I?"

Eric rubbed his palms on jean-clad thighs. "Oh. Do you think the elf?"

"I really don't know. But that's why I think it would be good if we stayed here for a while. These guys have seen everything, and if anyone can help us, it's them."

"You like the wolf guy, don't you?" He flicked the hair back from his face.

"Yeah, I do," she answered. "But if you don't want to stay here, we won't."

The noise in the hall alerted Janet the meeting had been adjourned.

"Hey, Eric," Ghost said. "You ever played the drums?"

"No." Eric answered.

"Wanna learn?"

Eric looked at Janet for permission. "Of course," she said. "But don't give Ghost any trouble, you hear?"

Eric followed after Ghost. "I won't."

"Hey, let's stop in the kitchen first," she heard Ghost say. "I think there is still some cherry pie left."

"Sweet," Eric replied and disappeared into the kitchen.

Janet shook her head. "Well, that was easier than I thought."

"What's that?" Fergus asked.

Janet gulped. What was it about this man that made her so nervous? Was it the fact that he never seemed to smile? Was it the fact he had a way of walking into a room and filling it up although he wasn't more than six foot or so? Was it the fact she could see him ripping people from limb to limb and not batting an eyelash. Ah, yes. That was the one.

"Are you in love with my brother?"

"Excuse me?" she asked when she found her voice.

"I do not stutter, and I do not take the welfare of Saint lightly. Are you or are you not in love with him?"

Pulling herself to her full height, Janet squared her shoulders. "I don't see where that is any of your business."

"My brother, my pack, my business."

Wow. This is what they mean by alpha wolf.

"Yes. I'm in love with your bother. It just would have been nice to tell him before telling you," she said.

"I see," he said, placing his hands on his hips. "Then I feel I need to tell you that Saint has decided to continue his last few days as a wolf. He will go into the forest and call when he is ready."

If Janet hadn't been seated, she would have fallen. Surely she didn't hear Fergus correctly. "What do you mean 'his last few days'?"

Fergus released a long, slow breath. "Saint has contracted a rare form of rabies. CJ's blood test told us as much, and when confronted, Saint confirmed it. The disease has already taken hold of his body, and soon he will no longer be the brother I have known for two hundred years."

Janet grabbed Fergus by both arms. "You're wrong," she said. "Saint's just tired. A little rest, he'll be fine."

He looked down his nose at her. "I wish it were that simple,"

Fergus said. "Before he goes, he wishes to speak with you."

"But...."

"There are no buts. There is nothing more that can be done. Saint is dying." Fergus pulled away and walked to the door.

Tears stung the back of Janet's eyes. This can't be happening. There had to be a mistake. There were vaccines for rabies, weren't there? CJ was smart. She could figure something out.

"There is one more thing," Fergus said, stopping in the doorway. "Saint has asked for your protection and that of your son. As such, Haven is now your home for as long as you wish, even until your death."

CHAPTER 36

Saint wandered through the gardens, stopping to look up at his old friend the griffin, Liam. "Too bad you can't save me now," Saint said. He breathed in the cool morning air, enjoying the scents of incoming rain. He liked running in the rain. Too bad he hadn't been able to do very much of it anymore, but now he would have his chance.

It was for the best, really, after what he did in the infirmary yesterday. In the whole of his life, Saint had never lost control, not like that. He was usually the one making sure everyone else kept control of their temper. There was so much he wanted to say to everyone, but his mind was slipping faster than he thought it would. No longer could he tell his memories from his imagination.

He had asked Fergus to have Janet meet him. The sooner he said his goodbyes the better it would be. Confession is good for the soul, or so they say. Maybe Janet was right. Maybe absolution was exactly what he sought that day in her shop. For a man whose every move was as it should be, he felt extreme guilt, guilt he wouldn't be around take care of the others, but mostly he felt guilt at what he had done to Janet.

He watched as she walked down the steps toward him. He wanted to smile, but his heart was too heavy. Bridget used to tell him how serious he was. She would often try to make him laugh. *I should have smiled more.*

"Hello, Aidan." Janet said, stopping just beyond his reach.

"Did you sleep well?" he asked, but he could tell by the dark circles under her eyes she hadn't.

"Not really," she said.

Saint motioned to a nearby bench. "Shall we?"

Saint could tell Janet was upset and confused. Still, she did as he asked and took a seat near him, being mindful not to touch him. He felt the myriad of questions bouncing around inside her. He only hoped at the end of his confession, she understood him and his decision.

This was wrong. This whole thing was wrong. He choked back the swelling in his throat. It was hard to tell how much had to do with Janet and how much had to do with the disease.

"Where to begin?" Saint took his gaze out over the hedgerows, across treetops and mountains, peering back through time itself. "I have always held a fondness for New Orleans. It's not simply the food, the people, or the architecture. New Orleans has a pulse and a thrum all its own. It was a place I once wished to call home.

"Long ago we, Fergus, Mika, Ghost, and I were given the job of being the security detail for a wealthy family of shifters, the LeCœurs. The family had traveled from France to New Orleans. Fergus, of course, watched over the father, Mika and Ghost watched over his wife and younger children, and I the eldest daughter, Bridget."

He could see Janet visibly stiffen at his mention of Bridget's name. He turned away from her, only to be brought back by the warmth of her hand on his.

"We met for the first time at the opera, *Les Huguenot.* After that night, we became inseparable. At the time, it seemed Bridget and I had a great deal in common. Many hours were spent strolling along the grounds of her family's estate. If there was inclement weather, I would read while she embroidered."

Saint paused in his remembrance of those days. He could still hear the hiss and pop of Bridget's needle pulling through taut linen as the sweet scent of magnolias drifted in through an open window.

He even remembered the sampler she worked on— two rampant wolves, one facing the other, between them a fire burning in hues of bright orange and yellow. The embroidery still hung above his bed. He wasn't one for mementos, but the tapestry was the only surviving relic from his first and only relationship.

"Please, Saint, continue," Janet coaxed.

He didn't need to look at her or search her mind to know her feelings. Janet's pain at his words was a tangible thing. "Maybe it would be best if I stopped. What possible good could come from this?"

"Consider this your confession." Janet squeezed his hand.

"Will you give me absolution?"

"If that is what you need, then yes." She said, tears forming in her eyes.

"Janet, I...."

He brushed away a tear from Janet's cheek with the pad of his thumb. His heart slowed when Janet pressed her cheek into the hollow of his hand.

"Don't, Saint. Don't tell me you're sorry about any of this. Just go on."

"Bridget loved her position in New Orleans society. She especially loved all the parties and being the center of attention. Over time, we came to realize Arturo had little thought in returning to France, and Fergus became increasingly suspicious of Arturo's pack and his business dealings."

"Shocking," Janet said.

"No. It's true. Fergus had no tangible evidence Arturo was doing anything wrong. Only a feeling he had. He tried to warn me something wasn't right with the whole of the LeCœur clan, but I refused to listen. I was so determined to prove him wrong, I didn't hesitate when Bridget proposed marriage."

"Hold it. You're telling me she asked you to marry her? You must have been pretty hot back then."

"It is always hot in New Orleans, but with the advent of air conditioning, it didn't seem quite so bad this time."

"That's not what I...never mind. It's not important," Janet said.

"In all honesty, I can remember every day of my life except for that one. But nonetheless, we became engaged to be married. The wedding was to take place on the LeCœur plantation within a fortnight."

"That was rather quick, don't you think?"

"Maybe, but at the time, it seemed logical. We had spent well over three hundred hours together. That is more than some people see each other in a year."

"You actually added up how many hours you two spent together?"

"Of course," Saint answered.

"Really? So what happened? Who called it off?"

"Fergus."

Janet raised an incredulous eyebrow. "I know he is the big dog and all, but he has that much authority over you?"

Saint coughed into his fist. "Big dog?"

"I got it from Ghost," Janet shrugged.

"Ah...well, be that as it may, Fergus was correct in what he did. Bridget was too agreeable. I could tell it was not within her nature to be so complacent and malleable. Naïvely, I believed she did so because of her love for me, not because she was ordered to do so by her father."

"Oh, Aidan." Janet took both his hands in hers, sending warmth coursing throughout his body. "How did you know?"

"Many truths are spoken in anger, and so it was with Bridget. But I digress." Saint kissed the tips of her fingers, inhaling the scent of her, locking it away in hopes he would never forget it, not even when he took his place in Helheim.

"Two nights prior to the wedding, I was invited for a hunt with Arturo and members of his pack. It was not something I wished to do, but Janet explained it was a rite of passage, a way to be accepted into her family.

"Much to Fergus's dismay, I was mandated to go alone. No other members of Delta pack were allowed to participate. After all, they were not the one seeking entry into Bridget's family. I was.

"The moon was almost full that night, allowing plenty of light to see by. I had been over every square inch of Arturo's estate and knew exactly where we were headed. As wolves, we raced through the trees, heading toward a creek where Voodoo rituals were performed. Smoke wafted in the cool night air. Of in the distance, I heard chanting and drums. I was sure we would veer from the creek and go deeper into the woods." Saint's voice broke as his memories came crashing back.

He could still see Arturo's pack as they tore through the tree line. Teeth bared and snarling, they had attacked the unsuspecting worshipers. Screams of horror and panic had filled the night air as one by one the humans were taken down.

At first, he had stood there, shocked by the carnage that lay before him. How could this be happening and how did he not know Bridget's pack ate humans? A flash of white had caught his attention. A young woman had run with all of her strength along the river bank toward the trees. Finding the closest and largest tree, the young woman had climbed as high as she could.

Saint's senses had returned, and he vowed in that moment to save at least one. Planting his body at the base of that tree, he had fought off every wolf that challenged him, but he was one against many. Bridget's pack had attacked en masse, pulling the lone wolf away from the tree and into the open.

By the time Fergus and the others had arrived, Arturo's pack was gone and Saint lay near death.

"I tried to shift to human form, but my injuries were too severe," Saint heard himself say. "Fergus was beyond enraged. That night he swore no matter how long it took, he would see each and every member of Bridget's pack dead. Unfortunately for Arturo, Fergus always keeps his promises. Had it not been for my intercession, Bridget would've been among the casualties."

"You should have let him kill her," Janet said, her voice shaking in anger.

"I could not let that happen."

"Because you loved her?"

"Because I believed all life was precious. Because I thought she loved me. I allowed my vanity to get in the way, thinking that I could change that part of her."

"And now?"

"I have known for a long time Bridget never truly loved me. As for Fergus, I will not be around to stop him. Even if I were, I doubt I could stop him this time."

Sharp pain pierced Saint's skull. If he didn't know better, he would have thought someone stabbed him with an ice pick. He pressed his hand to his temple, trying to push back the searing agony. Saint shook his head back and forth as the pain subsided.

"It is time. I must go." he said, moving away from her.

"No, you can't. I won't let you go."

"You saw what I did to Mingon yesterday. I cannot take the chance it could happen again. What if that was Eric I grabbed or you?" He looked down at her. "I will not take that chance."

Janet grabbed the sleeves of his coat, not allowing him to walk away. "But...but I love you," she whispered between sniffs.

Saint pulled her close. Bowing his head, he placed it against hers. "My sweet princess, you are now and shall forever be my true-mate."

"I don't know what that means."

Saint kissed her forehead, allowing it to linger there, etching into his memory the softness and warmth of her skin. "It means I shall love you throughout eternity."

CHAPTER 37

Michael Gray paced back and forth in front of his desk. It was only nine a.m., and he was well into his third pot of coffee. He hated waiting and waiting and waiting. He needed to speak with Freyja, and he needed to speak with her now.

"Did you ever think of switching to decaf?" Kel asked, stretching his arms over his head with a groan.

"No."

Kel settled back into his original spot and closed his eyes. "Maybe you should."

"How can you sleep at a time like this?" Michael paused.

"I'm a cat. It's what we do."

Michael sat in a chair opposite his desk, giving him full view of the mirror Freyja used as her portal. This way he would see her as soon as she arrived.

"That's the trouble with the gods, they only show up when they want to, not when you need them to," he said, taking another sip of coffee.

"Making others wait is a privilege of being a god. We are at no one's beck and call."

Michael heard Freyja's voice. "Goddess, I apologize for disturbing you, but we must speak," he said, talking to the invisible owner of the voice.

"Very well, speak." Little by little, the obsidian surface of the mirror turned clear as the image of the goddess came into view. Dressed from head to foot in thick pelts, Freyja appeared to be returning from a hunt. The top of her quiver along with the hilt of her sword peeped out from above her shoulder. Although it couldn't be seen, Michael was sure her bow wasn't far away.

"Is that Kellas?" Freyja asked, looking past him.

"Yes, goddess," Kel said, adjusting his position.

"To what do I owe this meeting?" she asked, as she removed the quiver and arrows from her back and passed them back through the mirror to her waiting servant.

"There is a problem or problems that you might need to be aware of."

"Problems? Is that not what I have you for, Gray? To handle problems when they arise?"

"Yes, goddess, it is, but as humans are fond of saying, this is above my pay grade." Michael said.

Removing the last vestiges of her hunting attire, Freyja waved her hand, dispensing with the barrier between her and Michael's office. "Explain, cat." She pointed to Kel.

"It seems our friend Loki is up to something, but I don't know what or why."

Freyja took a seat behind Michael's desk. "What do you mean? And," she added, "get straight to the point. Remember who you work for."

"Of course, straight to the point. Where do I start?"

Michael caught him looking his way for help.

"We are pretty sure Loki sent Scarlethand and Calamus after Eric Beesinger," Kel said.

Freyja raised a pale eyebrow. "Why do you think it was Loki that sent the elves?"

"Because Saint spoke to Calamus, and we know for a fact Scarlethand was at My Spicy Cauldron threatening Janet and Eric, who, by the way, is beginning to show his powers."

"Interesting. Where are they now?" she asked.

"They are at Haven," Kel said.

"Everyone?" she asked.

"Everyone. Including Bridget LeCœur's son, who she had somehow allowed to fall into the hands of the Alliance."

Michael noticed the subtle shift in Freyja's demeanor at the mention of the Alliance. It seemed no matter how many times Delta Pack destroyed one of their facilities, another was found. Once this whole mess was settled, Michael would once again ask Fergus to find and destroy yet another.

"Although distressing, there is nothing here you cannot handle. So tell me what was so urgent I was called from the hunt?" She propped her forearms on Michael's desk. "If everyone is with the guardian, then all should be well."

"Not quite," Michael said. From the look on the goddess's face, he could tell she already considered their story too long. However, he knew his final bit of information would gain her attention. "Saint was given a lethal injection of rabies by Loki. According to Kel, the disease has spread so rapidly, Saint has retreated into wolf form and gone into the forest to die."

Using her hands, Freyja pushed herself out of the chair. "You are positive of this?" Her tone was barely above a whisper.

"Yes," Kel said. "Saint was kind of kidnapped by Loki. We have no idea how much longer he has."

The electromagnetic charge within the room began to grow,

causing a marked drop in temperature. Neither Michael nor Kel knew what was coming. They just knew it wouldn't be good.

"How dare he!" she said, throwing her hands before her body. Lightning zapped across the room, singeing everything in its path and burning a hole through the opposite wall. "What right does he have to mess with my children?"

Michael shielded his face and head with his arms, and waited until Freyja finished barbequing his office. He debated whether or not to tell her his other little bit of information. However, he had come this far. "There is one other thing, goddess," he said, slowly lowering his arms. "It is thought Loki did this to facilitate Saint's agreement with Hel."

She turned her fiery gaze upon him. "What agreement?" she asked.

"The only way for Saint to get the guardian back from Helheim was to agree he would take her place when the time came. We believe Loki didn't want Hel to have to wait, so he rushed the process, not knowing Saint had found his true-mate."

Freyja dropped back into the chair. She sat in silence, staring at a blank spot on the desk. No one moved. Michael was pretty sure Kel hadn't taken a breath since the lightning zinged above his head.

"Very well," Freyja said, straightening a piece of hair that had come lose from the tight bun atop her head. "You were correct in calling me," she said, returning through the mirror. "I will handle this."

Michael rose to his feet. "Goddess, what would you have us do?"

"Nothing," she said over her shoulder.

Michael couldn't believe what he was hearing. "Nothing? But Freyja...."

"You are to do nothing," she commanded. "This one is mine to handle."

CHAPTER 38

It had been less than a week since Saint disappeared into the forest. In the beginning, Janet was able to carry on conversations with him. It seemed he spent a great deal of his time communicating with her or his brothers. It was as if he wanted to tell them everything he could remember in hopes that no one would forget.

But day by day, his thoughts became more jumbled and sporadic. The only way they even knew he was alive was by hearing his panicked howls at night. For Janet, her tears had been replaced by anger. How dare the Universe finally give her someone who was a good kind person, only to snatch him away from her? She was angry at the world and at the gods. Where were they now that she needed them the most?

Staring out across the gardens, Janet hoped to catch a glimpse of Saint. He may be in wolf form, but just getting that small visual would give her a small sense of relief. She thought her prayers were answered with the rustling of the hedges. Holding her breath, she waited to see what would emerge. Disappointment overwhelmed her as a rabbit jumped out of the foliage.

CJ still tended to Mingon's wounds, which were healing nicely. He was slowing beginning to understand he was truly free, but just like Saint, he chose to spend most of his time in private.

Ghost and Mika had started Eric's home-schooling, and whether Ghost wanted to admit it or not, Janet could tell he actually enjoyed teaching. He even looked good in those wire-framed glasses he insisted on wearing. It wasn't until she asked about them and learned they belonged to Saint that she understood Ghost's attachment to them.

Fergus had told her Haven was now her home for as long as she wished. But what was a home without the man she loved? Janet could hear the others as they wandered through the rambling manor house, trying to carry on with life as usual, which was a monumental task. They all knew what was to come.

But the person that broke her heart the most was Fergus. He had locked himself in his room, refusing to come out or eat. Most of the day, the only sounds coming from his room was the low, soft tones of a cello.

Janet tilted her head, listening. Yes, there it was. Closing her eyes, she gave into the music, allowing it to permeate her soul. She had never heard the composition before, but its melancholy echoed her own. Note after note, the cello sang. In her imagination, she could see Saint. He looked the way he had when she first met him. Not a hair out of place or speck of dirt anywhere.

She smiled in memory of him in her shop. Their first cup of tea, how he hit his head on the lamp in her reading room. *Too few memories.*

The sound of heavy footsteps pounded over her head and down the stairs. She opened her eyes in time to see Fergus leap over the sofa and tore out the door, heading toward the garden. The house filled with the sounds of running as everyone piled onto the terrace. No one spoke. They all watched as Fergus sprinted toward the reflecting pool and the dark red mass that lay nearby.

"Saint!" Ghost said, starting down the stairs. He turned back when he realized no one followed him. "What are you doing? It's Saint."

"No, my brother," Mika said. "That is Saint's body, but the Saint we knew is no longer there."

"Screw you, Mika." Ghost waved him off. "You do what you want. I'm not going to let our brother die alone," he said, running after Fergus.

Janet agreed with Ghost. There was no way she would allow Saint to die alone. He needed his family around him. Janet tried to hold her tongue but found it impossible to do so. "I know we all deal with death in our own way, but it doesn't matter if he remembers you or not. What matters is you remember him." Gripping the concrete bannister, Janet rushed down the steps and toward the fountain.

Fergus cradled the large, red wolf in his arms, rocking it back and forth like a child, weeping. Janet had no idea if anyone had ever seen Fergus cry, but no matter where her life ended up, she would never forget that he did on this day.

Ghost went to his knees. Janet could hear him whispering as he stroked the back of the wolf's neck. She could only make out snippets of what he said, but she had no doubt of his intentions. With trepidation, Janet approached. She could see Saint's body shake as he labored for every breath, whining with each exhalation. His body was shutting down.

Lifting her gaze, she fought back the urge to scream. She wanted to yell at the top of her lungs, to rail at the gods for what they had done. Her hair whipped before her eyes, frustrating her all the more. The clouds clumped together, blocking out the sun, and casting a cold shadow on the scene below. The winds picked up, bending the limbs of the trees and bushes, as if bowing them in sorrow.

Janet stumbled back against the force of the wind. She didn't know if they had tornados in the mountains, but that was exactly what this felt like. "What's happening?" she asked Ghost.

"Haven," he yelled over the roar of the wind. "Haven is mourning."

Haven in mourning? It wasn't possible for a place to mourn. Was it? "We need to get out of this weather," she said.

"No," Fergus demanded. "Let the sisters take me. I do not wish to be the last of my kind." Fergus stood, easily lifting Saint's limp body from the ground. "Do you hear me, Darkness?" he yelled to the sky. "Take me. I am the sinner. I am the one who deserves to die for all the death I have caused. Not him." Fergus lifted his brother's face close to his, hiding his tears against Saint's neck.

Lightning spider-veined across the sky, an answer to Fergus's plea. He stood steadfast as night engulfed Haven. "Come on, Darkness! Is that all you got?" Fergus said. "You do not scare me. If you are so powerful, take me now!"

Janet didn't know whether to try to calm Fergus or run for cover. Instead, she held her position, clinging to Eric and Ghost. In Haven's final act of defiance, a single bolt of lightning struck the statue of the griffin, crumbling it into the fountain, the light blinding everyone close at hand. Then the storm was gone.

"Coward!" Fergus yelled toward the heavens. "Death is nothing but a coward."

"I would not use that term lightly, wolf, especially where I am concerned."

When Janet's vision finally cleared, she beheld a woman standing at Fergus's side. Clad in a blue-frosted gown, the woman was a striking figure. Yet Janet could see through the beauty to the monster that lay beneath. "Death," she whispered.

"You know me," Hel said, gliding passed Fergus.

Janet refused to flee from the Queen of the Underworld though her legs screamed to run. "You're the reason for Saint's coldness. You had met before."

"I do have quite an unforgettable touch." Hel scanned Janet from head to toe. "You are Saint's human. I never understand why the fates choose what they do, but they have their reasons, I'm sure. Give him to me," she said, placing her arms out to receive Saint's body.

Resentment rose in Janet at Hel's familiarity with Saint causing her to form an instant dislike for the goddess. There was nothing likeable about Hel. Not her accent. Not her haughtiness and especially not her presumption that she could just waltz in and take Saint's body away.

Enraged, Janet lunged toward Hel. Without touching her, Hel sent Janet flying backwards and onto the ground. Eric went to her side, posting himself above his mother as her protector.

Hel dropped her arms to her sides. Blue flames extended out from her hands, engulfing her body. "Do not test me, Halfling," she said. "Not even your father has dominion over me." Hel turned to Fergus. "Now, place him on the ground."

Fergus hesitated. Janet caught a minute shake of Ghost's head. She wasn't sure if he was telling Fergus don't do it, or don't do what he was thinking about doing.

"I have been rather patient," Hel said. "But I will play no longer. Do as I say, or I will take you up on your offer."

With resignation, Fergus did as she commanded and placed Saint on the ground at Hel's feet. She waited until Fergus stepped away before bending down. Janet couldn't help the pang of jealousy that tore through her as she watched Hel rub her hand along the ridge of his back.

Removing a silken cord from around her neck, Hel held out a small, silver vial. "Do not take this is a dismissal of your debt, sweet wolf." Mist wafted from the open ampoule and into Saint's nostrils as he took what seemed to be his last breath. "One day you will take your place at my side, but the time will be on your terms, not my father's, unless, as we agreed, you find another to take your place." Hel placed a kiss on his muzzle. "Until we meet again, sweet wolf," she said, and shimmered into nothingness.

When she was sure Hel was gone, Janet scurried to the wolf's limp body. Placing her hand gently on his side, she felt for any signs of movement. Tears filled her eyes, making it difficult to see more than a blur of red and gray fur.

"Aidan, please," Janet nuzzled her face against the velvety fluff near his ear. "Please don't leave me," she whispered. "Don't let your beautiful heart and soul be taken from me. Not when I have just found you."

Janet waited for the sound of a breath or the thump of a heart beat, only to be met with disappointment. There was no way she was giving up on Saint, not yet.

"Did I tell you my guides told me my life would change that day, the day we met. I had no idea what they meant, then I saw you and I fell joyously in love with you. Do you hear me, Saint? I love you."

A gentle pressure weighed down Janet's shoulders, and she didn't have to look to know that CJ was behind her, comforting her.

"I can't leave him," Janet said.

"I know, sweetie," CJ whispered.

Janet wiped at her eyes and cheeks. "This isn't right. It's just not right." She watched for signs of movement from her beloved but, as far as she could tell, he still hadn't taken a another breath.

Stroking the curve of Saint's neck, Janet thought she felt a slight twitching of muscle. She stopped her motion and waited. Nothing. Could it have been her imagination? Did she want him to live so badly that her mind played tricks on her?

The grief of those around her was almost unbearable. Dropping her head, Janet fought to block out the swirl of emotions of those nearby. Her injured heart sought for a moment of solace. *How could the gods bring me such a perfect man, only to take him away?*

I have been taken nowhere, my princess.

Janet's eyes flew open at the sound of Saint's voice. "Saint?" She lifted the wolf's head. "Please tell me you heard that." She turned and searched the confused faces of the others.

"Saint, say something. Anything," she pleaded.

I would fancy...a cup of tea.

From the shouts and whoops behind her, Janet knew the others had heard him also. She couldn't stop the huge smile that spread across her face. Her Saint was alive, and no one, not even a Norse goddess would ever take him from her again.

EPILOGUE

Janet circled her arms about Saint's waist, snuggling closer to his back. She loved his scent and the way his lean, taut body made her feel feminine and protected, two things she never really thought she could be. To think she almost lost him, to never have known a man such as he or his crazy family.

"Why are you sad, my princess?" he asked. "Today is supposed to be a celebration."

Janet smiled. She still wasn't used to the fact Saint knew most of what she was thinking, but she was growing accustomed to it. "I'm not sad. I'm just overwhelmed. I guess," she said poking her head around his side to look at his reflection. *Oh my, but I am a lucky woman.*

"I believe it is I who am the lucky one." Saint finished buttoning his vest and adjusting the cuffs of his sleeves.

"You look very handsome." Janet spun under his arm, her embrace never releasing him.

"It's bad luck for the groom to see the bride before the wedding," he said, kissing her on the nose.

"You're a funny man, Saint Wolfe. This is not your wedding, and I am not your bride."

He hugged her tight against his body, his head resting atop of hers. "This is kind of my wedding."

"You're officiating, not getting married."

"Still my wedding."

Janet sensed his smiling. It was good to see him smile. It wasn't a common occurrence for Saint, but she hoped to rectify that situation.

"We need to go," Saint said, trying to pull away from her.

"What if I don't want to let you go?" Janet teased.

"I suppose I could perform the service telepathically, but that could prove embarrassing."

Janet pursed her lips in thought. "And why is that?"

"Because if we stay in this room, I will have to fulfill that little fantasy running around inside your head, and that I do *not* wish to share with them."

Flames seemed to shoot from the top of Janet's head to the bottom of her feet. To be honest, it was tempting to see if she could hold him to it, but Saint needed to be with his family. Today wasn't just a celebration of Mika and CJ sharing their lives together. It was a celebration of family, home, and love. Janet couldn't stop the tears of joy that rolled down her cheek.

"I can't help it," she said when she caught the way Saint looked at her. "I'm just so happy."

"Come on," he said, taking her by the hand and leading her from the room. Saint pulled to a stop as they neared the stairs. "I forgot my notes. I won't be a minute."

"Notes?" Janet called after him. "I thought you remembered everything."

Saint rummaged through his desk drawer. "Almost. I just want to make sure. Ah, there they are," he said, grabbing the notecards. His attention was drawn to movement outside the window. For a moment, he thought his eyes deceived him, but there, just beyond Haven's gate, stood Bridget. He rubbed his eyes, hoping she was simply a figment of his imagination, but she was still there, looking up at him.

Saint nodded in acknowledgement. Bridget waved her hand, creating a wormhole, and, stepping inside, disappeared.

www.ingramcontent.com/pod-product-compliance
Lightning Source LLC
Chambersburg PA
CBHW021334250626
47155CB00002B/691